A Sevenfold Trouble

A Christian Novel

Grace Livingston Hill

Pansy

Printed in the United States of America

ISBN: 978-1-62943-016-4
eBook ISBN: 978-1-62943-017-1

A Sevenfold Trouble

CONTENTS

A Sevenfold Trouble

Grace Livingston Hill

Pansy

PREFACE

Do you know, dear friends, we feel like calling your special attention in some way to this story of ours? So many questions have been asked during its writing, that I am sure you do not fully understand.

In the first place, it is really and honestly written by seven people, and not by one person pretending to be seven different ones, as some of you have thought.

In the second place, it is an honest record of what we, who are all writers, and all very intimate friends, have seen and heard as we looked on at the lives of certain people in whom we are deeply interested.

We used to talk about these people when we sat together after the day's work was done. "They don't understand one another," said one of the ministers, "else there wouldn't be much trouble."

"I think the little girl means better than she is supposed to," said Grace.

"And I know the two boys are not half so mean as they are made out to be," declared Paranete.

"They are like a great many people in this world," interposed the other minister, "working at cross purposes; making failures of their lives, just because they do not try to put themselves in one another's places."

"Making failures, also, because they are trying to carry their own burdens without the help of the only real Helper," said one of the ladies.

"O, yes! of course," spoke out both ministers; "that is really the foundation source of their troubles, as of most others."

Said Faye Huntington: "Let's write a book about them! One that will help others, as well as them. We can tell their story, but tell it in such a way that they won't even recognize themselves; they will only know that it fits, somehow, and helps."

"We might do that," said Grace. "We all know them so well; I'd like to write up the little girl, and suggest to her what to do. If I did, I'd call her Margaret; I like that name."

"It's a good idea," said the wife of one of the ministers. "I just long to give that mother a hint."

Said Pansy: "Let us do it. I like the thought. I'll mother the whole thing, arrange the chapters, and plan out the work, if you will each take the people in whom you are most interested, and be as plain-spoken as will do, and be as helpful as you can."

"Agreed," said they all; and we have honestly and earnestly done it.

Because the family whom we knew so well, were not named Moore, and did not live in a town like the one described, and did not name their children Margaret and Weston and Johnnie, they may not know that we mean them; but if they will see that the Moore family of whom we wrote made the same mistakes that they are making, and got out of trouble by the very road that they may take if they will, it is all we ask.

No, one thing more. Dear friends, every one, we call on you to help us. Read the book carefully, lend it to your friends, ask the Lord Jesus to make it helpful to every boy, or girl, or man, or woman who touches it; and may His blessing be upon us all in our effort to make less trouble and more sunshine in this world.

Your friends,
PANSY.
Grace Livingston Hill.
Paranete.
Mrs. C. M. L.
Faye Huntington.
C. M. L.
G. R. A.

CHAPTER 1: AN UNHAPPY HOUSEHOLD

MARGARET was washing the dishes; making a vigorous clash and spatter, and setting down the cups so hard that had they been anything but the good solid iron-stone which they were, they would certainly have suffered under the treatment.

Margaret was noisy in all things, but to-day the usual vigor of movement was manifestly increased by ill humor. There was an ominous setting of a pair of firm lips, and all her face was in a frown. The knives and forks, when their turn came, seemed to increase her ire. She rattled and flung them about with such reckless disregard of consequences that there landed, presently, a lovely tricolored globe of foam in the centre of John's arithmetic; over which he was at this moment gloomily bending.

"Look here," he said, half fiercely, half comically, "quit that, will you? This thing is dry enough, I know; but it will take more than soap suds to dampen it."

"Take your book out of my way, then. What do you s'pose she would say to its being on the table and you bending double over it?"

"She may say just exactly what she pleases. It will stay on the table until I get ready to take it off."

"O yes! you're very brave until you hear her coming, and then you are as meek as Moses."

"Now I say, Mag, that's mean in you, when you know well enough that all I'm after is to try to keep the peace."

"Peace! there isn't enough of that article left in this house to make it worthwhile to try to save it. I'm sick to death of the whole thing." And the knives bumped about against a plate in the dish-pan with such force that the plate rebelled and flew into three pieces in its rage.

"There goes another dish!" exclaimed West, from the window corner where he was busily whittling; "that makes the seventeenth this week, doesn't it? Mag, you are awful, and no mistake."

1

Then Margaret's face flamed and her angry words burst their bounds: "I wish you would just mind your own business, Weston Moore! You think because you are eighteen months and seven days older than I, that you can order me around like a slave."

"Whew! bless my eyes! How you do blaze out on a fellow! Who thought of ordering you around? I should as soon think of ordering a cyclone. I was only moralizing on the sweet and amiable mood you were in, and the nice comfortable times we have in this house."

"Well, you may let my moods alone if you please; and my dishes too. I've a right to break them all if I choose, for all you. I'd rather blaze up in a rage, than be an everlasting tease and torment, like you."

"Father'll have a word to say about the dishes, I fancy, my lady; you might now and then think of him: he isn't made of gold, I s'pose you know, and dishes cost money."

"I do think of him a great deal oftener than you do, you great lazy, whittling, whistling boy! If it wasn't for him I'd run away, and be rid of her and you, and all the other nuisances, dishes and all."

She paused in her clatter long enough to dash away two or three great tears which were plashing down her hot red cheeks.

"As to that," said the whittler, as he slowly closed his jack-knife, "perhaps you better seriously consider it. I'm not sure but it would be more comfortable for all concerned; especially the dishes." Then he spied the tears; and seizing upon the dish towel which had been angrily flung across the back of a chair, he rushed toward his sister, exclaiming: "Here, let me wipe away those briny drops."

Margaret's hands were in the dishwater again, but she drew them forth all dripping with the greasy suds, and brought the right one with a resounding slap, about the curly head of the mocking boy.

Just how he would have received it will not be known; for the sudden jerk backwards of the left arm, came against the full dish pan, already set too near the edge of the table, and over it went, deluging table, floor, and Margaret's dress not only, but pouring a greasy flood over the rows of bread tins carefully covered, and set in a sheltered comer for the dough to rise.

Margaret's exclamation of dismay was suddenly checked, and the angry color flamed back into her eyes as the door leading into the hall opened, and a woman appeared on the scene.

A tall, pale woman in a plain, dark, close-fitting calico dress, without a collar, and with dark, almost black hair combed straight back from a plain face. She gave a swift glance at the confusion, and took in the situation.

"Quarreling again! I might have known it. Were you three ever together in your lives, without it? John, let the book alone until it dries; if it had not been on the kitchen table where I told you never to have it, the dishwater wouldn't have ruined it. And the bread too! I declare! This is too bad!" These last words came in detached sentences as the extent of the misfortune grew upon her.

A quick snatch of the carefully tucked cloth, now holding little pools of dishwater, a comprehension of the utter ruin of the many loaves of bread, and she turned upon the wrathful girl:

"Margaret, go upstairs this minute, and don't venture down again until you are called. I'm sure I wish you need never come."

"You can't begin to wish it as I do." This was Margaret's last bitter word as she shot out of the door.

John stood dolefully surveying his soaking arithmetic, and his great sheet of now ruined examples, carefully worked out. The woman was already tucking up her calico dress ready for work, but she had a message for him.

"Now you go somewhere; don't let me see you until dinner time. And mind, I shall tell your father you have disobeyed me again."

As for Weston the tease, he had slipped swiftly and silently from the room with the entrance of the mother.

Yes, she was their mother. At least, she was their father's wife, though none of the three had ever called her by the name of mother. A curious position she held in the home, bound by solemn pledge to do a mother's duty by these three children, yet receiving from none of them a shred of the love, or respect, or true obedience, which the name mother ought to call forth.

Poor Mrs. Moore! I do hope you are sorry for her. Sorry for the children, are you? Well, so am I. Indeed it is true, they every one need pity and help. The question is, Will they get what they need?

Upstairs, angry Margaret made haste to remove her much soiled dress, eyes dashing, and cheeks burning the while. Something more than the scenes we watched in the kitchen had to do with Margaret's mood.

A green and prickly chestnut bur came whizzing into the room, landing in the middle of her bed.

It called forth an angry exclamation. Here was some more of that tormenting West's work. She would not stand it! She made a rush for the window, but a low, merry laugh stopped her. This was not West's laugh.

"Well," said Hester Andrews, from under the chestnut-tree, "can you go?"

"No; of course I can't. I should think you might know without asking. Do I ever go anywhere now days?

"It is just too mean for anything!" declared Hester. "What reason does she give this time?"

There was a peculiar emphasis on the word "this," which was meant to indicate that here was only one of the numberless times in which Margaret Moore had been shamefully treated. Margaret answered the tone as well as the words.

"Oh! father says he can't have me out so late in the evening; it isn't the thing for a little girl, and he doesn't approve of sail boats, anyway. As if I didn't know where all that stuff came from!"

"The idea! I declare, it's a perfect shame. Wouldn't you like to see your own mother keeping you at home from places, and treating you like a baby, or a slave, as she does?"

"Don't you speak my mother's name the same day you do hers" said Margaret, with fierce voice and flashing eyes.

"Well, I'm sure I don't wonder that you feel so," was Hester's soothing answer. "I'm just as sorry for you as I can be; I wonder sometimes that you don't run away. Everyone says it comes harder on you, because you are a girl: the boys can keep out of her sight. O Mag! I'm so sorry you can't go. If your mother were only here, what lovely times we could have."

And this was the help which Margaret's most intimate friend brought her! In point of fact, these two knew no more of what the mourned mother would have done, than did the squirrels up in the chestnut-tree. She had been lying in the cemetery for a year when Hester Andrews' family moved into the town, and Margaret was only a busy little elf of not quite six, when she received with gleeful laughter her mother's last kiss. Could she know how the mother would treat the thirteen-year-old girl's longings for sail boats and evening parties?

Downstairs, Mrs. Moore left to solitude and bitter thoughts, worked with swift, skilled fingers, and set lips. Not long alone; someone came to help her — a sister, married, and living at ease in a lovely home a few streets away; a younger sister who was sorry, so blindly and unwisely sorry for the elder's harder lot, that she could not keep back her words of indignant sympathy.

"It's a shame!" she said, "just a burning shame, the way you are treated by those children. The idea of your being down on your knees mopping up the musses which they have made, on purpose to vex you. If I were you, Sophia, I wouldn't endure it another day. It is a wonder to me that their father permits such a state of things. Henry and I were speaking of it last night."

"Their father doesn't know the half that goes on," Mrs. Moore said, speaking quickly in defence of her husband. "What is the use? We live in an uproar all the time, as it is. And after all, Emma, they are his children."

"I don't care. You are his wife. You owe something to yourself respect. Henry thinks so too; he thinks it is a shame. Why do you go on the floor and clean after them? Isn't that girl as able to mop up her dishwater as you are?" Mrs. Moore wrung the wet, greasy cloth with a nervous grip, letting some of the soiled drops trickle down her arm, in her haste, and answered with eyes that glowed:

"To tell the truth, I would scrub the floor after her all day, for the sake of getting her out of my sight for an hour."

And this was the help Mrs. Moore received.

CHAPTER 2: FRENZY AND REMORSE

MEANWHILE she — not the one in the kitchen, but Margaret — was busy as forty million bees with her thoughts. Not one of a dozen lunatics did more wild thinking than this raving girl. Had she — of the kitchen — come in just then, there would have been a scene more tempestuous than ever disturbed a dozen dish-pans. Fortunately, the disaster below was too widespread and serious to permit the stepmother's absence. Margaret was left severely alone to manage her own mental world. She managed it after this fashion:

"I hate her; I hate her; I h-a-t-e her. I wish she'd never come here. What'd we want of her? 'Zif she could fill my mother's place! Wish there was spooks, and one of 'em would come and haunt 'er and haunt 'er till she was scared out of her senses, and would pick up her duds and get out of this house. What business has she got here in my mother's house, using my mother's things and talking and acting zif she'd always been here and owned everything? commanding me to go here and there in my mother's house and stay till she calls me! Guess I'll do as she says! Let her come in now if she dares, and command me, and I'll throw this book at her head."

And our lunatic, at that, sprang like a tiger to the little stand near her bed and, seizing a small Bible, struck a defiant attitude, facing the door, her eyes flashing fire, her hand clutching the trembling little book and drawn back to its utmost as though making ready to deal a deadly blow the moment the first sound was heard approaching her room.

"Let her come now, and — " At that the door opened enough to disclose an eye, when the enraged girl, thinking it belonged to her, hurled the book with all her pent-up power. Then came a shrill cry of pain, a backward heavy fall upon the stairs, and, "You've put my eyes out; oh! I can't see; I'm killed; help!" followed by quick steps from the kitchen and sharp words.

"Now see what you've done to your brother! What if you've killed

6

Weston and you'll be hanged for it? What'll you think, then, you wicked girl? What you think your mother'd say if she was here and had seen you trying to kill your own brother! My lady, if you hav'n't got yourself into trouble now!" said the mother, lifting the groaning Weston and giving his face a searching look to make sure that a really blind boy was not added to her misfortunes. "Just a little more, my lady, and instead of this black and blue spot on his nose you'd a put his two eyes out, and then your father'd seen to you, and he will as it is. Come, don't stand there, shaking your head at me. Shut the door, and don't let me hear a sound from you. Your father'll settle with you," and she pulled the door sharply to and locked Margaret in and turned to dispose of Weston.

That person, however, in spite of his wounds, gathered himself up and got away, preferring to bear the pain rather than try the treatment of his step-mother with the usual accompaniment of a lecture on the evils of mischief and the punishment sure and sudden to follow.

West had really meant no mischief in this case, but rather to extend a bit of sympathy to his imprisoned sister, with what result the reader now knows.

If Margaret was frenzied before it was now frenzy and wretchedness combined. What if she had indeed forever blinded her brother?

"I wish I was dead — yes, dead, dead! then I'd see if she could torment me. Oh! if I had put his eyes out; poor West! poor West! what if he did tease me? He meant it for fun, and — but—I won't be teased — teased too, when I'm washing her greasy dishes! West'd no business to come up squinting into my room to see how mad I looked. I thought it was her old eye there at the crack, and I almost wish it had been, and I had knocked her down stairs and let her see how it feels to be hit once, hard. Doesn't she keep hitting me every time she can with her hateful old tongue till I'm so mad I could scream? Oh! oh I What shall I do? I wish I was a bird, I'd fly this very minute; or even a grasshopper, and I'd jump out of this hateful room and out of her sight, if I jumped into the well and drowned myself."

And Margaret looked from her window and saw a swallow. It skipped through the air and then would dart down the chimney and twitter and leap out again, and away it would whirl after its kind.

Margaret would really have exchanged her humanity, nay, her very soul, to be a mere chimney swallow and twitter a day or month and then be no more forever! She even envied an ugly toad that at that moment was vainly trying to get over a small root rising across its path. Anything to be away from her!

Ah! if only her auntie would just then drive up and stop under her window and see her there, and say, "Come, Margie, put on your hat; make ready quick, I've come to take you to spend the winter with me. I know your father will say yes!"

Oh! why couldn't it be for her this once, as books often have it in the story; "I go away from her and never see her again, and live with good Aunt Cornelia, and she pet me and not scold my life out of me, and not always make me wash the dishes, and let me have nice things to wear, and never say 'Margaret, my lady, I'll tell your father?' Then after two or three years perhaps I'd come home, riding in uncle's carriage like a fine young lady, and I don't know whether I'd speak to her or not. But oh! Auntie won't come, or anybody, but that old thing."

And she strained her eyes out the window, looking up and down the road, wishing she were old enough to be engaged, or something, and someone would come with a ladder and carry her off to some island of the sea — no matter if one of the Fiji.

Then a thought struck her "I'll run away. I'll make a rope of my bedclothes as I've read they do when the house is on fire, and let myself down, and be gone where they'll never find me, and go and take care of myself, and then she'll see what she's done, and father'll hate the very sight of her, and wish she was dead too."

And the excited girl began to measure with her eye the height of her window from the ground, to see if she couldn't safely jump; then she started toward the bed to tie the clothes for a rope, when her eye fell upon the leaf of her Bible, at her feet, that was torn from its place as it struck against the partly opened door where West's eye had appeared.

It seemed to look up with a pleading gaze.

She stooped and took it up tenderly; then went to the door for the Bible. It was not there. It had probably swept through the crack out upon the stairway. In vain she tried to open the door. It was locked. Margaret was a prisoner, and this torn leaf her only seeming companion and friend. May be it could speak some word to her poor stormy spirit.

She read: "Come unto me," the other portion was torn out, except "find rest."

How strange it seemed, those words, "Come," and, "find rest." Rest! rest! Oh! if she could have rest. Then came that scene in the Sunday- school, when her teacher, after all the class was gone, drew her to her arms and whispered, "Now, Maggie, won't you — for Jesus' sake at least—won't you be patient and good to your new mother?" and the little Bible was presented, and several passages marked, and these very words, " Come," etc. Ah! that scene. It was the last between Margaret and her teacher. The angels came soon after and carried the faithful Miss Barrett to the skies.

Margaret remembered it all now, and how she promised to be good and patient for Jesus' sake. Then she burst into a flood of bitter weeping.

Falling upon her bed, she continued to sob till in weariness and sheer exhaustion she sank into a troubled but deep sleep.

The dream of battle, blood and groans that came to Margaret was at length broken by a fierce blast of wind, accompanied by thunder and frequent lightning flashes. A wild storm had burst from the sky almost as suddenly and madly as that from her lips.

She started up in terror, yet defiant as though still in strife with someone, and that one her step-mother. Fiercely she gazed, expecting to hear her cold, sharp words. But the room was still and dark as death. Then came a flash, and her eye fell upon her stand, and she thought she saw a salver with bread and a cup of milk, possibly other edibles; then all was black as night. Now another brighter flash, setting the room aflame, revealing her father near the bed with sad, but tender face.

"O, papa!" she cried out, "is it you, papa? I thought — I — where? Don't let her; don't let her; you won't; oh! I will be good; I promised Miss Barrett — I — O papa, take me!"

"My daughter, there! there! be quiet. It can all be well if you will."

"I? papa, I? but she! what shall I do? I can't, I can't, she won't let me, she hates me — she hates us all, I know she does. The neighbors all say so — "

"My child you must — "

"Oh! they do, papa; you don't hear what we do; and they say she said we should all be bound — "

"Hush, Mar—"

"—out," finished Margaret with a great effort. "O, papa! I want to go away from her. Take me somewhere?"

"From me, too?"

"Can't we all go, papa? Anywhere, anywhere, and be just as we used to. I'll take care of the house and be good and patient as Miss Barrett said I must; and you'll come up from the mill and find the dinner all ready, and everything so nice, and a good fire, and the boys good — oh! won't you, papa? only don't — oh! don't let her ever, ever, EVER come where we are. Oh! I—I—I—" and the child clung convulsively to her father, while peal after peal of thunder followed blinding flashes till the house seemed about to fall.

And then the clouds rained a tempest, until it seemed to Margaret that a second flood was upon the earth — and all because of herself. God seemed angry with her; the storm was his words. Maybe the house would fall with the next flash or be burned up and all be consumed, may be the end of all things was near, and soon she would stand at His bar to give account for that day's doings. What should she say? What if it should appear that she was not so bad a stepmother, after all, and that if she, Margaret, had tried to be good and patient as she promised Miss Barrett, her home would have been happy and her papa's face would not have been so sad. Oh! if she could but begin that awful day again, she would do better, no matter how sharp "she" might be to her, and —

At that instant there came into the room such a light and terrific explosion that Margaret dropped back upon the bed as if shot. A groan escaped her, and all was still save the quiver as of one in dying agonies.

Mr. Moore bent over his child, begging her to speak just one little word to her father, but answer came only from the raging storm.

CHAPTER 3: CALM AFTER THE STORM

THE morning dawned clear and bright; the skies gave no token of the fierce storm which had raged. Nature, calm and smiling, seemed to have forgotten the tempest of the previous night. The air was pure and sweet, the grass and foliage had put off their dustiness and were fresh and green in the sunlight. Yet there were many evidences of the strength of the storm. Wrecks were visible — from the despoiled home of a pair of robins, to the forest trees which lay prostrate, having yielded to the power of the tempest. On the shore of the little lake lay a wrecked sail-boat; the very boat in which Margaret, but for her step-mother's wisdom, would have gone out for an evening's pleasure. And her friends? Hester? Oh! God was merciful, and this morning Hester lay weak and faint upon her bed; thankful for her own deliverance from what had seemed certain death, and wondering if, after all, Margaret was not glad that she had not been allowed to join the sailing party, shuddering to think how it might have turned out, had there been two instead of one to be saved from drowning. As for Margaret herself, she too lay upon her bed, worn and weary. The storm of passion had indeed spent itself, as had the tempest in the physical world, and Margaret had been the victim of both. Dr. Perkins came, and looked very grave, though to Margaret he spoke cheerfully, saying,

"You must keep yourself quiet, and I trust we shall have you up and around soon."

To Mr. and Mrs. Moore he said:

"Your daughter has received a severe nervous shock. The thunder-bolt which struck the tree in the yard, affected her. It is often the case that persons out of the path of the electric fluid receive a shock, and I should say that there was considerable previous mental excitement."

At this last remark Mr. Moore gave a little start of surprise and alarm; however, he calmed himself as the doctor went on: "Probably it was occasioned by fear of the storm. I judge your daughter to be of a highly excitable temperament, and counsel you to avoid all exciting topics, and keep her as quiet as possible, but of course in a quiet home like this there is little occasion for giving words of caution about excitement. Margaret is fortunate in having a mother's tender care; that is what she needs more than anything else. I will look in occasionally, though, as I have suggested, rest and quiet will do more for her than medicine."

Whether these severe thrusts were given consciously or not, Mrs. Moore could not determine, though in her peculiar state of mind she was inclined to think that his remarks had double meaning, and were intended, too, as a rebuke. The truth, however, was, that Dr. Perkins was a comparatively new-comer, and was quite unacquainted with the previous history of his patient's family; but, all the same, the thrust struck home, and had a sharp edge.

The kitchen was very quiet that morning. Mrs. Moore went swiftly but quietly about the work. The boys were hushed; and stepping softly, tried to help, but when the school-bell rang they were glad to escape from the "gloomy old house."

"Tender care!" Mrs. Moore repeated when she was left alone. "I can't be a hypocrite!" Did you ever notice how often people make that statement as an excuse for not doing their duty? "I can't pretend to love the little minx when I sometimes almost hate her! I can and will do my duty towards my husband's children. But as for loving any of them, that is out of the question. They have not treated me in a way to win love. I can get along with the boys, but Margaret! If her father could afford it, I would persuade him to send her away to school. But I know what he would say: that our schools here are first-class, and that home is the proper place for a young girl. What a perfect whirlwind she is! Who would have dreamed it! A regular tornado when her temper is up. I do not know but she will be too much for me. It would be rather humiliating not to be able to manage a child like that, when I ranked among the first as to discipline when I taught in the district schools. Ten o'clock! I must go now and give her the beef tea the doctor ordered. I suppose I might as well make up my mind to wear myself out for them. Certainly I will never shirk my duty."

Mrs. Moore carefully prepared the prescribed nourishment.

Taking from the top shelf of the china closet a dainty china cup, and from a drawer below a solid silver spoon which had belonged to Margaret's mother, she was about to go up-stairs when Weston appeared, having returned for a forgotten school-book.

"Here!" he said, "let me take that up." Relinquishing the tray, she said, "Now, take care! Don't break that cup!"

"Bother!" exclaimed West as the door closed behind him. "Does she think a fellow can't do anything right? I suppose she imagines I'll smash it purposely! She must have a remarkably good opinion of me. If she would let us use the front stairs instead of this old steep, narrow, crooked ladder way, there would be less danger for necks as well as cups."

Meantime Margaret had been lying in a sort of dreamy tranquility, perhaps induced in part by the doctor's potion. Too weak to think much, she was only dimly conscious that there were dishes to wash; and wondered a little if "she" would not rather wash them herself, than to have her, Margaret, around in her way? She remembered, with a nervous shudder, the last time she washed the dishes, and wondered what became of that bread; it all seemed so long ago! Was it only yesterday? Then came the memory of the storm, and she recalled her father's face as the lightning flashes revealed its sadness; poor father! She opened her eyes and let them rest upon the portrait of her own mother which hung at the foot of her bed. For the first time in her life that face seemed to wear a look of reproof. "She looks just as if I had been very wicked I" thought the child. "But, O, mother I you cannot know what a hard time your Margaret is having with her! She doesn't love me one bit!" Then it seemed to Margaret as though the lips moved and whispered, "But for your father's sake, can't you be patient?"

"I will try," she said aloud, as if answering a spoken message. Did someone whisper that motto, "For Jesus' sake?" Something like peace came into the child's heart; the unrest and anger, the rebellion and wilfulness of the last few months seemed about to give way to better feelings; a ray of hope had entered into one of the almost despairing hearts of that apparently ill-assorted family. And soothed and quieted, the child fell into a light slumber, broken by West's entrance with the tray. Margaret roused herself to take the refreshment.

"Are you lonesome?" asked West, by way of entertaining the invalid.

"Not very; I've been thinking!"

"Whew! That's new business, isn't it?" Margaret smiled faintly. "West, suppose I had died last night; do you suppose she would have cared?"

"O, Mag! don't talk of that."

"But I might have died; people do: and I wouldn't want to die and have folks glad I was out of the way. I've been an awful trouble; and made father unhappy; I mean to turn over a new leaf; when I get downstairs I mean to be very patient and good to her. Of course I don't love her, and I don't suppose I ever shall, but while I am a little girl I will mind her, and be pleasant, all the time."

"Mag, you can't do it!"

"Yes, I think I can; I know I have an awful temper, but people do get good, sometimes. One day Miss Barrett said that— Say, West, don't you wish we were all Christians? "

The conversation was becoming too serious for Weston, so he answered, "See here! the doctor said you mustn't talk. Just take this last spoonful and I'll go. I declare, I almost forgot that I was in a hurry."

Margaret obediently drained the cup, saying as she lay back upon her pillow:

"Wasn't it nice of her to send it in that cup? And one of mother's spoons, too!"

"O well," said West, "I suppose she was afraid you would bite one of hers, so she sent this instead!" and thus Margaret's softened feelings had a bitter turn given to them.

"What did she say?" asked Mrs. Moore as Weston re-appeared below stairs.

"Nothing to tell of," said West carelessly, as he went out the door.

"Nothing to tell of!" repeated the poor woman; "just as I supposed, they say things when they are together that would not do to tell of. I know they hate me; but I am determined to do my duty." And Mrs. Moore set her lips more firmly, and worked with feverish haste.

Little did Weston think that by his careless reply he had widened the river that already flowed between this mother and daughter.

He did not think Margaret's remark about the cup and spoon worth repeating, and never dreamed that just that little sentence would have helped to bridge the chasm, nor did he mistrust how his own words could be misconstrued. He had not meant to convey the thought that the conversation had been private, but that it had been insignificant, so lightly did he look upon Margaret's repentance and resolutions of amendment; surely the way was being ill prepared for Margaret's unaccustomed feet! Must the child make a path for herself, climbing the mountains of difficulty? Will she lose herself in the darkness which will sometimes surround her, or because of the crookedness of the pathway? Will she be dismayed and discouraged because of the heights to be surmounted? Yet Margaret seemed to be reaching out for the Hand that can make straight the crooked places. Oh! if only she would rest upon One who has the power to make even the mountain become as a plain!

Mrs. Moore stopped in the midst of her preparations for dinner, and, leaning against the kitchen table, read a note which a boy bad just left at the door.

It was from her sister, and ran thus:

DEAR SOPHIA:

Henry has just sent up word that in consequence of some break of the machinery he will have the rest of the day off. He will come up with the carriage, in about an hour, and take us out to mother's for the afternoon. I suppose you can lock up, or tie up, those young animals of yours so that they will keep out of mischief while you are away. If it were not for yesterday's performance I would suggest that we take Margaret along, but I presume you will enjoy the afternoon better without her; be sure you are ready.

In haste, Emma.

Out to the old home! It had been such a long time since she had been there! She was actually pining for a sight of the home faces. It seemed as though a draught from the spring under the hill would cool her fevered brain; and as if to rest in the old arm-chair would calm her troubled heart. Mrs. Moore was not a woman of much sentiment or imagination, yet as she stood there twisting the note in her fingers, she seemed to catch the odor of the white lilies that bordered the garden path, and hear the hum of the bees about the hives in the orchard. She could see mother bringing out the old-fashioned gold-band china, in honor of their coming, and could guess at the list of good things with which the supper-table would be spread. O yes! it would be delightful if only she could go: but it was out of the question, of course. Such things were not for her nowadays. Stern duty stood in the way. If Margaret were well — but, even then, she was not sure that she could go. According to late developments the children could not get along peaceably even when she was in the next room. Emma and Henry would be disappointed, but that could not be helped.

She walked over to the stove and threw the note into the fire, saying as she did so, "Now if only they would come and go before Thomas comes home, he need know nothing about it."

You see this woman was capable of making a sacrifice for the sake of what she considered her duty, without making a fuss about it, or parading the fact. Some of us are not equal to that! But she failed, in that she lost her serenity of manner and gave quick impatient replies; and, when John upset a glass of milk at the dinner-table she sent him away, his dinner unfinished. Then, when West, very unwisely considering the circumstances, remarked that he "hated baker's bread," she said "that both he and his mater deserved to have only baker's fare, and for all effort she would make in the future they might eat it," adding, "I do not consider it my duty to make bread to throw away!"

Upon this West followed his brother, leaving his plate uncleared. Forgetting Margaret and the quiet enjoined, he banged the door as he went out, causing his father to look up in troubled surprise; it was such an uncommon thing for Weston to be out of temper. He did not come home as usual at four o'clock; neither did he appear at tea-time; and at nine o'clock his father was asking, not for the first time,

"Where can the boy be?"

CHAPTER 4: A TRIP WEST

WHEN Weston banged the door as he left the dining-room, he had no idea what he was going to do. He only knew he was tired of "that woman," and wanted to get away from her as fast as possible. As he was walking down a narrow street, he met one of his school-friends, Rob Stewart.

"What's the matter?" asked Rob, seeing his friend's face had lost its usual cheerful appearance. "Have you been eating vinegar?"

"No," said Weston, "but I've been eating some bread just as sour, and she is just — " Here he paused, perhaps for lack of a word, and perhaps because he realized that he was talking to a mere acquaintance of his father's wife.

"I know," said Rob sympathetically, "but she can't be worse than my aunt. She won't let me do a thing, and keeps scolding me all the time. But I've got a plan."

"What?" asked Weston.

"I've just been reading a book Tom Morton lent me, called 'The Step-son's Revenge,' and it's about a boy that had a horrid step-mother, you know, just like — all of 'em, and he ran away, and sailed around Cape Horn to California, through lots of dangers, and all that, and then he turned miner, and got — oh! ever so rich; and came back, and lived in a magnificent house, with a carriage and horses, and everything, and wouldn't have a thing to do with his step-mother, and she died, bemoaning her wicked life. Wasn't that fine?"

"Very," said West briefly, evidently not seeing quite so much felicity in the career of the heroic step-son as did his friend.

"Now what do you think of it?" continued Rob. "Think of it?"

"Yes; of running away and getting rich, and coming back, and — well, we, I guess," — with philanthropy beautiful to behold, — "would support our step-mothers and aunts."

"I think," said Weston, "that it wouldn't work at all."

Rob's face fell. "Why not?"

"Well, we might not get rich, and we might get kicked and cuffed more than your hero, and it wouldn't do for me, because father and Sis would feel bad, and I wouldn't like to disappoint them." Weston remembered his sister's words that morning, and felt that perhaps he ought to make it a little easier for her to carry out her new resolves.

"Well," said Rob, "if you won't do that, what do you say to just going somewhere for a day or two, and scaring them a little, so they'd treat us better when we came back?"

Weston hesitated. But his adventurous, fun-loving nature, with his dislike of his step-mother, conquered. "Yes, he said, "that might do."

"Then," said Rob, "let's go down the canal to the fair."

"The fair" was that of the county, and was held in a field used for games, races, circuses, and other purposes, some distance down the canal which passed through the boys' home.

"Have you any money?" asked Rob. "Between one and two dollars," said Weston. "Well, I have a little too. You get yours, and I'll get mine, and we'll walk down to the lock, so that nobody here will see us go," replied his companion.

It was with some difficulty, however, that Weston visited his room without being observed, procuring the money, and a few small articles he wanted. As he tiptoed noiselessly past his sister's room, he felt almost sorry he was going away, even for so short a time, but as he heard his step-mother's voice in the kitchen, his dislike for her again urged him onward.

He found Rob waiting at a corner they had decided upon, and together they walked through the woods for three quarters of a mile, coming around the opposite side of the lock, so that it would appear as if they came from the country. Very soon the noisy shouts of the driver were heard, and the dilapidated-looking horses were seen dragging along the tow-path. The boys turned to speak to the driver. His clothes were very dirty; his face and hands were in the same condition. His dirty yellow hair was long, and appeared to have been combed, if ever, at some time so far back as to be recorded in ancient history. His hat was of felt — that is, what there was left of it; for a ragged strip of that material, with no brim, was all there was on his head. He stared at the boys as if they were cariosities in a muse am. Awed by their appearance, he was prevailed upon to get the boat where they could speak to the captain, and to call his attention to them.

"What d'ye want?" asked that individual. "You young scoundrel, why don't you mind your business!"

This last remark was not addressed to the young strangers, but to the aforesaid driver of the team, who, turning away, and closing his mouth, which had been wide open as he gazed at the boys, proceeded to get the fresh horses in waiting for him.

"We want to ride down to the fair," said Rob. "How much would you charge us?" The captain meditated. The canal was only used as a means of locomotion for goods which it was not necessary to hurry, and therefore he had few passengers, though before the railroad had invaded that county, there were passenger boats also.

"I reckon," he remarked, finally, "about two dollars apiece." He evidently thought, from the appearance of the boys, that they had plenty of money, and would know no better than to waste it in this way.

"Oh!" said Weston, "we haven't that much to spare. Have we, Rob?"

"No, sir," said Rob. "Can't we work some for you, and pay our way so?"

"Wall, dunno but you might," said the captain. "One of you could drive, and the other pile up some old boxes below. I've got somethin' for Tim to do there too, so he could be company for one of you," and the speaker laughed grimly, as the difference between "Tim" and the boys before him struck his mind as rather ludicrous.

The boys were not pleased with this proposition, but did not want to turn back, having come so far, and therefore consented, and went around to the other side of the lock till the boat should arrive there.

"You," said the old man to Weston, "can get on that there horse, and take this whip, and drive. And you," turning to Rob, "can come below and I'll show you what to do."

Weston hesitated. "That there horse" looked savage to him; he was as unused to horses as he was to walking far, and the whole situation was unattractive. But he took the whip, and with some difficulty got on the animal.

"You can't stay there long," said the captain. "Pretty soon you'll have to walk. But seeing you've been walking, and look kind of tuckered out, you can ride a piece."

Weston did not tell the old captain that he would have much preferred walking, but thanked him for his intended kindness, and taking the reins, said, "Get app!"

The captain roared, whether in rage or amusement, Weston felt in doubt. "You can't start the animal without the whip. Lick him, boy!" So the boy applied the whip, but so much more gently than the horse had ever felt before, since the days of his youth, that he took about three steps, and stopped again. Weston began to feel that he was not a success on the tow-path, and applied the lash a little harder, being partially successful, for he persuaded the creature to move, and lead his companions; yet at a pace which seemed to the inexperienced driver exceedingly slow.

It was not long before the captain called to him to get off and walk, and as he dismounted he wondered why he might not as well have walked to the fair in the first place. It was not such a long distance, and though it would have seemed so to him — for he was unused to it — he certainly couldn't call this riding.

The summer day seemed to grow warmer and warmer, the flies and gnats swarmed thicker about the poor driver of the team, and the tow-path stretching away in the distance, seemed a path of misery to him.

The tears came into his eyes, and one or two dropped into the dust, at the thought of home, his father, and his sister. He was sorry he had started, but it would certainly seem cowardly to turn back now. Besides, he was too tired to return — or to walk on, for that matter.

You may imagine he was very glad to see Rob appear on the deck of the canal-boat, and he called out to ask him to change places awhile. Rob explained that he should be glad to do so, as it was very unpleasant "below," but Weston thought it could be no more disagreeable than the place and position he then occupied. So with some difficulty the change was made, and Weston proceeded to split apart, and pile in a corner, some old boards and boxes which the captain furnished (apparently for the purpose of giving his victims something to do) from every nook and corner of the boat; sometimes from the most unexpected places. The nails the boy drew from the boards he was to straighten and sort. This was not very unpleasant work, but the air was so stifling in the dark region known as "below," and filled with such obnoxious odors, that Weston almost thought he should smother. But he was thankful for anything which would keep him from driving those slow and tail-whirling horses, and from the hot sun and flying insects outside, though many of these latter found the way "below" themselves.

At last the boy finished the work which he thought at first would never come to an end, and climbing up on deck, lay down in a shady spot, with his head on a coil of rope, and soon was fast asleep. Rob, seeing him, envied him, but was too kind-hearted to disturb him, and whipped the horses harder than the sleeper had done. The captain liked him better, therefore. He — the captain — also saw the sleeping boy, but said, "He ain't used to it—he ain't, and it's right hard on him." Before long he called Rob in, and sent Tim out to drive, who whipped the horses harder than either of his predecessors had done.

So the afternoon wore on, and the clock in the four-by-six cabin ticked on and on, and the sun set lower and lower, and the horses dragged along slower and slower, and the gnats sang softer and softer, and the mosquitoes sang louder and louder, and bit deeper and deeper, and the captain smoked his pipe with less and less energy, and the dog and the cat who resided on the canal-boat slept sounder and sounder, and all five, the captain, Weston, Rob, the dog, and the cat, snored louder and louder, till —

"Whoa!" roared Tim, who had awakened from a slight doze on the horse's back (to which he bad privately jumped when the captain went to sleep) to find the boat opposite the fair grounds. So the captain awakened, and in turn awakened his passengers, and stepped on the dog's tail, and he awakened to give such a bark as awakened the cat. The party gazed at the tents and buildings of the "Shelby County Fair." The boys bade good evening to the captain, Tim, the dog, and the cat, and went up the hill to the gate.

"Now what are we going to do?" asked Weston.

"That's the question," said Rob.

"Maybe," said Weston, "we could find someplace where they keep the horses during the day."

"The boy, in 'The Step-son's Revenge,' went out in the woods and spent the night in a hollow tree," said Rob, rather mournful at having a less adventurous career, "but I suppose we shall have to put up with the horse stalls." "What are we going to do for supper?"

"We can get that at the lunch counter just outside here."

The boys procured a frugal meal at the said counter, and then examined the stalls for the horses and wagons, finally selecting as beds two wide shelves above the mangers, intended for piling hay to be used for the horses.

"They're worse than the upper berths in a steamer or a Pullman sleeper. We must look out that we don't fall off."

"The boards at the edge will keep us from that," said West, "and now I move we go to bed. At least, I'm going to."

"Agreed!" said Rob. And they climbed up, hung their hats on nails, took off their shoes, and turned over and went to sleep.

Weston awoke in the middle of the night. The moon was shining down into his stall, and lighting up the world outside with a light which seemed ghostly, and made the tall trees look like giants, stretching out their long arms to catch the unwary passer-by. It was certainly very lonely. Weston reflected, and came to the conclusion that he should feel a good deal happier on his bed at home, than in a stall on a fair-ground. He thought of how his father must be troubled about him, and how Margaret would feel. He had always been very fond of "Sis," despite his propensity for teasing her.

"I shall go home to-morrow, as sure as I live," thought he, "and I'll never run away again, if it is only for a day."

Then he turned over once more, and fell into a sound sleep. The moon and stars shone brightly and clearly down upon him, as if they would help and protect him, or rather, as if they would tell him of the great Helper and Protector who guided them and him, and who loved him, and asked for his love. And the stars and the moon told him a great truth, which in after years he came to realize.

In the morning the boys got another not very hearty meal at the lunch counter, then wandered through the fair-grounds until they were tired.

"Come over in the woods here and have some fun," said Rob.

Weston wanted to say that he preferred to go home, at once, but he thought it would appear cowardly to be in such a hurry, so he walked along with Rob. The woods were quite thick, and a good many times the boys found branches suitable for canes, and deserted them for better ones. Finally, however, two good stout canes were selected, and the travellers moved on, swinging and twirling them as they walked, scaring the wild birds from their nests.

"West," said Rob suddenly, "shall we make for a railroad, and go West, or what?"

"Go home," said West, shortly. "I'm tired of running away, and I should think you'd be. I'm sorry we ever begun this business."

"O well," said Rob, "it hasn't been very pleasant so far, but in 'The Step-son's Revenge' —"

"If you please," said West suddenly, and he turned entirely around and faced his companion, "I'd like to hear no more of 'The Step-son's Revenge.' In my opinion, the step-son generally has the worst of the revenge! And as for the book, I don't believe it was worth reading." Rob was silenced by this outburst, and much surprised at hearing it from West. I do not fully commend that person's way of stating the case, but I am inclined to think his philosophy was pretty correct, and his opinion of the book in question coincides with mine.

"Very well," said Rob coolly, after he had recovered from his surprise. "If you are so anxious to go home, I'm willing."

In after years he was heard to say that he was rather more willing to go home than he expressed at the time, but of course it could not be expected that he should so suddenly change his views on any subject, so he merely acquiesced in his companion's desires.

He and Weston agreed to walk back, and soon they came to a road through the woods which Rob said led to their home. They had walked but a short distance, before they came to a dilapidated bridge of logs, over what was probably a brook in the spring or fall, but what was then merely a stony channel. Rob was just about to step down to get a curious-looking stone he saw, when he heard an exclamation from Weston, which made him turn around.

West had stepped close to the edge of the bridge, when the end of one of the logs had slipped, and he fell down between it and another.

Rob hurried over, and offered his help, and West succeeded, apparently with much pain, in getting on the bridge. But as he tried to rise, he said, with a groan:

"I can't do it, Rob. I've hurt my leg. I'm sure I don't know what we shall do!"

CHAPTER 5: A BLACK FRIDAY

WESTON had not all the troubles to bear. His father paced the floor far into the night thinking sad thoughts. Not that he was worried lest Weston was not safe; he supposed him to have stayed with some of his friends over night because he was angry with his stepmother and wished to spite her. He had never gone away without permission before, and it was this that worried his father. Had he made a great mistake in marrying again? He had thought he was doing the best thing he could do for his children in giving them a mother, and they all hated her, and the house was made a perfect bedlam. What was he to do? Life must not go on in this way, his children at war with his wife. Weston had gone away in a fit of anger and stayed overnight without permission. It was very evident that something must be done. Weston most be punished. It would not do to have the children rising up in rebellion.

But the father's heart ached for his boy even while he acknowledged that he had done very wrong. He half-hoped that Weston would come back late after they were all asleep and steal up to his room, and so he stayed up half the night pacing the floor and waiting for his son, but no son came. In the morning he went to his business with a haggard face and a heavy heart. The night of watching had brought no solution to the problem of how to harmonize his ill-assorted family. Johnnie reported at noon that Weston was not at school, and the lines of care on the father's face deepened. He told Johnnie to find out if his brother had been with any of the boys over night, but he came back to tea with no intelligence of the missing boy.

Mrs. Moore set her lips firmly when she heard this; her eyes snapped and her cheeks were very red, —

"Mr. Moore, I think that boy ought to be severely punished when he does come back."

Before Mr. Moore had time to answer this, Johnnie burst out with,

— "You're a mean old thing to talk about punishing my brother when mebbe he's dead or drowned or something, and you don't care a bit, and he'd never a'gone away at all if you hadn't scolded him all the time, and Rob Stewart has gone too, and they're afraid he's drowned, and if anything happens to West you'll be a murderer!"

These last words were almost a shriek. His eyes flashed and his face was crimson. He stood up as he spoke, brandishing his fork in the air and looking straight at his step-mother. So excited was he that it would have been difficult to stop him if they had tried; he only stopped now for want of breath.

Mr. Moore's face was white and his voice stern as he said, "John, go up to your room immediately, and do not come down again until you are ready to ask your mother's forgiveness for the wicked way in which you have spoken to her."

He was about to reply that she was not his mother at all, but a glance at his father's face frightened him and he left the room as he was told. He had never heard his father speak in such a stern tone before.

"I hope you see how your children treat me. That is a common specimen of what I have to bear from them almost every hour in the day. I'm sure I can't see why they have taken such a dislike to me; I've tried to do everything for them."

Mrs. Moore did not usually complain to her husband about the children, but to-night she was very tired, and probably her conscience troubled her a little as to whether she had treated the boys quite right, after all, although she wasn't aware of it. Indeed, I think if you had suggested such an idea to her she would immediately have asserted, and thought she was honest too, that she had done all for those children that anyone could have done. But I think she would not have spoken so even this time, if she had looked at her husband's face first.

She received no reply. Mr. Moore left his supper untasted, took his hat, and left the house. He came back no more that night. Instead he began a weary, fruitless search for his boy, following up this and that clue, but a second morning dawned with no trace of Weston, and the worn-out father came home to swallow a cup of coffee and start out on his search again. He was now thoroughly alarmed, and could scarcely stop to eat. More from habit than because he cared to have his morning mail, he stepped into the post-office as he passed. There were several business letters, which he read hastily and thrust into his pocket. Two letters were left, the upper one a small, dirty, much-crumpled yellow envelope, addressed in a cramped hand, misspelled, and with no capital letters where they should be. The postmark was of a town a few miles away. His first inclination was to put it in his pocket unopened, but he finally tore it open.

It ran as follows:

mister moReyooR boy is heeR he fel in the Rayveen I founde himan
tuk him home, i liv on hukeR Rode ennybudy wil tel yoo wer tiz yoor
Survent job atkinS

It took Mr. Moore some minutes to make out this queerly written
letter, and when he understood it he pulled out his watch and saw that
the train going East left in half an hour. There was not a moment to be
lost. The other letter went into his pocket without so much as a
thought, and he strode toward home. He told his wife that Weston was
in Salemville somewhere, hurt, or sick, how badly he did not know, and
threw the letter down upon the table for her to read. Mrs. Moore put
together things for him which she thought might be useful in sickness,
and she knew just what was necessary in such emergencies as this.
While she gathered and packed bandages, arnica, a sheet, a blanket, and
many other little things that might be a great comfort, and which many
another woman would not have been able to think of in such a hurry,
much less get together,— Mr. Moore questioned her about Johnnie.

"I took him up some breakfast this morning, but he said nothing to
me. He would not open the door, so I put the tray down on the floor.
I'm sure I don't know what to do with him, but I guess he'll soon get
tired of staying in the house."

Mr. Moore would have gone himself to talk with Johnnie about his
misconduct, but the whistle of the incoming train warned him that he
had no time to spare, and catching up his satchel he started, telling his
wife as he closed the front door that he did not know when he would
be back, or what he would do; he would let her know as soon as
possible. He manage to step on the train just as it was moving out of
the depot.

It seemed to Mr. Moore that the train moved very slowly, and
stopped an unnecessary number of times on the way to Salemville, but
after many haltings they reached that village. The station, which was
not much more than a box set up on end, was a forlorn place indeed.

Mr. Moore inquired of the sad-looking man in the ticket-office
where Mr. Atkins lived, but he answered that he didn't know any one,
he had only just come there to live, and had never even heard of
Hooker road.

The next individual he accosted was a barefoot boy with a rimless
hat, a very dirty gingham shirt, and tattered trousers held up by one
suspender.

"I never heerd o' no Mr. Atkins in this yer town," was the
encouraging reply. Mr. Moore went on up the street toward a small
grocery store, the steps of which held a few forlorn specimens of men
— poor, run-down creatures with nothing to do but hold up the door
of the grocery and smoke. They all looked puzzled when asked if they

knew where Mr. Atkins of Hooker road lived, until one said, —"Yeh don't mean ole Job, do yeh?"

"Why, yes," Mr. Moore said, "that is his name, — Job Atkins."

"Wal, he lives out 'bout tew mile. You go up that there road yonder till you come to the ole red schoolhouse, an' turn to your right, an' the first house on the left-hand side is his'n." Mr. Moore found there was no way but to walk the two miles, so he started. As he passed the red schoolhouse with its monotonous hum of voices, he saw the restless little feet hanging from the high benches, and it reminded him of the days when he used to go to an old red schoolhouse and swing his feet from a high bench and eat his dinner from a tin pail. He sighed, and half-wished he were back in those old days with his mother to put up nice lunches of apple-pie and doughnuts for him. He noticed the white weary face of the teacher through the open door, and thought that this world was full of trouble, — everyone had plenty of it; that teacher had a good deal by the looks of her face, and the station-master looked sad too, and -he was sure he had more than his full share of it. Poor man! he had no Refuge to which to fly in trouble. He had never placed his confidence in the Heavenly Father. If he had only been accustomed to go with all his cares and troubles to Him who careth for us all! But instead he went on drearily thinking how very heavy his burdens were, and that he must bear them all alone.

The first house on the left-hand side proved to be a little weather-beaten, one-story shanty, the outside being covered entirely with shingles. The ground around was overgrown with weeds and partially covered with last year's cornstalks.

Mr. Moore had no need to open the gate, for it had been off the hinges for a long while. Indeed the fence itself was broken down in many places. The whole place wore an air of dejection, as though all its friends were dead and gone long ago and it would like to be gone too.

One wild white morning-glory, struggling to live by the pathway, smiled up at him as if to cheer and tell him of the pitying love of his Heavenly Father.

But Mr. Moore passed the flower without even a glance. His sharp rap at the door brought a long lank woman, broom in hand. Her dress was scant and dirty, and her coarse gray hair was gathered into a hard knot at the back of her head. She stood leaning on her broom surveying the stranger while he inquired if Mr. Atkins lived here, and whether this was where his boy was.

"Yas, he is," replied Mrs. Job, "an' a powerful lot o' trouble he's ben to us tew. Job, he's so soft-hearted. He's allus bringin' some ole sick cat or lame dog fer me tew take care of." With these sympathizing remarks Mr. Moore was ushered into the Atkins domain. There on an old home-made lounge, his head perilously near the hot stove, the bright sunlight glaring full in his eyes, lay his eldest son.

He certainly did not look much as though he were enjoying himself. The room was small and low and dirty-looking, and there were suggestions in the air of the departed breakfast — pork mingled with onions.

Mrs. Job continued her interrupted sweeping the minute the door was closed, and raised such a dust that father and son were both set to coughing. Mr. Moore mildly suggested that she suspend operations for a season, but the indignant woman declared that she couldn't be interrupted in her work "for no one," and swept on the harder.

The dust and heat and odors were unbearable, and Mr. Moore stepped to the door and threw it wide open before he attempted to say a word to his son. This was no time to reprimand him, and if it had been he would not have chosen to do it before this woman, so he merely questioned him about his fall, and how badly he was hurt. He found that his back gave him a great deal of pain, and that he was unable to move his ankle, so great was the pain. Nothing had been done for him by the ignorant old couple, so that his ankle was very badly swollen. As his father knew nothing whatever about sickness he thought it best to go back to the village for a physician, and also for a carriage in which to remove Weston, for he never would get well in such a place.

While Mr. Moore was tramping back and forth from Job Atkins' house to the village of Salemville, Mrs. Moore had quite as much on her hands as he.

Left alone in the midst of a room all confusion she stood still a moment to take breath after her rush. The clothes-press door stood open and a pile of blankets had slipped to the floor in the hurried pulling of them about. A soiled collar lay on a chair, a coat on the bed, the bureau drawers all stood open.

Mrs. Moore was not one to stand looking long in such a state of things, and she presently set to work with energy to right them.

In the course of clearing up she noticed the forgotten letter and took it from the little table where her husband had thrown it in his haste. She thought it strange that it was not opened, but her well-regulated mind at once came to the truth of the matter, and decided that the wrong letter had been taken out of his pocket. She studied the postmark for some time, but it gave her no help. Her husband's letters were never kept secret from her, so she went to the bureau, took the scissors from their place, and carefully cut the end of the envelope open. She never by any means tore open an envelope.

Perhaps you can imagine her dismay when she read that letter. It began, —

My DEAR NEPHEW:

At last I am coming to make you a short visit. I have made up my mind that I would like to finish my days at the old homestead, so I have written to my agent to have it put in order at once. He tells me that it will be some time before it will be ready, so as I am prepared to start I shall accept your many kind invitations to visit you.

I shall leave here on Wednesday of next week, arriving there as nearly as I can make out about three o'clock Friday afternoon. You needn't bother to meet me at the depot, as it is uncertain when I shall get there, and I can take a carriage right to the door.

If it is not convenient for me to come now, let me know immediately. I take the liberty of announcing myself thus suddenly because you have so many times urged me to come. Give my love to your wife and children. I hope soon to see them all and get well acquainted with them.

Your most affectionate aunt,
CORNELIA MERWIN.

Mrs. Moore's face had darkened as she read the letter, but when she glanced a second time at the date and saw that the letter had been delayed for more than a week, and that this was the Friday on which she might be supposed to arrive, she actually looked troubled.

Company coming at three o'clock, Margaret sick, the house in disorder, Mr. Moore away attending to his runaway son, who for aught she knew might be brought home in a few hours more dead than alive, Johnnie shut up in his room on a course of bread and water — all these things passed through Mrs. Moore's mind like a flash, and then she looked at the clock. Ten o'clock! The house must be swept from top to bottom, the spare room put in immaculate order, biscuits baked, and at least two kinds of cake; all this to be done before three o'clock. Her house had been swept carefully only two days before, but she was an inveterate sweeper, and would sweep and sweep whether there was a speck of dust to be found or not. There was a very nice sponge cake in the house, and the bread was fresh, why could she not be satisfied? But she wasn't.

Mrs. Merwin was Mr. Moore's aunt whom he had not seen in several years. Mrs. Moore had heard her husband speak of her many times in the highest terms. All she knew about her was, that she was very rich. Now to be very rich was in her eyes to be very particular, proud and hateful. It was therefore not to be supposed that she would have looked forward to her visit with pleasure under any circumstances.

And so Mr. Moore walked to Salemville; and Weston lay still and bore his pain and discomfort as well as he could, and thought how hard the way of transgressors was; and Margaret lay and moaned as the steady sound of the on-coming broom drew nearer, feeling that she should positively go crazy if it did not stop soon; and Johnnie stood by his window and sulked, and thought hard thoughts about that tired woman down-stairs, and the clock fairly galloped, and the Western train drew nearer and nearer, and still Mrs. Moore swept and swept.

CHAPTER 6: THE RETURN JOURNEY

IT was no easy matter to find a comfortable carriage in which to remove the lame boy from that dilapidated hat to the box of a station. What was to be done? The sad, tired father could learn of no hack or spring-wagon within many miles. While standing near the comer grocery holding a council with the small crowd gathered around the door, he heard the crack of a whip, and a "Gee up!" from the driver of a pair of ancient oxen.

Said oxen were drawing a queer-looking old cart which held two or three bags of apples resting on a goodly pile of clean oat straw. I would not say that there were not thistles and briers mingled with the straw, but the whole thing presented the first hopeful prospect he had seen for the transportation of his homesick son.

It stood to reason that one who would be willing to take a long drive for the sake of selling a few apples, could be induced to go a little farther, for the sake of the price of said apples, added to what he could get for them.

As for expense, it began to seem to this father that, poor as he was, he was ready to give almost any price for the sake of getting his suffering boy safely to the cars.

The driver was not given time to dismount from the bundle of hay on which he was perched, before the request was made that he would drive to Mrs. Joseph Atkins' and bring a lame boy to the station.

The team was a slow one, and was in that particular exactly suited to its owner. To drive to "town," as that bit of a place with its one store, and blacksmith's shop, and half-dozen houses was called, was an event that took at least a week for Zabed Williams to plan for. To come from his hiding-place on the other side of the mountain, with such climbing and descending and fording as the intervening space required, was a task, which, however much enjoyed by Uncle Zab, was no easy experience to his "steers," as he persisted in calling his team, though he had driven them when he was a very much younger man than he could now be called.

So, in view of the distance which his team had come, and the pleasing prospect of a smoke and a chat with those benevolently inclined friends of his who so patiently helped to hold up the door-posts of the store and post-office (two in one), and to hold down the floor of the piazza, it was not strange that much time was consumed and much persuasion was found to be necessary before a bargain could be made.

"You see, stranger," he began, after getting his old clay pipe well fired up, — and it took almost as much time as it does to stoke the furnace of an ocean steamer,—"them steers of mine has had a right smart tramp this morning, and a pretty good load for boys, as them is, and a 'merciful man is merciful to his beast,' or ought to be, that's my way of lookin' at it."

"But, Mr. Williams, think of the trouble I'm in; if I could carry my boy to the cars, or if I could get a team anywhere else before train time, I would not trouble you; but as it is — come now, put yourself in my place and do as you would be done by. I'm not afraid to leave it to your heart to decide the question. Of course I don't expect you to go so far out of your way, nor take your valuable time without paying for it. I'll pay whatever you ask, if you'll get us to the station in time for the next train."

Love in the father's heart, and the vivid picture in his mind of what his boy must be enduring on that old lounge in a dirty, smoky, steaming kitchen, made him forget alike his own poverty and the disobedience which had been the cause of all the trouble, and plead most skilfully.

It must be, he thought, that old Zabed, ugly as he looked, had a heart. Perhaps it is the heart which moves the head. It is the heart which moves the heart, anyway; if you do not believe it, try the experiment.

Old Zab was quiet and thoughtful; he had been made to sit in judgment on himself, and little as he liked to do any more journeying, he did not wish to bring in a verdict which should read, even in his own eyes, "Heartless."

Oh! I don't say that the prospect of being liberally rewarded did not help to turn the scales in favor of the suffering boy. Suppose it did! He was a poor man; poor in a sense which you and I might find it hard to understand.

Whatever influenced him, as soon as his apples were handed over to the grocer, and his orders taken on a bit of brown wrapping paper, and he had been assured three times over that his "things" should be ready for him by the time his steers were baited, he turned their heads in the desired direction, to the father's great relief, and would have gotten under way, had not his burden-bearers seen a brook nearby, which in their younger days had often slaked their thirst; seeing it they "went for it" with such persistence that no amount of "Whoas" could stop them.

"All right, boys," said Uncle Zab at last, when he found they meant to go whether he would or not, " take in all the water you need for the trip; that's the way the old engine does, and I reckon you need it just as much. Jump on, Mr. What did you say your name was?"

"Moore, my name is; Thomas W. Moore. No, thank you, I'll just go across lots, and be ready for you when the team arrives, so that there need be no delay. I hope we can get back in time for the train."

This last was spoken anxiously, in the hope that he might possibly stimulate the old man's actions. Perhaps he did; at least, a loud crack of his whip, which to Mr. Moore looked more like an outfit for catching fish than for driving oxen, had an encouraging sound.

Meantime, it seemed to the boy, Weston, that his father had been gone almost long enough to build a railroad from the station to the hut. But his weary waiting had perhaps helped him to bear the pain of removal better than he otherwise would; at least, he realized that he was not in a condition to find fault with anyone but himself; so his father found him outwardly patient.

If his hostess was not very tender of tongue, her vigor of body came in good play in helping to carry him to the cart and "load him up," as Mr. Williams expressed it.

As to comfort, the cart, with its depth of soft straw, was paradise compared with the old lounge; the fresh air, too, had a reviving effect, and this and the hope of at last reaching his own clean room and bed, helped Weston to feel somewhat encouraged. But what a coming back it was, compared with that which he had planned!

They reached the station nearly a half-hour before the train was due, but by this time Uncle Zab had become so interested in the injured boy that he volunteered to wait, and let him rest in the cart until he could be removed to the car. On the whole, the slow-moving cart had proved to be quite an easy ambulance, and Mr. Moore's heart was full of gratitude.

"Well," he said, "we need not wait for the 'unloading,' before we settle our bill. How much do I owe you, Mr. Williams?"

Slowly the old man puffed his pipe, a dreamy, far-away look m his eyes, and for some seconds said not a word. Mr. Moore began to doubt whether his question had been heard. At last the old pipe was taken out, its owner stooped down and carefully knocked the embers and ashes from it, returned it to its place in his hatband, took another look at the boy on the straw, then turned to the father.

"I reckon I ain't done no more than I'd want done for me, s'posen my Jake had been in his fix; if I can make it all right with the steers, —

and I guess I can, — I don't see as any harm's done. I kind of think the boy has paid for it in aches, though I druv as careful as the pesky stones would let me, so we'll call it square."

Then, as Mr. Moore began a demur, "Well, if you think it ain't quite even, and you ever see my Jake, and he needs a lift, why, just you remember the steers; that's all. I dunno where that boy is, nor how he's goin' to git home." And the poor father furtively wiped away a tear with his soiled sleeve; his Jake, like Weston, had run away, and his father had not been able to go after him, nor find him.

During all these hours, Mrs. Moore had wasted not a moment in her nervous preparations for the aunt whom she expected would introduce herself before her husband could reach home with the runaway. As she flew about her house in nervous haste, having Margaret to care for, with all the rest, and deprived of even the help of naughty Johnnie, I do not know that she can be blamed for thinking her lot a hard one. But if she had heard the howl which poor Weston gave as they were lifting him to the platform of the car, I don't think she would have envied him, or his troubled father.

Weston's outcry, caused by a sudden wrench of the injured foot, of course drew on him the attention of all the passengers, much to his dismay. One of them was an elderly woman in a neat plain dress, and wearing a kind, motherly look on her quiet face. By the time Weston had been brought to the vacant place near the centre of the car, she was there, busily engaged in preparing a bed for him. Toward this, she contributed a large soft shawl, a rubber pillow, and a trim flat bundle; Mr. Moore had not turned his head in her direction until his son was made as comfortable as possible. When at last he had time to thank the stranger for her kindness, instead of doing so he stared in amazement, and then exclaimed — "Aunt Cornelia!"

The exclamation made Weston open his eyes, and he felt a little flush creeping over his face. He had heard about aunt Cornelia; what a state of things in which to meet her!

There was a little confusion, and embarrassment, not lessened by the attention and interest of the other passengers.

The truth is, Mr. Moore was not quite sure whether to be glad or sorry to find his aunt so near his home, and evidently on her way there.

His recollections of her, years ago, were pleasant ones, and her presence thus far had certainly been helpful; still he could not get rid of certain ugly pictures which imagination would force upon him. Thought outran the locomotive, and reaching home, showed him a state of things not pleasant to look upon. Some things he did not know, which only made his picture darker. He did not know that in Margaret's room a little spirit of regret and penitence had crept; nor did he know that Mrs. Moore had been informed of the coming guest and was doing her best to make ready.

What he saw, was, his daughter ill with nervous excitement, and waiting only for returning strength to exhibit still more opposition toward her step-mother; Johnnie a prisoner in his own room with a heart full of hatred toward that same step-mother; and she, tired, nervous, overanxious, and withal, perhaps just a trifle cross; certainly very unready for company; least of all for the aunt with whom he had spent his childhood.

So much Mr. Moore believed he could see as well as though he had been at home. Then that torturing "What — if" put in an appearance; what if there had been more trouble in his absence? What if Johnnie had defied his authority and tried to escape? and Margaret had attempted to interfere between him and the mother? What if he should introduce aunt Cornelia in the midst of some such scene as that! What if Mrs. Moore in her wrought-up state of mind, should say something to hurt the aunt's feelings! Or perhaps receive her so coldly that she could not help being offended!

Truly imagination can succeed in making people very miserable! Of course all these thoughts painted themselves more or less distinctly on his face; enough so to make him appear reserved, and sadly ill at ease. Altogether, the interested passengers had food enough for curious thought, and to judge by the constant attention which they gave the three, they worked over the problem industriously.

Fortunately the distance, to travel was not great, and so the time for this embarrassing state of things was short.

There was time enough, however, for Weston to have additional proof that "the way of transgressors is hard." As often as he opened his eyes and caught a glimpse of his father's troubled face, there would seem to appear before him a commandment which he had known almost since his babyhood:

"Honor thy father and thy mother, that thy days may be long on the land which the Lord thy God giveth thee."

Was it possible to get away from the thought that he had broken that commandment hundreds of times, and that his present condition was the direct result of its flagrant violation?

The pain of his strained limb and injured back, the glimpses of that sad face bending over him, the thought of all the trouble he had caused, and the haunting fear that perhaps he would never be able to walk again, made sorrow for the consequences of sin an easy matter.

He did not understand it, but this feeling lacked the first element of genuine repentance; for he was at that moment arraigning the woman whom he had been told to call "mother," as the prime cause of all his trouble.

Instead of resolving to do in the future all he could to help his father, and make home a happy place, he was strengthening his resolution to "have nothing to do with that woman if he could help it."

At last the familiar name of the home station was called, and the bustle of removal began. Some suggestions from the wise-eyed auntie made this a less painful task than the coming on board had been; as for a conveyance, the roomy omnibus was close at hand. A loud "Whoa!" from its driver was the first announcement to the Moore family that the travellers had arrived.

When Johnnie peeped from his chamber window, he saw his father in the omnibus, bending over his brother, who was stretched upon one of the seats, his head in the lap of a stranger; an old lady.

"What in the world is the matter?" said Johnnie, and, "Who can that old woman be? She is getting out, too! O dear! how I wish I could go down-stairs."

CHAPTER 7: AUNT CORNELIA

"PLAINLY dressed," Mr. Moore had called aunt Cornelia, but his wife knew at a glance that her black cashmere dress was very fine and soft, and that her bonnet, though destitute of feathers and flowers, had a certain something about it which people call "style." Then she wore gold spectacles and carried a gold watch, held herself erect, and moved with dignity. Mrs. Moore took in all these little points as a woman will, and a man does not, and at once decided that it was just as she had feared, she was an uppish, fault-finding woman who had come to their little overflowing house, and come, too, in the nick of the wrong time. She would likely set the children up to act worse than they did. She didn't look in the least like an old lady either, as her husband had said she was. If now she was only a nice old body like aunt Betsey, who would sit by the fire and do up all the mending and nurse Margaret for her. How she wished it were instead of this cityfied lady who would expect the whole house to rise up and wait on her. She shouldn't put herself out much, though.

These thoughts did not make her welcome very warm as she met aunt Cornelia in the hall.

However, that lady was so taken up contriving the easiest way for Weston to be carried in, that she had no time to think how she was received. She could not but notice, though, that her nephew's new wife was a trim tidy woman with clear dark eyes and a face that might be amiable if it were free from a worried, irritated expression. She noticed, too, that she moved about in an energetic, capable way, as if she understood the best ways of doing things. Then she did not exclaim, or pour out a storm of questions about Weston.

When the poor boy was at last established on the wide lounge in the sitting-room, it was she who brought cool water, bathed his face and head, and asked him — in a voice that was a little stiff and constrained, to be sure — if the pain was very bad.

Weston was not at all the penitent boy he should have been after all that had happened. It irritated him to be obliged to receive care from his step-mother, and so he was surly.

After Mr. Moore had brought the doctor to care for the swollen ankle, he went to the kitchen to ask his wife about John.

"He has not shown himself since you left," she said. "He has locked his door, and when I went to carry him some bread, and knocked on the door he told me to go away and mind my own business."

Now Mrs. Moore was not a hateful woman who wanted to have revenge on the boy, neither was she hard-hearted. She felt very sorry for her husband. He looked haggard and troubled, and she pitied him; but she was a truthful person and tried always to be straightforward, besides, she had good sense, and thought it was better to face the thing as it was, and not try to cover up faults to make trouble in the future, for the sake of sparing anybody's feelings.

Mr. Moore did not say anything. He went on, out into the back lot, walked straight over to the old elm tree, took out his jackknife, and, reaching up to a branch, cut a long elastic switch and trimmed it as he walked up to the house.

His wife saw him from the window and we must do her justice to say that she was sorry that such a resort had become necessary. Johnnie was a hot-headed, roguish little fellow, but he was not really bad. He had never before given her so much trouble as the other two. He had actually crept into her heart a little way. Perhaps it was because he had a round chubby face and a merry nature, and being the youngest did not rebel so often against her authority.

She went to the hall-door, thinking to intercede for the boy, but his father was already half-way up-stairs with such a look on his face as made her feel that she had better not interfere. He stopped a moment in his own room first, because he dreaded to do what he thought he must. He was a nervous, tender-hearted man, and always shrank from inflicting punishment, especially in this way. Perhaps if he had not been too much so when his boys were little fellows they would not have needed it when they grew older. He had tried other modes of punishment whenever it became necessary, but now they had failed apparently and things were in a desperate state. John must be kept from following his older brother's example at any cost, and he must have such a lesson as would prevent any more rebellion and disrespect toward his step-mother.

I should not wonder if boys sometimes think when they are punished that father is only venting his anger. Sometimes fathers may, but most of them would prefer to be scourged themselves rather than strike a blow on the shrinking forms of their dear boys, and so this father was far from being angry. He was sad and in despair. He hid his face in his hands and groaned aloud.

Johnnie in the next room had heard his father come up-stairs, but his stubborn spirit was not yet subdued. He was just then resolving that he would never ask his step-mother's pardon. He would just stay there in that room. He wouldn't eat any more bread and water either, and some day he would be dead, then his father would come in and find him still and cold. There would be a funeral and everybody would send flowers, and his father would feel dreadful bad when he saw his poor little starved boy buried in the ground. How weak and faint he felt even now. What a cruel father and wicked mother he did have to treat him so, and the tears rolled down his cheeks as he pitied himself.

Just then he heard that groan in the next room. There was a stove-pipe hole between the rooms and the sound was quite distinct. His father felt bad about something. He had noticed his face was pale when he got out of the wagon.

"He has lots of things to trouble him," thought Johnnie. "There's West been acting just awful, and maybe he's most dead. O, dear! and what if father should die? and then there wouldn't be any more father in this house."

As this idea surged over Johnnie he began to cry. That is a good sign when a boy has been naughty. As the tears rolled down his cheeks he thought what if he should go and tell his father that he would beg his step-mother's pardon. He needn't be any different to her, and he never should love her, never! But he could do so much to make his father feel better, so he rushed into the next room.

His father had thrown himself into a chair. His head was in his hands and the switch lay on the floor. Johnnie saw it the first thing. He ran across the room and did what he had not done since the day his mother died — flung himself into his father's arms and sobbed on his bosom.

"I'm good," he said, "I'll tell her."

Then his father brought his arms about him and hugged him close, half wishing he could hold the little fellow so forever and keep him safe from temptation.

"You must not say 'her,' Johnnie," he said at last, "you must say mother, and you must be a good boy or I shall go distracted with everything going wrong."

"I will," Johnnie sobbed again, ready to promise anything as he saw his father's pale troubled face and heard him sigh.

The doctor had made Weston's foot comfortable and he had fallen asleep, so aunt Cornelia asked to be taken to see Margaret.

Now she was the last person in the world that Margaret wished to see. She stood in great awe of this aunt and had meant to tell her stepmother not to let her come into her room, but she had forgotten to ask her the last time she was up-stairs.

Margaret had no reason for feeling so. It was just one of those foolish prejudices people get up sometimes for someone they have never seen. Then she had that other silly idea, that because a person has more money than some others, of course she is proud and haughty, and thinks herself better than those who have but a little, which is often very unkind and unjust.

Margaret had been nervous all day. She was improving slowly, but was just at that stage in recovery that you were, those days you felt so wretched and irritable; when you cried if anybody looked at you and you couldn't wait a minute for what you wanted. If your dear mother or sister had not given up everything else and waited on you and amused you, the days would have been forlorn enough.

Margaret had tossed restlessly about all day; her step-mother's hands had been so full that she had scarcely been in the room except to take her meals, so she had tossed about, groaned and fretted, and twisted the bed-clothes into heaps. She had wished somebody would come and tell her about Weston, but now when her step-mother and a stranger appeared at the door she resolutely turned her face to the wall, and all that aunt Cornelia could see was a tumbled bed, and the back of a brown head, tangled and curly.

"Margaret, here is your aunt Cornelia. You aren't asleep, are you?" her step-mother said.

It was a very cross face that the girl on the bed turned to the visitor. She did not attempt to make any reply to her aunt's pleasant "How do you do to-day, my dear?"

But aunt Cornelia acted just as if she had received a most polite reply.

"Sick, aren't you?" she said, "and don't want to talk. Let me sit with you a little while, dear, and you need not speak a word if you do not like."

Mrs. Moore went down to busy herself in preparation for tea, and aunt Cornelia went across the hall to her own room and took from her satchel a large gingham apron, saying as she tied it on, —

"Now, Margaret, play I am a nurse just arrived to take care of you. You are to tell me exactly what you would like done and I am to do it."

Margaret turned in surprise and looked her new aunt full in the face, for the first time. What pretty soft grey waves her hair lay in over her smooth forehead; how kind her eyes were; and her mouth was pleasant; too big, Margaret decided in that instant of survey, but so pleasant. It was smiling, and in spite of herself Margaret smiled too. It was good to see somebody who did not look worried, and whose month did not shut tight and hard.

"Now for my orders," said aunt Cornelia. "A nurse is just for

39

nothing else but to wait on her patient, you know. What have you wanted most all day?"

Margaret was an imaginative girl, and the conceit of playing nurse pleased her. She used to play all sorts of things with her own mother when she was very young. Aunt Cornelia had struck a right chord. Her lip quivered as she looked into the kind face. If she had spoken the truth she would have said she wanted somebody to love her and pet her. She did not know then that her step-mother, though she seemed cold and precise, really had a warm heart and would have loved her if she had not been so fiery and rebellious. Then things would have been different. She had not the least idea of it. How should she have, being only a foolish little girl who had not yet learned to read character.

Aunt Cornelia saw the wistful look and bent down and kissed her, murmuring, "Dear child," then she began gently to straighten and smooth the disordered bed.

"There are two flies," said Margaret, emboldened by such kindness, "that torment me so much, and the light conies in my eyes through the slats, and my face feels all prickly."

"That's right," said the sympathetic voice, "tell all your troubles."

Then aunt Cornelia moved softly about, darkening the room and arranging for a circulation of cool air. She brought water and washed her patient's face and hands, putting a few drops of some delightful fragrance from a bottle in her bag, into the water. After that, she patiently brushed the tangled locks, first getting them into smoothness and then brushing on with even, gentle strokes which was very soothing in its effect, talking meantime in low quiet tones, answering some eager questions about Weston and his accident and then drawing Margaret's mind off to other things.

"Your hair curls prettily, Margaret," she said, as she wound the glossy locks about her finger; "it is a nice simple way for young girls to wear it."

Unfortunately her step-mother had often said, "I wish you would braid up that mop of hair and get it out of your way." And Margaret had hardened her heart against her on that account. But there are two sides even to curls. Margaret sometimes loitered unnecessarily over the arrangement of her hair, and her stepmother thought it would take less time if braided.

When everything was done, she felt so quiet and refreshed that she fell into a sweet sleep, and did not wake until after tea. Just as she opened her eyes she saw aunt Cornelia coming in at the door with something for her on a tray. It was such a nice delicate little supper—a slice of brown toast, a tiny cup of hot chicken broth, and a dish of blackberries and cream. Who could not eat such a nice tea as that? Margaret felt bright after her sleep, and partly sitting up in bed really relished her supper for the first time in many days.

"Your mother is an excellent cook," said aunt Cornelia, and then she noticed that a little frown gathered on Margaret's face which she tried to straighten out at once as she answered with a sigh, "Yes, she knows how to cook" with an emphasis on the "cook" as if there were numberless things she did not know how to do.

Margaret decided after two or three days that being sick was not such, bad business if one had a kind pleasant nurse. It was so delightful to be taken care of and to have everything done for you in such a dainty manner. Aunt Cornelia had given her whole time to nursing her and the improvement had been marked. Mrs. Moore had done all she could, but there is a limit to what one pair of hands can accomplish, besides, when she was in the kitchen she could not very well be up-stairs at the same time. And when she did come she had to hurry with all speed.

Aunt Cornelia had been busily sewing some pretty sprigged cambric every spare moment since she arrived. When Margaret asked her what she was making, she answered "A wrapper," and while Margaret lay watching the needle go in and out she thought how nice it was to be rich and have every pretty thing you wanted.

The next morning after the patient and the room were made tidy, and Margaret had had a nap, aunt Cornelia drew the large old rocking chair near the bed, and brought out the pretty wrapper.

"Now, my dear," she said, "you are going to slip yourself into this wrapper and creep out on to this chair. I will draw it near the window, and you shall sit up awhile. You will like that, I am sure."

Aunt Cornelia was a tall woman and rather large, so Margaret was quite surprised that the wrapper fitted her nicely.

"Oh! how pretty," she exclaimed, "and it fits as if it had been made for me."

"And who should it have been made for, but yourself, my dear?" aunt Cornelia said as she buttoned it up, and smoothed the little frill at the neck.

Sitting by the window with the sweet morning air coming in, with the breath of honeysuckles and the song of birds, Margaret leaned far back in her chair and gazed out at the trees and sky, taking in all the sweetness and enjoying it.

"How good you are to me, aunt Cornelia," she said. "I didn't know there were any such good people in the world."

"There are more good people than anybody knows for, my dear," aunt Cornelia said, while she carried the pillows and blankets out into the next room to air.

When she had come back and seated herself at her knitting, Margaret rocked back and forth contentedly, saying, ---

"Oh! I wish I was as happy always as I am now"

"What is to hinder your being always so happy, dear?" aunt Cornelia asked.

"Why, don't you know?" Margaret said, opening her eyes wide. "You won't be here always, and she will. It's a different house since you came. I feel as if I had known you always, Auntie."

Aunt Cornelia looked at her a moment and hesitated. The fever had turned Margaret's face into a pale thin one, and her eyes were large and hollow. The good auntie's heart was full of pity, but she felt as if she must help this young girl in the best, truest way. She had good eyes for seeing all that went on about her, and she had drawn her own conclusions. She had been down-stairs as well as up, and she had marked the faithful, conscientious way in which Mrs. Moore tried to do all her duties; how she never spared herself in order to make things comfortable for the family.

"Is it so bad as that, poor child — does your mother abuse you?" she said, looking straight at Margaret.

Margaret was a truthful girl and she could not

honestly say "yes" to that, so she was silent a moment, then, in a hesitating way, said, —

"Why, no, not exactly. She isn't my mother, you know, Auntie. My own dear mamma died, and I remember her very well. She wasn't a bit like this woman."

"What does your step-mother do that you do not like?"

"She scolds me and makes me do things all the time that I hate!"

"It must be a very cross woman who scolds when one is doing the very best they know how. And that is the case with you, then, is it, Margaret?"

Aunt Cornelia's eyes were very soft, and yet when they looked straight into Margaret's, the little girl felt, without putting it into words, that they had a clear penetrating look different from some eyes, and that they saw away down into her very heart. Margaret's pale face turned pink then, and she said:

"Why, Auntie, of course I don't always do right."

"It is when you have not done right that you have trouble then, is it not? Why not do right, dear?"

Margaret was tracing the course of the vine in her wrapper with the point of a pin, her head bent low over it. She was silent again.

"Nobody does right all the time, besides, this was my home before it was hers. She isn't my mother, and she oughtn't to try and order me around. I wish she could go away," Margaret said, forgetting the good resolves she had made a few days before, and jerking out the sentences in a painful way while the tears came to her eyes.

Aunt Cornelia did not notice it, though she said, —

"Do you have very bad, uncomfortable times? Is the cooking so bad you cannot eat it? Is the whole house filthy and untidy, and your stepmother a sloven? Is that why you wish her to go?"

Margaret glanced up then. There was a twinkle in her aunt's eye and she laughed in spite of herself.

"O no! I didn't mean that at all. Everybody knows she is a great housekeeper."

"Suppose she were to go away. Could you do all the work and make the house as comfortable and nice as it is now?"

"I could learn," Margaret said, feeling that she was in a comer.

"Yes, you ought to learn by degrees, but would you be willing to leave school now and work hard in the kitchen all day? My poor child, it makes me ache to think how tired you would be. Think of makings bread and having it turn out sour and heavy and your father and brothers not able to eat anything you cooked, what a gloomy time you would have. Let us look at things just as they are now, my dear. Your father is not a rich man, but he makes a comfortable living for his family. With economy and good management you will have a comfortable home. Now your step-mother, because she cares so much for your father, is willing to come here and take care of his home and his children. She is an excellent housekeeper and a fine manager. She will make one dollar go farther than some people would three. One cannot have a pleasant home, dear, unless there is somebody at the head who knows the best ways of managing and who is a good cook. A better one than your step-mother cannot be found. Now that is one reason why you should be glad to have her here, and why you should respect and love her."

"Love her!" Margaret exclaimed. "People never love step-mothers. How can they when she has got your own mamma's place?" Margaret said, in her excitement mixing pronouns. "And they always hate you and try to torment you. What should I love her for?"

"My poor child," said aunt Cornelia, "I fear you have been listening to some gossiping mischief-makers. It sounds like their talk. Margaret, dear, do you love your father?"

"Yes, I do," Margaret answered.

"Well, that is another reason why you should love your step-mother. Your father selected her from all other women to come here and help him take care of you all. He thought he had made a wise choice, but his children do not think so, and it troubles him. He brought her here a stranger, and I think she meant to be kind to you all, and try to make everything pleasant, but, perhaps, she saw that you did not want her, and you did not give her a warm welcome, and so things have not gone smoothly. I suppose she feels badly about it too."

"What makes her try to boss us about so, then? It isn't her business.

We belong to father."

"My dear, when you grow up and marry a man who has three children, will you let Mollie and Sammie and Bob run wild, or will you make them behave themselves and grow up good and respectable?"

That was so funny to think of her, Margaret, ever marrying anybody and being a step-mother, that her troubled little face straightened out and she broke into a laugh.

"Now we'll not talk another word about this to-day," aunt Cornelia said. "You will get too tired, and besides, I have a nice story to read you. Some day we will talk more and try to straighten out this tangle."

CHAPTER 8: A RESOLUTION THAT FAILED

WHAT a world of trouble this family is making for itself!" Aunt Cornelia said these words with a sigh, as she moved slowly about, putting away books and work, after one of her talks with Margaret.

"They are not doing it all alone, either," with an emphatic nod of her head; "I wonder if every member of the family has an adviser who is bent on mischief?"

It is not surprising that aunt Cornelia wondered just this. The day before, when she was having a little confidential chat with Weston, he had turned restlessly on his lounge, thereby twisting his foot in a way to make him scowl, and said, — "Rob Stewart says his aunt says she knew just what kind of a life we would have, when she heard father was going to get married."

Aunt Cornelia's face burned. She felt like telling Weston that he was an unprincipled boy; worse in every respect than she had imagined him, if he had stooped so low as to allow his father's wife to be discussed before him, by outsiders; but she controlled herself; nothing was to be gained by putting Weston in ill-humor.

"Rob Stewart," she said pleasantly, "who is he? I do not remember to have heard his name before; he must be a very intimate friend, of course. Why hasn't he been to see you?"

Then Weston's cheeks burned, he could hardly have explained why; but he looked down, and fitted the toe of his slipper to a red stripe on aunt Cornelia's gay afghan which was spread over him, before he answered, speaking low, — "Why, Rob isn't much of a boy; he's that fellow who was along with me the day I got hurt."

"Oh!" it is astonishing how much meaning some people can put into those two letters. Weston's cheeks burned harder than before.

"Does he live with his aunt? Poor fellow; perhaps he is more to be pitied than blamed, if he has had that sort of bringing up."

"What sort, aunt Cornelia? Do you know her?" Weston's tones

were eager, and he twisted back again and looked at his aunt. He was quite ready for a bit of gossip.

"Never heard of her in my life, until you gave me a glimpse of her character, just now; a woman who can say hard words to a toy, about the father and mother of another boy, for no other object than to talk, is not the sort of person, as a rule, to trust and respect."

Talk about red cheeks! Weston felt as though his were made of flames; and not his cheeks, only, but his ears.

"I'll give you a good rule, my boy; never respect a boy or girl who says anything to you against your father and mother; and never respect yourself so long as you allow any boy to speak such words to you." Then aunt Cornelia gathered up her work, and left Weston to his flaming cheeks and startled self-respect. As she went, she murmured: "Rob Stewart indeed! and Rob Stewart's aunt; if people could only hold their tongues!"

So when Margaret, this morning, returned to the subject which had been gently put away a few days before, seeming anxious to talk about it, and began her line of defense by saying, —

"But, aunt Cornelia, Hester Andrews says that people never do get along well with step-mothers, and folks never expect them to," aunt Cornelia was prepared to appreciate the situation.

"How many step-mothers has Hester Andrews had, my dear, and what amount of age and wisdom has she acquired to make her a safe adviser for my little Margaret?"

Then did Margaret hang her head.

"Who is she, dear?" persisted aunt Cornelia. "Why, Auntie, you know she is the girl next door, who comes in to see me, sometimes."

"Not the girl who stayed all the evening, once, though she admitted that her mother had told her to come home at dark; and who had to be sent for, twice, before she started? You surely cannot mean that Hester Andrews!" But Margaret, with head drooping still lower, was obliged to admit that she did.

"Well!" said Aunt Cornelia, "such a girl as that would not get on well with some mothers I know, to say nothing of step-mothers! What a strange child, to be willing to insult you, her friend, by talking to your face against your father and mother. It is bad enough to say these things of people; but very few persons get so far as to speak against us to our faces."

"Aunt Cornelia, she never said a word to me against my father; never in the world! and she'd better not, I can tell her!" Margaret's eyes were blazing now. But aunt Cornelia was neither alarmed nor awed.

"Hasn't?" she said inquringly. "I don't see how she has avoided it; I should call it quite a serious insult to your father, to suppose him not capable of selecting a wife who could be trusted to do her duty by his children. I know I should not have liked such words said of my father when I was a girl. I'll tell you something, my little Margie; I had a step-mother, the truest, dearest friend a girl ever had; I loved her so, that when she died I thought my heart was broken; and I have never learned to do without her." Aunt Cornelia's voice was trembling, and a great tear dropped on the white sack she was making. Margaret looked at her with a kind of awe. A grown-up woman, like aunt Cornelia, actually crying because her step-mother was dead!

"I would love to be like her," said impulsive. Margaret to herself; "I would like to love my step-mother, a great deal, and astonish everybody; but I don't believe I cam" Then she thought of all the things which she and Hester had said to each other about step-mothers; dreadful things I It made her feel ashamed to think of some of them; and this thought reminded her of what aunt Cornelia had said about her father being insulted, and the shame deepened in her heart as it occurred to her that Hester might never have said a word if she had not begun the talk; had she, Margaret Moore, insulted her father? Margaret was very uncomfortable. She made crooked stitches in the bit of ruffling she was getting ready for that same white sack, for she had so far recovered as to be able to work a little each day.

"Auntie," she said, after a few minutes of silence, and her voice was low and gentle, "do you think anybody could begin to — that is — well, could learn to like a person very much whom she didn't like a bit, and thought she never could?"

"I understand you, Margaret; we cannot make ourselves love a person as we can make ourselves learn a lesson by saying, 'I'm going to do it;' but what we can do is, to make ourselves in word, and action, and thought, careful, respectful, obedient; and we can learn to pray; and praying daily for any one, and treating her constantly with the respect which our consciences tell us belongs to her, is almost a sure road toward love. In fact, if the object is at all worthy, with such a line of conduct, love will be sure to come. But, Margaret, the first thing, after you have made your own tongue, and hands, and thoughts obedient, is to permit no other tongues to say to you what you know to be wrong."

Margaret gave a little sigh, which she did not want her auntie to hear. What a long road it was, and hard. How was she ever to keep Hester Andrews from saying things! And then there was aunt Frances! What would aunt Cornelia say if she should hear aunt Frances talk? If only this little girl could spring at once into such a character that people would say of her, "What a perfectly angelic creature that Margaret Moore is!" she would be delighted to do so. But she shrank from the uphill road. Part of her thought she spoke: "Aunt Cornelia, I wonder what you would say if you could hear aunt Frances go on!"

Aunt Cornelia sighed; but she said, "You and I will not 'go on' at least, dear, about her, nor anyone else, shall we? I think you have sewed quite enough for one morning; suppose you see how Weston is getting along?"

Yet she treasured that hint about "aunt Frances" and wondered if there was anything she could do. This was a younger sister of Mr. Moore, who lived in the same town, but who had been away from home ever since Mrs. Merwin's coming. She had returned but the night before, and Mrs. Merwin was to make her an all-day visit on Thursday.

"I don't go there at all," said Mrs. Moore, with eyes which flashed something like Margaret's when aunt Cornelia suggested that she plan to spend part of the day with her. "Mrs. Irving has never even called on me. She has Margaret there whenever she feels like it,—and Margaret is twice as hard to manage after a visit there, — and the boys go when they like; and Thomas goes in to see his sister, of course; but I am never noticed any more than if I weren't in existence. I have some things to bear, as well as the rest of 'em; but there! I didn't mean to say a word!"

So Mrs. Merwin went alone to the handsome house at the west end of the town to visit her niece Mrs. Irving. All the long bright day while all sorts of luxurious attentions were being lavished upon her, Mrs. Merwin studied as to what she could say which would do any good. At last, the niece herself opened the way: "I hope Thomas will come to tea; I told Mr. Irving to be sure and bring him if he could."

"I don't think they can," said Mrs. Merwin, taking pretty stitches in the soft gray shawl she was knitting. "I spoke to Sophia about it, last night, and she said she couldn't." Now "Sophia " was Thomas's wife, and the step-mother of Mrs. Irving's niece and nephews.

That lady looked disturbed for a moment, then said stiffly, — "Oh! I do not expect Mrs. Moore; of course she couldn't come, when I never invite her; but I have Thomas here as often as I can."

"But, Frances dear, you don't expect a husband to go out to tea very often, without his wife, do you?"

"He can come to his own sister's I should think; besides, Thomas is peculiarly situated, and I feel sorry for him, poor fellow."

"Yes, I know he has a great deal of care; he told me something about his business worries in a long talk which we had the other day; I wish I could help him; by and by I think I can; at present all I have is tied up, so I can't get hold of it; but I hope I will be in time to give him a little lift. I am glad he has so good a wife." Mrs. Irving surveyed her in silence for a full minute, while she quietly knitted the soft gray shawl, then asked coldly,—

"Aunt Cornelia, what do you mean?"

"Just what I say, of course," speaking cheerily. "I like Sophia very much; she is a good faithful woman; I never knew one who tried harder to make a neat, comfortable home, with small means, and to do her duty by the children. How does it happen, Frances, that you have never become acquainted with her? I should suppose your love for the children would have made you anxious to know her well."

Mrs. Irving twitched so hard at her thread, as to make a rent in the lace collar she was sewing, and said: "It is because I love the children that I keep myself aloof from that woman; I was out of all patience with Thomas for setting her over them, but one cannot quarrel with an only brother, so I make the best of it, and do all I can for him and the children."

Mrs. Merwin laid down her gray shawl, took off her gold-rimmed glasses, and looked full in the face of her niece. "Frances!" she said solemnly, "you distress me beyond measure. I was told that she was an excellent and highly- respected teacher in the town where she lived, and that not a whisper had ever been breathed against her. What is it she is accused of? and, Frances, have you undoubted proof that it is true? So many stories are utterly false." Mrs. Irving uttered an impatient "Nonsense!" then spoke rapidly:

"Aunt Cornelia, I don't mean anything of that kind; I've nothing against the woman, except that she is Thomas' wife. What I do not believe in, is step-mothers; and I am just as sorry for those children as I can be; I've said so from the first, and nothing can make me change my mind."

"Then," said aunt Cornelia, grimly, "we will hope that you will never have a step-mother; but I think Thomas must have believed in them, when he brought a good woman home to assume the hardest duties which, in my opinion, ever fall to a woman's lot; and as nothing you can say ought to make him change his mind, now that the thing is done, it becomes you and me to help her bear her burden in every way we can."

It was not what she had meant to say; aunt Cornelia was like many other people, and had let her indignation get the better of her judgment; she must now Work more carefully than ever, if she hoped to accomplish any good results here. She resolved not to mention Mrs. Moore again for a week or two, and in the meantime to see an much of her niece Frances as she could.

That is the Way we plan; the facts were, that on reaching her nephew's house that same evening, she found a telegram which had just come, summoning her to the bedside of her dearest earthly friend, hundreds of miles away, and she made her hurried good-bys in the gray dawn of the next morning, leaving Johnnie whistling to keep his courage up, and Margaret crying bitterly.

"Good-by, Sophia," she said, giving the stepmother's hand a hearty grasp; "I respect and honor you; life isn't easy, live it where we may, unless it is 'hid with Christ in God.'"

"You have a good wife," she said to her nephew, as they rattled over the road, the only occupants of the great omnibus. "She is a good woman, Thomas, who is trying to do her duty; and the place isn't an easy one."

"I know it," he said, gratefully; "I think she does try; and the children are aggravating, and she hasn't been used to having children around her all the time."

"All children are aggravating, Thomas; not a mother but needs the patience of Job; more patience than the father, because she is shut up with them; and a woman who tries to take the place of a dead mother, needs all the help that outsiders can give her; and the trouble is, Thomas, they don't get it. If more people had been born deaf and dumb, there would be less trouble of many kinds in the world."

After that remark, Mr. Moore was dumb for sometime; he was wondering whether he had always answered his sister Frances' tongue just as it ought to have been answered; or whether he had sometimes allowed himself to be pitied, when he did not really need it.

As for poor Margaret, she had a hundred, excellent resolutions to live on, and if she had been even half so good as she had planned, I am not sure but she would have earned that angelic character I spoke of.

But it was a dreadful blow to have aunt Cornelia gone; above all things, she wanted her to see the improvement. However, in her lonesome little heart, she resolved to try her best.

It was with this idea strong upon her that she came to the kitchen one afternoon, just as the table was being made ready for tea. "Shall I set the table?" she asked, and her voice was very gentle.

Now Mrs. Moore was not in good heart; she missed aunt Cornelia more than she had imagined would be possible; so did Weston, and he had been correspondingly cross. Then her sister had that afternoon called on her and Mrs. Moore had said, speaking of their departed guest, "I liked her ever so much; I believe if she could have stayed, she might have done us all good; she had a quieting effect on Margaret."

"O yes!" said the sister, with whom matters at home had gone awry that day; "you are easily hoodwinked, Sophia; I believe the woman was deceitful; and she was making Margaret so; the child looks like her. Mrs. Paine told me that Mrs. Irving said she said now that Thomas was married to you and they couldn't help themselves, the only way was to make the best of it. Lovely talk that, for a friend!" This sentence was rankling in Mrs. Moore's heart when Margaret came with her offer of help; but the little girl's voice was so gentle, and her face so marked with recent weeping, that the mother resisted the temptation to say she didn't want any help, and instead, answered coldly: "You can if you like." And Margaret had at once begun the task.

There was a certain choice bit of china in the closet, Mrs. Moore's very own; a quaint and delicate treasure, which had graced the tea-table ever since aunt Cornelia's coming. Margaret admired it; she took it in her hands to say; "I won't put this on to-night, will I?" But she got no farther than the "I won't." How did it happen? Whoever knows how such accidents happen? Why do choice dishes perversely slip out of well-meaning hands at certain unlucky moments, and dash themselves headlong on the floor? I don't know; but it was just what this choice bit of china did! And the mother? — O dear! I am so sorry she said it; "I believe

you did that on purpose, you little—" Just there, she stopped herself, but not soon enough. Then Margaret, all her good resolution apparently crushed with the china,—"I didn't either, and you are mean! mean!" Then she rushed headlong from the room.

Next door to the Moores on the south side lived a young husband and wife; very near neighbors; only a narrow alley separating the houses.

The two families were not acquainted; Mrs. Moore had felt bitter against almost everybody about the time the new couple came there to live, and had not attempted to be friendly. Within a few days she had said to her husband, "Who is that handsome young fellow who has appeared, next door?"

And Mr. Moore had replied that he believed it was a brother of the wife; somebody said he had come here to attend school. This was all Margaret knew about him, save that he had merry eyes, and looked good-natured, and was always very neatly dressed. As she rushed up to her room, and her south window, and leaned over the low dill, and sobbed: "It's of no use, I can't be good and I sha'n't try anymore; and I almost know I hate her!" the "handsome young fellow" next door, was whistling, but the wind brought him Margaret's words, he stopped his whistling, and said aloud, after listening a minute, —

"Poor little thing!"

CHAPTER 9: AT THE SEASHORE

"OF course you will let the child go?"

Mr. Moore had dropped in at the Irvings as they were sitting down to supper and had yielded to his sister's persuasions to "Stop just a moment for a cup of tea and one of Hannah's nice muffins."

The half-interrogatory remark was in response to an item of information which Mr. Moore had given, incidentally, for he had not gone there intending to consult his sister; indeed, since aunt Cornelia's hint, he had been a little careful about talking over family matters with Mrs. Irving.

"Well, I don't know," he began, in answer.

"But I know," interrupted Mrs. Irving; "the child needs a change, and it seems to me that this is quite providential. Margaret has not been well since the storm, and I have been quite worried. I spoke to Dr. Strong about her—"

"You did!"

"Yes; he was in to see Bertie and it came about naturally enough. He said the child looked unhappy, and that perhaps if there could be a change in her surroundings—oh! you need not suppose that I stooped to talking over family matters; but of course I knew what he meant, and he knew that I understood. There is no use in trying to shut our eyes and not see what is plain to everybody—that the home atmosphere is uncongenial and unhealthful to one of Margaret's temperament — but we do not talk of it outside the family. It seems to me that this is just the thing for Margaret and that you ought not to hesitate a moment about allowing her to accept the invitation."

"But I cannot afford it."

"Oh! it will cost next to nothing."

"I don't know about that; there will be new dresses and spending money."

"I'll see to the dresses. She will need very little; a school girl is not expected to dress much; she has a pretty white suit, and a cambric; and the navy-blue flannel which she wears to church is just the thing for the seaside. Oh! I'll fix her off in a proper manner; you need not give the matter a thought."

"But," said Mr. Moore, "I do not know how she can be spared. Mrs. Moore is rather used up with taking care of Weston. It has been a hard spring and summer thus far, and Weston still needs considerable attention."

"Oh! She will be glad to have Margaret out of the way for a week. I have no doubt that if the truth were told, it will be a relief to her." All this, and much more, was over an invitation which had come to Margaret that morning. The girl had come to know the Duncans, the neighbors on the south side, very well. The acquaintance had come about in easy fashion, though Mrs. Moore thought that Margaret must have been forward and presuming to have become so familiar in so short a time as to receive an invitation from Mrs. Duncan to spend a week with that lady at the seaside. If Mrs. Moore had considered a moment she would have known that had the young girl been either forward or presuming, she would have been almost certain to have shut herself out from any such kindness on the part of a woman like Mrs. Duncan.

The way it came about was this: the boy, Elmer Newton, Mrs. Duncan's young brother, sat upon the veranda one sunny morning, watching Weston as he hobbled out upon his crutches. He noticed the discontented look upon the lame boy's face and heard him mutter,—

"O dear, if I could only get out of sight of this lonesome hole!"

Elmer said within himself, "I wonder if I ought to do it? I mean, 1 wonder if it would be the proper thing to do! Suppose Ella doesn't feel like making advances because Mrs. Moore has not called upon her; it's different with boys — and there's a lonesome fellow, and I could help him, I know I could, to while away the morning — and I'm going to do it! Ella said at breakfast that people ought to remember the verse which says, 'Do good as ye have opportunity,' so she can't scold me for overlooking the proprieties. Here goes!"

Crossing the veranda, he called out, —

"Say, old fellow! Don't you want me to come over there, and make you laugh? "

"You can come over if you want to, but I don't believe you will make me laugh; I don't feel like laughing, I can tell you," replied Weston as soon as he could master his surprise sufficiently to speak.

"Which shows that you don't know me? said Elmer, clearing the fence at a bound and running up the steps. "I expect you to laugh in five minutes, and forget that you ever felt sober! I have been just aching to show myself off to you ever since I came! But I have been hampered, hedged in, not daring to give utterance to my noble aspirations, lest my phlegmatic brother-in-law should give me a figurative shower-bath by making some common-sense remarks about going where I wasn't wanted. But I thought you looked as if you needed me if you didn't want me, and so I am here, at your service, sir."

Weston smiled in spite of his determination not to be pleased. It was refreshing to hear the stranger rattle on in that merry fashion, and although he felt cross at everybody he could not help admiring the free-and-easy manner and the well-fitting clothes of his new acquaintance. Surly as he felt he was constrained to be courteous; he had no need to ask Elmer to sit down, for that young gentleman had already perched himself upon the railing of the piazza, and swinging back and forth a foot encased in a shiny shoe, he continued his merry talk, not seeming to mind it that Weston was almost entirely silent.

"How did you get that sprain?" he asked presently. "It seems to be an ugly one; you have been laid up ever since I came, haven't you?"

"I got it playing the fool," said Weston.

"Well, now, that's honest; it isn't everyone who is willing to own up that he has been and made a goose of himself," returned Elmer, laughing, then suddenly changing the subject, he said, "Do you like games? I have some splendid ones. History and literature games. I'll go and get them; or, if you like, we might try a game of chess?"

"Oh! do you play chess?" said Weston eagerly. "I can play a little, but Meg does not like it, and I scarcely ever have any one to play with. She would like the history game."

That was how it began; after that morning the two boys were often together, and soon Margaret was drawn in to share in the companionship. Elmer had planned for this; he had been full of sympathy for the little girl ever since that afternoon when her sobbing, despairing words had floated down to him from the south window. Sometimes they sat upon the Moore piazza, but when Weston was able to hobble so far, they were oftener together at the Duncans; and Elmer's sister soon came to share his interest in the Moore boy and girl. Then Mrs. Duncan was sick for a few days and sent to ask Mrs. Moore to allow Margaret to come and sit with her for an hour now and then; and so in many ways the bond was growing strong, and two earnest-hearted, Christian people, without in any way meddling in family matters, were exerting an influence over these other two which would eventually be felt even in those same family matters; then a little later came the invitation for Margaret to spend a week with Mrs. Duncan at the seashore. This time everything was very properly done. Before speaking to Margaret about the plan, Mr. Duncan interviewed Mr. Moore, saying, —

"I have a favor to ask."

"I shall be happy to accommodate you in any way possible," said Mr. Moore politely.

"Will you lend Margaret to my wife for a few days?"

"Lend Margaret!"

"Yes," responded Mr. Duncan, laughing a little at Mr. Moore's bewildered expression. "Mrs. Duncan has not been well, lately, and I want to send her down to get a breath of the ocean. We thought we would not go, this year, and rented our cottage, in the spring; but the tenant will vacate next week, so the way is clear for her to go, if I can find a companion for her. She wants your Margaret; of course if you consent she will go as Mrs. Duncan's guest, and I assure you it will be esteemed a great favor if you and Mrs. Moore consent." "But Margaret is not accustomed to travelling, and I fear she would be a burden instead of a help to Mrs. Duncan," said Mr. Moore.

"That will be all right; Mrs. Duncan has taken a fancy to her and does not want to go unless she can have her."

After more talk, the two men parted with the understanding that Mrs. Moore should be consulted and the decision announced to the Duncans as soon as arrived at.

"I shall go with them, at least as far as New York, and Elmer will get around from his visit home in time to escort them back. Besides, my wife is used to travelling," Mr. Duncan added as he was saying good-morning.

And after much discussion, shared in by several people who might better have kept out of it, everything was settled as they wished. Mrs. Moore was somewhat opposed to the plan; not that she was unwilling to take upon herself the few household duties which usually fell to Margaret's share, but she was not sure that it would be a wise thing to do. The Duncans were, as she looked upon them, of a somewhat different world; she was afraid that Margaret would get "notions" and be more unmanageable than ever. Of course Margaret herself was wild to go, and Aunt Frances waxed indignant and talked unwisely and unkindly about the tyranny of stepmothers; Hester Andrews came over to assist Weston and Margaret in their council and to advise a rebellion in case permission was withheld. Since her talk with aunt Cornelia, Margaret had not been so intimate with Hester, and indeed since she began to run in and out at the Duncans so familiarly, she had scarcely seen Hester at all; but now in her anxiety and suspense she forgot herself, and after listening to Hester's— "It will be just horrid mean if she doesn't let you go!" and "I would go, anyway. I'd show my independence," Margaret exclaimed, unmindful of Weston's bitter experience, 'I declare, I almost think I'll run away and go, if she says I can't!"

"O, Mag!" said Weston.

"Well, I won't do that, but I shall hate her, I know I shall! I did not mean ever to say that or even think it again, but it will be so dreadful if I can't go! Just think, I never went anywhere in all my life, and now when I have a chance, to have to stay at home for her! I don't think I could bear it! "

"Of course she won't let you go," said Hester. "I am afraid she won't," said Margaret sadly. Just then she was thinking remorsefully of the fact that she had not always treated her mother in a way to deserve favors. Hester's next remark roused her.

"I don't see what she has got to do with it, anyway; she isn't your mother. I should think you could get around your father and make him say you could go."

"And, anyway," she continued, "if I couldn't go, I'd be just as hateful and ugly as I could be!"

Perhaps it was well that no word of this conversation reached the ears of their elders; Mr. and Mrs. Moore were both out for a little while, and the children had the house to themselves.

Mrs. Duncan had hoped that nothing would be said to her young favorite about the plan until it was decided. But the secret leaked out as a thing will, with half a dozen people to guard it. In spite of all the foolish and even wicked talk, Margaret got off and spent a very happy week at the Duncan cottage, in sight, and within hearing of the roaring old ocean. That week of companionship with a "real Christian," as Margaret expressed it, was a blessing to the young girl. In the course of one of their conversations Margaret said, —

"I have tried and tried to be a Christian; that Sunday that Mr. Wakefield staid at our house, I wanted dreadfully to be a Christian, and that night I prayed a long time, and I felt a great deal better; but it was only a day or two after that something happened to provoke me and I flew into a passion, and felt just as wicked as ever! Then I tried again. I asked Jesus to forgive me and make me better. But I can't be good when things go wrong," and she ended in a passion of tears.

"My dear child," replied her friend, "are you not depending too much upon 'feeling better,' as you call it? I think you are depending upon your good resolutions and upon your prayers, instead of looking away to Christ."

"That is what Mr. Wakefield said, 'look to Jesus;' but I thought I ought to pray a great deal, too."

"And so you asked God to take away your trouble and make you happy?"

"Yes."

"But suppose He wants you to bear it?"

Margaret looked up quickly. "I never thought of that!"

Mrs. Duncan left that word to do its work. She noticed that Margaret was thoughtful, and that after a while a new light came into her face, but she did not question.

The day before they were to return home Margaret sat alone upon the sands; she might have been watching the bathers, like everybody else, but her eyes had a far-away look, and it might have been doubted if she was at all conscious of her surroundings. Presently Elmer left the group where he had been sitting with his sister, and came and stood beside Margaret. They made a pretty picture, she with the flounces of her cherished white dress spread out, he in his jaunty seaside suit. Presently he spoke:

"Well, Margie, will you be glad to go home to-morrow?"

"Yes; I shall never forget this week here, and I shall hate to turn my back upon the ocean; but I want to see them all at home!"

"All, Margie?" The word slipped out; Elmer could have shaken himself for saying it, but Margie did not appear to notice the impertinence, and she replied without turning her eyes from the far-off gaze, —"Yes, all!"

CHAPTER 10: NEW HELP

THE train from the seaside steamed into the depot, and the Duncans and Margaret alighted, the latter to be received by her father.

"We are ever so much obliged for her," said Mrs. Duncan, heartily; "she has been a real comfort; and we are sorry to give her back. But she is glad to get home. Will you ride up with us, Mr. Moore?"

So they all came up in the handsome Duncan carriage, seeing Mrs. Moore in the doorway, and Weston, proud of his almost recovered strength, hobbled down to the gate.

"It is going to be very hard, Elmer," whispered Margaret, as the carriage stopped. The boy grasped her hand kindly, as he jumped out first, and nodded an assurance of help and sympathy.

"Well, little daughter," said Mr. Moore, "here you are home again. And we are all glad, I think."

"I am, anyway, father," said Margaret, and was received into the vehement embraces of Weston, who had, you may imagine, been very lonely without his sister or his new-found friend. "Think of it, Margie, how stupid this house has been, for a fellow like me!"

"Well, Margaret," said Mrs. Moore, "I hope these weeks of pleasure have not spoiled your love for home."

"No, indeed, mother," she said, reaching up her rosy lips for a kiss; "I am truly very glad to get back."

Mrs. Moore, bestowing mechanically the expected kiss, wondered what had happened, or if the millennium had come. And as for Weston, he almost tipped off the railing of the piazza in his amazement, and Mr. Moore, strange to say, sprang forward to assist him with an expression and exclamation rather of joy than dismay.

Then the family gathered around the tea- table. Johnnie was spending a week in the country, so Mrs. Moore had said to her sister that she had had a week of almost peace.

For Weston, until the last day or two, when he began to get

impatient for Margaret to come home, had been very contented with a set of stories of adventure, which aunt Cornelia had sent him.

"I should think," said Mrs. Moore, looking at the books severely, "that she would have sent you histories, or something instructive." But Weston "thanked his stars" that she had not; and said to himself: "That's just the 'dif' between her and you."

(I regret to say that he did say "dif," for he had been brought up among respectable people, who believed in using only words found in the dictionary, and not that new and extensive vocabulary, denominated "slang.")

"What is the news?" asked Margaret, as she disposed of her supper, with an appetite sharpened by the journey.

"I don't know of any," said Mr. Moore, "the town is going on in the same busy, yet quiet fashion. Oh, yes! the minister has gone away."

"Gone away!" repeated Margaret.

"Yes," said her father, "some of the people weren't satisfied, and he knew it—in fact, I guess they told him so. He handed in his resignation, and left almost immediately. That young minister who stayed here one Sunday, you know — what is his name? — is coming instead. He preached last Sunday, and the church voted to call him. For my part, I don't think there was much need for a change; though I suppose we shall be better satisfied."

"I am so glad!" said Margaret.

"Why," said her father, "what do you care, Margie?"

"Because — he was real nice and good, and I liked him."

(The young minister had had a talk with Margaret the Sunday he was there, which had helped her very greatly.)

"He's a jolly fellow," said Weston, "the boys all liked him. When he went to visit the school, he played ball with them at recess, just like any man, or boy"

Then they arose from the table, and Margaret busied herself in clearing away the dishes. Mrs. Moore said she "needn't," but apparently the young helper didn't hear, and both in dining room and kitchen helped very creditably. Mrs. Duncan had given her some lessons in housekeeping, while in their little cottage by the sea.

"I wouldn't," said Weston, as he came out, when Mrs. Moore had gone into the yard for a moment, "if you don't do things right, you'll get a scolding, and if you do, you'll have to help everlastingly. You're busy enough when you have to be."

Margaret turned a look upon him from her flashing black eyes, which showed her feelings, but only said quietly, "Mother is tired, Weston, and has a good deal to do. I want to help her all I can."

Weston retired into the hall, saying "Whew!" as he left.

When the work was done, and Mrs. Moore was sitting alone in the parlor, Margaret came up to her. "Mother," she said, softly, settling down on the floor beside the rocking-chair, "I am going to be real good, and help you all I can. And I'm real sorry I've been so—wicked." This quite used up Margaret's courage.

Mrs. Moore looked at her in surprise, and said,—

"Well! I'm very glad to hear it. I am sure I hope you will. I do get real worn out, with so much to do." The lady did not dream what a comfort it would have been to her little penitent, if she had taken the young head on her lap, and murmured loving, forgiving, helpful words, as Margaret's other mother would have done. As it was, she didn't know how; but she had a dim idea she ought to say something comforting, so she remarked: "You have been a great help to me this evening, Margaret. I was very tired." And Margaret went away, rejoicing unspeakably.

She found Elmer ostensibly hunting for four-leaved clovers in his yard, in close proximity to the Moores' fence, but really waiting for his young friend's appearance.

"How does it go?" he asked.

"All right, so far; but it's going to be awfully hard."

"Never mind, Margie, if you remember Who will help you. You and Weston come over as soon as you can, for some games, and all sorts of fun. I must go in now."

"Thank you, Elmer;" and Margaret returned to the porch, to find her brother in a very disconsolate condition. "You're always off with that boy now," he said, "I don't see anything more of you." This was such a very exaggerated statement that Margie looked surprised, but said nothing, and went up to where Weston lay, and pat her arm around him caressingly. The truth is, she felt she ought to speak to him about what she rather dreaded to talk of.

"Weston," she began, "I have made up my mind to be as good as I can, and help mother. She is our mother, and we can't deny it, and while she can't be so good to us as our very own, we ought to try to love her and obey her." "What has come over you, Margie?" asked Weston.

"Nothing, except that I am trying to do right and please Jesus."

"This is some of that boy's doing, isn't it?" "Why, Weston! Of course not. Elmer has helped me, though." She would have liked very much to have been able to say that Elmer had had nothing to do with her change of feeling, but such was not the case.

"Well," said Weston, "I don't see why you act so differently. You were always cross enough to her before."

"It was very wrong, I think now," said Margaret, "and I wish you would feel so, too." "Well, I sha'n't," said Weston, and he kicked the floor sullenly, "she's been awfully mean ever since you went away, and said—oh! such things about you! They make me mad if they don't you"

Now Margaret had by no means become a perfect little girl, and although she knew about how much to trust her brother's exactness in his reports, such words made her immediately angry; she went to her room rather discouraged, not realizing what a victory she had gained by not listening to Weston's highly-colored story, which he had all ready, and by not speaking crossly, and slamming every door through which she passed, as she formerly would have done. I say that at that moment our young friend was greater than Alexander the Great, or Julius Caesar the conqueror, and I have good authority for it: "He that ruleth his spirit is greater than he that taketh a city."

"I don't believe you will be a bit better than before," said Weston the next morning.

"Perhaps not," answered Margie, "but anyway I shall try, and that's something."

At the dinner-table Mr. Moore appeared with a letter in his hand and a puzzled look on his face.

"I have a letter," he said to his wife," from the new minister, and he wants to come and board here."

"Here!" exclaimed Mrs. Moore.

"Yes. Of course I haven't answered, without consulting you. He says: "I know you are not in the habit of taking boarders, but you have room in your house, and if you could accommodate me, I would be willing to pay a good price. I like your home; it is quiet and comfortable, and will be far preferable to a regular boarding-house, or a hotel, for me. I ask at a late hour, but I did not think of it till this morning, when it struck me as being just the place I want.' Well," said Mr. Moore, looking up from the letter, "what do you think of it?" "I don't know, I'm sure; if it weren't for the additional work" —

"Mother," said Margaret, "I don't want you to work too hard, but if you'll take him, I'll help you just as much as I can. It would be so nice to have him here."

That afternoon and evening the father and mother talked it all over.

"I'm not getting much money now," said Mr. Moore, "and as he is well off, and will pay a good price, you might make a profitable thing of it." So in the morning, much to the children's delight, a response was sent to the young minister, telling him he might come.

The rest of the week was a hard one, especially for Margaret, her only comforts being the near arrival of the new pastor and boarder, and her hurried talks with Elmer, besides her hour of prayer and Bible-reading every morning. Her temper threatened to forsake her, many times, but, on the whole, she did bravely. The day before the minister, Johnnie arrived, bumped and bruised, his clothes tattered and torn, yet he was rosy and good-natured. "Had a splendiferous time," he declared;

"fun all the time. Riding in the country wagons, rolling in hay-mows, teetering on see-saws. Didn't work much."

But the week in the country did not prove to have converted Johnnie's mischievous disposition. In vain were the scoldings of his mother, or the punishments of his father. Margaret seemed to be the most successful disciplinarian, and partially controlled his mischief.

On Saturday came the minister. He gave Margaret a cordial greeting, and that evening called her into his room as she was passing through the hall.

"How do you do?" he asked, and Margie knew he meant more than he had when he said the same thing at the door.

"Very much better," replied Margaret. "I took your advice, and it helped. Other friends helped me too."

"And can you trust Jesus," asked the minister, "with all your troubles?"

"Yes, sir; but I find it very hard to do right. I forget, and get mad — and it's all hard."

"I know," said the pastor, "but you have the best help, and so are strong, though weak. You have plenty of work to do, my young friend, besides conquering yourself."

"Work?" asked Margaret.

"Yes, indeed. Your brothers, my dear, and your father and mother, do not know Jesus. You must help introduce them. I do not mean," he added, seeing Margie's look of dismay, "that you must preach to them, or talk very much about it. You will do your best work by living patiently, and growing Christ-like. And you and I will pray together, and help each other."

"I am so glad," said Margaret, "that you have come here."

Just then a dismayed exclamation was heard from Mrs. Moore, and Margie hurried downstairs, followed by the minister. A group of men were entering the door.

CHAPTER 11: AN IMPORTANT STEP

WHERE am I?" came from Weston as he opened his eyes and looked around upon the anxious group, gathered in the room where he lay.

Then, with a wild gesture, he screamed, "Take him off! take him off! Oh! oh! he'll kill me! oh!" and with difficulty the doctor and friends calmed the poor boy, assuring him that he was safe in his own father's house.

After a long stillness and searching looks into each face and toward the door and windows to make sure that no danger was near, Weston began to recover from the shock he had passed through.

"You see I was out there by the post-office and Elmer came along, and I said to myself, 'West Moore, now's your time to settle with this young saint for getting Margie away from you so much.' So I went at him with my tongue. I didn't really mean it, you know; but nothing I could say provoked him to answer me back! That made me mad; I wanted him to show himself no better than the rest of us boys. But when he began to preach to me what's right and what's wrong, I just couldn't stand him any longer, and I drew back my crutch to give him a good lick over his head, when, before I knew what I was about, I didn't know anything. Elmer's big Newfoundland seized me just as I was going to strike, and that's all I remember till I woke up here; and the funny thing of it is that any two pieces of me are left together."

Thereupon he was about to stretch out his hand, but, to his dismay, it was heavy with bandages, and the least movement gave him intense pain. Then came a sob from the corner of the room. Weston knew the sound in a moment, and called, "Margie, Margie, are you there? Don't cry, Margie, I'll soon be over it, won't I, doctor? Come here, Margie, and sit by me."

She came, struggling with her tears.

"There, there, never mind now; don't cry."

"You tried to strike Elmer!"

63

"Yes, I did;" was the impatient reply of Weston. "But I didn't hit him and I got the worst of it; and I'm sorry for it."

"For which?" was the searching inquiry of the sister. "That you tried to hurt him, or got hurt?"

"For both, I guess," was the measured answer; and then, after a moment's thoughtfulness, "Say, Margie, did he get hurt?"

"Flame wouldn't let go of you for all the men could do, till Elmer actually choked him off, and they say he was badly hurt."

"He was?" Came slowly from Weston. "O, dear! what can he think of me?" sighed the poor boy.

At that moment came a message from Elmer, inquiring how Weston was doing and promising soon to come and see him and read something to pass the time away. Now it was Weston's turn. The big tears stole down his cheeks, and from his lips: "What a fool I've been! How came I to get so mad at a fellow who is worth so much more than I am?"

But Margaret laid her hand gently upon the forehead of her brother, and whispered some thing that quieted him; soon the troubled heart slept, the fingers of his sister moving through his hair soothingly.

It was now growing late on Saturday night. Weston was sleeping. Margaret had retired. The young minister was still toiling at his sermon for the next day.

He finished the last sentence and sat back in his chair. It was very still. He thought he heard a groan, and listened. The sound came again. Was it from Weston's room? No. His door opened into the hall. Silently he placed it ajar.

A voice came distinctly, "Oh! what's the use of trying?" Then sobs. "They don't seem to care. I thought they'd be so glad when they knew I was trying to be a Christian. But mother, she just eyes me from morning till night as if she thought me a little hypocrite. O, dear! it doesn't seem much better. And father doesn't scold as much, but he never comforts and encourages me. And here is Weston striking at Elmer and calling him a saint. O, dear me! what a world! I almost wish it was over and I was dead! And how can I join the Church, as the minister says I may, and should? Weston will laugh at me, and mother and father will only, expect more of me; and I can't be any better or more patient, no matter how much 1 try; and those girls will come to church to wink at each other about me.

"Dear, dear, how can I? Oh! if he'd only preach all about it and make it plain, maybe I could. His sermons are so hard for me to understand and — "

The minister heard no more. He went back to his room to think, and pray that he might know how to preach to such sad hearts as poor Margaret. The next day he saw one eager face turned up to his, while he told of Jesus and his tender care of the lambs.

On the way home he observed Margaret making several efforts to speak, but as often only failed, and he was troubled lest his sermon was too hard and heavy for her. That night he could not sleep for sorrow lest the hungry lambs had looked up, but were not fed. Then there stole to his ears from a child's voice, sweet and low:

"Jesus, lover of my soul,
Let me to thy bosom fly — "

And the minister listened and was comforted.

The Sabbath came, fresh and sweet. The church stood amid a maple grove. The windows were thrown wide open. Out rang the morning bell, and the birds on the trees joined in, while the flowers, arranged about the pulpit, filled the air with fresh perfume and seemed to smile as though they knew something beautiful and blessed was to come.

"Among the exercises of to-day," said the minister, "is the reception of new members. And, oh! how I wish many were coming into the Lord's blessed fold now.

"He invites you, dear children, and why will you not hear Him and come? I am so sorry at the way you treat Him!

"You treat Him worse than you do me; and I am only a person like yourself — a poor sinner.

"He died, my dear young people, to save you, and you do not seem to care. Only now and then one or two of you listen. But I am so glad there is one to care and come; that one a young girl. And she does not come because she thinks she is better than any of the rest of you, but because she wants to be saved from her sins, and at that last great day walk with Jesus in white.

"We have talked with her much, and believe she has truly repented of her sins, and now wishes to live a holy and beautiful life."

As he hesitated a moment, many eyes looked this way and that, and heads came together whispering who it might be. Others looked over where Mr. Moore's family sat, and nods were exchanged.

The minister went on:

"Margaret Moore will now make a public profession of her faith."

At which almost audible exclamations were heard from some of Margaret's former mates:

"Mag!" "She!" "Well, indeed!" "Don't believe she's converted any more'n I am." "'Member how she treated her mother?" "Little hypocrite!"

Whether the poor heart heard all this or not, yet bravely she came forward, and before a great crowd of witnesses took upon her the everlasting vows, and the minister gave her the right hand of fellowship, and looking up, prayed, "The Lord bless thee and keep thee."

Then they sang:

Jesus, like a shepherd lead me,
and the birds outside just then lifted up their voices, and —
There were angels hovering round
To bear the tidings home.

Many took the young hand after the benediction and bade her be of good cheer.

So she walked homeward, the young minister and the family near, conversing in an undertone, and she could occasionally hear her name mentioned; from her father, "I don't know," and from her mother, "I suppose the child's honest and means well enough; but it's one thing to say, and another to do." And from some passing schoolmates, "Just wait one month and you'll see where Saint Margaret is!"

From the upper window she thought she caught a look of scorn from Weston.

But as she was about to enter the house she heard a low voice saying, "Never mind it all, Maggie, be of good cheer. He who is for you is more than all that can be against you." Turning, she saw Elmer leaning from the window, waving his hand as if to cheer her on.

The door closed behind her, and in spite of the sunny day with its bells and birds and flowers, the sweet words of the minister, and the joyful hymns, a shadow stole over Margaret's heart.

The evening came with clouds as if to make the shadow upon the young disciple into darkness; and in the gloom there stole near the tempter, telling her to turn back.

Many have listened; what wonder if she was one of the many! But wait.

CHAPTER 12: FORGOTTEN RESOLVES

MARGARET threw an old shawl over her head and went out the side door. This had been a hard day. Weston had been very cross, and insisted upon having her run a great many errands for him, some of them unnecessary.

This, too, was the first day of the fall term of school, and Margaret had so wanted to be early at school to secure her old seat; for she had heard that Helen Marcy was going to try to get it first. She had almost forgotten her new resolves in the morning when her step-mother had told her she would have to stay home to-day and help her.

As the tears came into Margaret's eyes, Mrs. Moore had remarked: "Now's a good time to show your religion. A girl that's joined the church shouldn't go around pouting all day because she's asked to do a little work; especially when she's been off doing nothing at the seashore."

It was all true, Margaret knew it, but it seemed so hateful of her step-mother to say it. It had been so hard to bear.

After tea she walked down to the gate and stood staring out into the darkness.

It was a very hard life, all just as black and unlovely as that dark autumn evening.

She glanced back at the house. There was Johnnie bending over his books, the gaslight above him brought him out in clear relief against the dark room. Naughty Johnnie! How he had teased her every time he came near her that day! Nobody cared for her much. She gazed down the street. Here and there a light gleamed out. Across the way there was a bright fire in the fireplace, and the family seemed to be having a happy time, sitting around the table, sewing, reading, laughing and talking. The little girl was sitting in her father's lap. How Margaret longed for such a pleasant evening in their home. She turned involuntarily back to the house. Her father and Mr. Wakefield, the minister, had gone out just after tea, and Mrs. Moore had gone to her own room directly after the dishes were washed. The house was all dark, save Johnnie's one gas jet. It was just unbearable. No other girl in the world had such a hard lot. It couldn't possibly be any worse.

Yes, she really thought so, this poor silly little girl.

But she did not altogether forget her Heavenly Father. She remembered presently, with a glad thrill of joy, that she belonged to the rich King of all the earth. He could help her. She would ask Him.

Down went her head on the gate-post, and she told her Father in Heaven all about it, and how she could not possibly stand it.

Then she raised her head with a confident feeling that now all would be well, and fell to planning different ways in which her prayer might be answered.

She didn't exactly want her step-mother to die! She was rather shocked at the thought. That was a very wrong thought for a Christian girl to have.

Poor little Margaret! She thought she loved Jesus, and was trying with all her might to serve him, but she still had to learn the command: "Honor thy father and thy mother."

Throwing that disagreeable thought aside, she went on. How could it all be changed? Perhaps some rich, unheard-of relative of her mother's would die and leave a vast fortune to her as her mother's only daughter. Then what would she do? She would give her father enough so that he wouldn't have to work anymore. She would — yes, she would show a very Christian spirit toward Mrs. Moore. She would refurnish the house, and hire several servants for her, and give her enough to buy beautiful dresses. The boys should be sent to college, and she, — she would go off to boarding-school and study as much as she liked, and never have to stay home and wash dishes. She would have plenty of money to give away. She would buy a great many flowers to give to poor sick people. Her room should be beautifully furnished, and she would invite all the poor girls in school there and give them nice times.

She was just treating those imaginary girls to chocolate creams and marshmallow drops, when she heard her father's step coming swiftly down the street, and his voice say: "Margaret, you should not be out in this chilly night air." Then she turned and followed him into the house. She had to give up her musings for a while and help Johnnie with his arithmetic lesson, but she promised herself more castle-building when she went to her own room, before she slept.

But presently her father called her. "Margaret," he said, "I have a letter here from your Aunt Cornelia. She wishes you to come and spend the winter with her and attend school. Would you like to go?"

Margaret's heart bounded with joy. Not alone with the pleasure of going to Aunt Cornelia, but with a sort of triumphant feeling that her prayer was answered, and that so soon. She resolved complacently that she should always pray for everything. Poor child! She thought her faith was very great.

It was quite dark in the room and Margaret could not see her father's face as he said this, but his voice was very kind. The door into the hall was partly open, and the streak of light which came from it fell upon the sofa, and showed the dim outlines of Mrs. Moore lying there.

There was an odor of camphor and vinegar pervading the room and Margaret's conscience smote her as she remembered her hard thoughts out by the gate. Perhaps Mrs. Moore had been suffering all day from a sick headache, and that was why she was so severe. The young girl's heart softened and she resolved to pray that the headache be cured, which, however, she forgot to do. You must remember how full her heart was of excitement, and pity this poor young Christian.

It was all settled that evening that she should go in a week, and she went up to her room to write a letter overflowing with thanks to dear Aunt Cornelia, and then went to bed to dream of the new life.

How easy it would be to be a Christian, living with Aunt Cornelia, she thought, while she was dressing the next morning. God must have seen how utterly impossible it was for her to serve him truly here in her home, and so planned this for her. But her thoughts were interrupted by a knock at her door, and Johnnie called out:

"Say, Mag, she's sick, an' father's gone for the doctor, an' he said you must come an' get some breakfast, an' West's cross, an' it rains like sixty, an' the wood's all wet, an' I can't make the fire born. Can't you come quick?"

Had Margaret known all the trials that were to come to her that day, she would have stopped, and that little minute that stood between her bright hopes of the night before, and the unknown future, to ask her Heavenly Father for strength for what was to come. But she did not. Perhaps it was some shadow of coming trouble that made her reach out her hand and push the letter she had written into her upper bureau drawer. Then she hastened down-stairs. Desolation reigned there. Johnnie's books and slate were scattered over the dining-room table, just as he had left them the night before. Weston had added to the confusion by spending his evening in cutting bits put of several newspapers for his scrap-book, and little white snips were scattered thick over the floor. Margaret remembered that the dining-room always before looked nice when she came down in the morning. It did make a difference to have a mother around, even if she was only a step-mother.

Out in the kitchen Johnnie was rattling the stove and the smoke was pouring out of every crevice.

It was late that morning before the new minister got his breakfast.

The steak was smoky and the coffee muddy-looking, but he smiled pleasantly at Margaret's red face and told her that she had done well for the first time.

While they were at breakfast, Mr. Moore came in with the doctor.

They went directly up-stairs, but soon came down again, the doctor taking out his medicine- case and calling for glasses and water. Mr. Moore looked anxious and worried. Margaret tried to hear the doctor's replies to her father's troubled questions, but she only caught words now and then:

"Inflammatory rheumatism." "System completely run down." "Rest for several months." These were the bits of phrases that came to Margaret through the open kitchen door, as she stood by the faucet drawing water for the doctor. The rest of the sentences were drowned by the rush of the water, but Margaret could, easily imagine it, and her heart stood still.

She knew that this meant many things that the doctor did not say.

It meant that she could not go to Aunt Cornelia's; that she must spend the winter at home; that she must be the one who must constantly wait on the sick woman. She could even now hear the irritable words which she imagined her step-mother would use to her when she didn't do everything just rights

Then a great rebellion arose in her heart.

"God hasn't answered my prayer at all," she said to herself, and the great disappointment made her hand shake as she set the water-pitcher down before the doctor.

Mr. Moore didn't think his little girl had heard the doctor's words, and he looked after her with a troubled sigh as she went back to the kitchen. How should he tell her? Would she storm and cry as she had been wont to do when her will was crossed? He decided that he would not tell her that day.

The breakfast dishes washed, Johnnie at school, and her father up-stairs, Margaret betook herself to the kitchen to wail out her sorrow and pity herself. She dared not go to her own room, lest she should be heard. Rebellion was in her soul, and the more she cried the more she pitied herself and cried again. Mr. Wakefield, coming to the kitchen to ask for some warm water, found Margaret with her arms on the table, and her head on her arms, sobbing great angry, disappointed sobs. He stopped in dismay.

"Why, Margaret, what is the matter? Is there anything I can do for you?"

"No, there isn't! God hasn't answered my prayer! You said he would! Now I've got to stay at home and wait on her! I don't believe he heard me at all!"

Margaret fairly screamed this out. She had worked herself into such a state that she scarcely knew what she was saying. Was this the gentle, humble Christian he had received into the church but two days before? This thought passed through the minister's mind, but he was too wise to express it to the excited little girl. He only asked quietly:

"Margaret, does your father always say 'yes' to you when you ask for something?"

"Why, no; of course not!" she said, in surprise.

"And suppose you should ask for something, and he should say No, would you come and tell me that your father would not answer you?"

She did not answer this time, and Mr. Wakefield went on:

"Suppose your father knows that what you ask would be very hurtful to you, would you think him cruel to refuse you?"

"But this isn't hurtful! It's best for me! God wants me to be a Christian, and I never can be one in this house!" she burst out.

"Margaret, who do you think knows best? you who know so little, or God who made you, and who sees all things that ever have happened or ever will happen in your life? My little friend, I am afraid you didn't pray in the right spirit," —

"O, yes, I did!" she interrupted, eagerly. "I believed. I thought of course He would give it to me."

"But believing is not the only thing. You forgot to put one little sentence in, 'Thy will be done.' If you had put it in words your prayer would sound something like this: 'Our Father, who art in heaven, hallowed be Thy name, Thy kingdom come, Margaret Moore's will be done,'" —

At this Margaret couldn't help smiling through her tears.

"Your kind Heavenly Father didn't give you just what you asked for, because he saw that it would not be best for you. Perhaps he saw that his servant must learn patiently to serve him at home, among trials, before she would ever make the right kind of servant out in the world. He will answer your prayer in some other way than the one you had planned, Margaret. He loves you a great deal better than you love yourself. Can't you trust him?"

And then the minister went away without his hot water. Went back to his room to pray for the poor little troubled disciple down-stairs. And Margaret sat and thought. She saw now just how foolish and wicked she had been. She had a long struggle with her rebellious heart, kneeling on the bare floor with her head on the kitchen table, but she conquered at last, and the peace of God filled her heart. She was resolved now to give up her own way and try to do God's way. "But, dear Jesus," she prayed, "I'll have to be helped a great deal, for I can't do it alone, and I know I shall cry if they say much about Aunt Cornelia."

Margaret had found the right way to do all she could herself and trust in Jesus for the rest, and to give up her life, her will, her whole self into his keeping.

But she remembered that she had other duties and that her father might be down-stairs at any moment, so she hastened to her room to wash away the traces of tears.

Half-way down the stairs she paused. "Would not it please Jesus if she were to knock at mother's door and ask if there was anything she could do?"

She retraced her steps softly and gave a very gentle knock. Her father came from the darkened room, his face so careworn that it almost startled her. "Father, please don't look so worried. Everything will be all right. I can keep house," she said.

Her father regarded her with a tender, sorrowful look.

"Does my little girl know that she cannot go away this winter?"

"Yes, sir; I know it. Never mind that. It's all right, father."

Mr. Moore was so amazed and pleased at this new character exhibited by his daughter that he scarcely knew what to say.

"I am sorry it is so, Margaret, but your mother is very sick. She has been under a great strain this summer. You will have to wait on her and be a general help. I would hire someone else to do it if I could afford it, but I cannot. Your mother's sister, Amelia, who has been living in Brierly with her brother, will come, I think, and keep house, and then the minister need not go away, for we need all the money we can get now to pay the doctor's bills."

Margaret's face fell.

"Must we have her? Isn't there some one else we can have?" she said, lowering her voice.

"Not without paying for it," said her father, sadly.

"Couldn't I do the work?" she asked.

"No, Margaret; you will have all you can do to wait on your mother, and," he added, "I am afraid you cannot even go to school here at home, — for a time, at least. I am sorry, but I don't see any other way out just now."

Margaret felt very much like bursting into tears again, but a glance at her father's worn face changed her feelings.

"Never mind, father, I'll do all I can, and be as good as I can." And she wound her arms around her father's neck and kissed him.

If she only could have known how much that kiss comforted her father. He went back into the darkened room with a lightened heart and a feeling that there must be something in religion, for it had changed Margaret wonderfully.

Margaret snatched the first hour that came to her to write a letter to Aunt Cornelia, telling her how impossible it was for her to come to her, and how very sorry she was, and soon there came a long, sympathetic, helpful answer, and with it a little book bound in green and silver. "To help you when you feel discouraged," the good auntie wrote.

On the first page Margaret opened, her eyes met these words:

"God's will is like a cliff of stone,
My will is like the sea.
Each murmuring thought is only thrown
Tenderly back to me.
God's will and mine are one this day,
And ever more shall be,
And there's a calm in life's tossed bay,
And the waves sleep quietly."

And they sang a little tune in her heart as she thought of all she must bear that long winter.

CHAPTER 13: A NEW DIFFICULTY

THERE is no denying that it was very hard for Margaret Moore to give up spending the winter with Aunt Cornelia, and, instead, stay at home and wait on her step-mother through a tedious illness. When once she had made up her mind to it, she thought the battle of life was ended and all would hereafter go smoothly with her. Surely she could meet and conquer anything after that. And who can tell what she might not have done if she had kept close to Jesus? but young disciples — and old ones, too — wander from him and forget that it is he they are to trust, and not their own good resolutions.

Margaret forgot this, and so fell into many snares. In the first place, she began to feel she was very good. Instead of thinking about Jesus, what a wonderful Saviour he was, she thought about herself and wondered if everybody did not think she was a self-denying, noble girl to bear disappointments and perform disagreeable duties so patiently. She felt very strong and was sure she should never be cross or angry again. And indeed for a time everything went well. She was patient when waiting on her step-mother and kind to her brothers. Even Johnnie had not power to put her into a rage, although he put burs in her hair and untied her apron strings. There was one thing Margaret chafed under, and that was having Amelia Barrows, her step-mother's sister, come to keep house for them. Her good resolutions in no wise extended to that person. She had made her mind up very hard that she should not call her "Aunt Amelia." "She was not her aunt, and never could be," and "she should not be under orders to her;" not that she would not treat her well, but she should be dignified and give her to understand that she was not such a very little girl. "Thirteen and a half was nearly fourteen — almost a young lady, she was."

Amelia Barrows was a young woman with eyes and brows as black as Margaret's own, and a will quite as positive. So it was to be expected that there would be some jarring.

The hardest part of it all to Margaret was that she was obliged to share her room with Amelia. It was a large old house, but there were not a great number of chambers, because they were all large except the hall bedroom. When the minister came Mrs. Moore gave that to him for his library. So there really was no other place for Amelia. Margaret knew it could not be helped, and yet it was so hard to feel that her room was not her very own private room any more. She prided herself greatly on it, and she really did deserve great credit for its cheerful prettiness.

It was only a plain, square room with whitewashed walls and a straw matting on the floor, but there were two pleasant windows with cheap white muslin curtains, and the bed was daintily dressed in white and blue. The rocker was covered with blue cretonne, and there were blue mats on the bureau. A bright home-made rug on the floor, small pictures on the walls, and a set of shelves in the corner filled with books; then, in winter, there was always a pleasant sense of warmth because the stovepipe came through from the sitting-room. Altogether, it was quite a cosey place and Margaret was always glad to flee to it and shut herself in from all annoyances. She thought it the prettiest, pleasantest room in the world, and one reason was because it was always in order. Carefulness, when once learned, becomes a habit, and is easier than carelessness. Young as Margaret was when her mother died, she had been taught by her to sweep and dust her own little room, and to hang her clothes at night on hooks placed within her reach, and always to put a thing in its place after using it. She had, besides, inherited dainty tastes and neat ways from her mother, so it was not such a task for her to be orderly as it was for some others.

And so it was with a pang that she saw Amelia walk into her room and take possession with the air of one who had a right there.

It is not easy work to wait upon a sick person, so you must not suppose that Margaret had nothing to do but sit within call in her stepmother's room handing her something occasionally. She had to take the place of a nurse, young as she was, in the best way she could, for Amelia had her hands full with the housekeeping. It was hard work, and Margaret was often very tired. There was the room to be put in order every morning, and Mrs. Moore was a very particular housekeeper; not a speck of dust, or spot on window or mirror, escaped her keen glance. There was much running up and down-stairs, too, for hot water and cold water; there was liniment and mustard and draughts to be applied by turns to the aching limbs, and sometimes nothing helped; the pain grew worse instead of better, and the patient was not patient, but let fall sharp words at Margaret's blunders, whereupon poor Margaret blundered still more, and did not give soft answers. Some days, though, everything went well, and her step-mother felt that Margaret really was very different from what she used to be. She was gentle and patient and tried hard to please. The reason was plain; those were the days when she remembered to get her verse from the Bible and think about it, then asked Jesus to keep her, and remembered, too, when temptation came to call to Him to help her. But some mornings she forgot all about it, or she spent too much time curling her hair, or trifling in some way till it was too late, and she had to hurry down-stairs with all speed. There would be time for it after breakfast, she thought, but then it was put off from hour to hour, and perhaps she ended by not doing it at all. When this happened she was fretful and unhappy; nothing went right with her. God made the body so that it cannot go without food at regular times, and keep in order. He made the soul in the same way. It must get food from the Bible, and by thinking about God and speaking to him, or it cannot be a healthy soul. This poor little Christian knew she must eat her breakfast or she would feel faint and weak by ten o'clock, but she had not learned that she must not starve the other and better part of herself. So it was no wonder that she did not always do right.

One reason why it was particularly hard now was that two of her best friends were away. Elmer Newton's older brother was obliged from ill health, to spend the winter in the South, and wished to have Elmer with him. Mrs. Duncan felt anxious about her sick brother, and at the last decided to accompany them and remain a few weeks, which lengthened into months. This made a lonely, gloomy time for Margaret, she had come to depending so much upon their help and counsel. She felt as if there was nobody to go to with her troubles and doubts. Mr. Wakefield was always kind, but she stood in a little awe of him because he was the minister, and so, unless strongly excited, was too timid to talk freely with him.

When a girl of thirteen resolves to be dignified toward anybody it means that she is going to make herself very disagreeable whether she knows it or not. Amelia Barrows was not an ill-natured young woman, and if Margaret had tried she might have made a friend of her. As it was, Margaret forgot that she was herself several years the younger. She assumed airs of importance, and found fault. She laid down laws about her room, and called Amelia to account if a brush or a chair was not in its exact place.

"See here, young woman!" Amelia said one day, losing all patience, "you'd better stop your high airs. A piece of this room belongs to me while I stay here, and I'm going to do exactly as I please in it. I don't want to be in it, or in this house, either, but I'm here, and we've both got to stand it. I never wanted my sister to marry your father any more than you did, — not as I have anything against him, — but I told her she might as well pat her head into a hornets' nest as to try to manage three saucy young ones. No wonder she's sick!"

There is no telling what Margaret would have said then if Amelia had not gone out and banged the door after her. She was angry enough to have said anything. To be called "a saucy young one" when she had borne everything, and was almost as tall as a woman; it was too much!

"O, dear!" she sighed, bursting into tears, "I wish she wasn't here. She's perfectly horrid!"

When she went down to the well-cooked dinner a couple of hours afterward she forgot to ask herself how they could possibly get along comfortably without Amelia.

There were afternoons when Amelia had leisure to stay with her sister and Margaret was at liberty. One day she went to take a walk, and was sauntering slowly along when Hester Andrews tapped on the window and beckoned her in. Margaret hesitated. She had not been going much with Hester of late, but she finally went into the house. "You poor thing!" Hester said, meeting her with a kiss, "I wonder if you have got out at last! It is just too bad for you to be shut up in the house all winter, waiting on somebody who's nothing to you; all the neighbors say it's a shame, and mother says that it is entirely too hard for you." Poor Margaret! She had been trying all day to get the better of her discontent and ugly feelings. Now, they sprang up anew. She looked about the pleasant parlor where Hester sat at her fancy work. Hester seemed to her to have everything she wanted, and to do just as she pleased. How different it was with her! How hard her life was! It had not occurred to her how hard till Hester put it into words.

"If it was your own mother, now," Hester went on, "why of course you would expect to do all you could, but now, it's just dreadful. I'd like to see my father put a step-mother over me if my mother was gone — and make a slave of me waiting on her! I'd go out and scrub for a living first."

Margaret ought to have known, by this time, that Hester always did her harm and not good, and have had courage enough to shun her company. She went into that house in a good frame of mind; she came away feeling that she was a much-abused girl: one who had a bitter lot; and she pitied herself.

If Satan had hired Hester to do some ugly work for him, to spoil Margaret's peace and draw her away from God, it could not have been better managed, for, besides all the wicked things she had said, she did something more. As Margaret was about to leave, —after having poured into Hester's sympathizing ears a long story about Amelia and all she had to bear from her, — Hester said, "Wait a minute, Mag. I've got a perfectly splendid book, and I'll let you take it, if you haven't read it. You've got to have something to cheer you up or you'll die."

Margaret seized it eagerly. She saw at a glance it was a novel. She had read enough of them to spoil her taste for more solid reading, and to know that she liked them far better than anything else. She felt guilty in taking it, because she had promised Elmer when he went away to read only what would be of benefit. How did she know, though, she told herself, but there was something good in this book? She remembered, too, with a twinge of remorse, that she had not yet touched the books Mrs. Duncan left for her to read, except to look through them and pronounce them "dry." She meant to read them before the lady returned, but just now she must have a real story to cheer her. Anybody who has read "Madam How and Lady Why," "A Family Flight," and "Harry's Vacation," knows of what delightful reading Margaret had deprived herself all this time.

The next morning when the room was in order and Mrs. Moore was taking a nap, Margaret brought her basket of work and drew up to the fire, planning for a good time, not with her mending, though. "The Deserted Wife" — Hester's book—was in the bottom of the basket, well covered with stockings. The fact that it was so hidden, and that she drew a tall rocker between the bed and herself, proved that her conscience was not altogether clear. However, she was soon lost in her book. She did not raise her eyes or move a muscle, except to turn over the leaves for a long time; she even forgot to breathe except by irregular gasps; she read with feverish haste, because her stepmother might waken at any moment and require her help, and she must know what happened next.

If Hester had but placed a live coal in her hands instead of this book! She would have dropped that instantly and have burned only her fingers. This tale of sin and shame and crime might leave scam on her soul forever.

Mrs. Moore had an unusually long sleep, for two hours had passed away when Margaret was startled by her voice, saying, —

"Scents to me it is cold here. Has the fire gone out? Where are you, Margaret?"

Sure enough, the wood tire had burned to ashes, and the room was quite chilly. Margaret hid away her book and went for kindlings. They were wet, and the fire smoked and sulked, but did not burn for a long time. Her father came in to dinner before the chill was off the room. He noticed it, for it was a raw, windy day, and told Margaret, rather sharply, that her mother's room ought not to become cold like that, and there was no need of it if she had attended to the fire as she should. Margaret could never bear to have her father speak sternly to her. She went off to her room in a tempest of tears, telling herself, amid sobs — as foolish girls do at such times—that there was nobody to love her.

This was only one of the many difficulties she brought herself into during the next few weeks. She plunged into a perfect whirlpool of novel reading. As fast as one book was devoured Hester provided another. She read "The Fatal Marriage," "The Terrible Secret," "A Bridge of Love," "Lady Gwendoline's Dream," and "Lord Lynn's Choice," besides many more. She read while she was dressing, and snatched every moment through the day. She even sat up nights and pored over those fascinating books, when she should have been sleeping. Sometimes she stole out in the evening and walked up and down the street with Hester, and talked them over. So she constantly lived in another world. She was in a frenzy of eagerness to get through whatever she was doing, and drown all her senses in a book. As a natural consequence, nothing went well with her. She hated her lot and its duties. She longed to get away and live with the beautiful, unreal people she had read about.

Novel-readers are usually cross. Poor Margaret was very cross. She disputed constantly with Weston, and boxed Johnnie's ears when he teased her. He turned everything into rhymes, so when he had succeeded in putting her into a rage, he would leave off singing,

"Aunt Ameliar,
She's a pealer,"
and would dance about Margaret, shouting in her ears,
"Mag is mad,
And I am glad. "
This would make Margaret very angry, and sometimes the two had what Amelia culled "a scuffle." She would interfere at last and declare, as Johnnie ran off laughing, that Margaret was the "worst of the whole pack if she was a church member. She would rather be nothing than a hypocrite."

And Margaret in these days was impertinent to her step-mother and jerked things about in a way that is very trying to a sick person. She left undone all she possibly could, allowed great holes to come in her stockings, and went about slip-shod, with the buttons nearly gone from her shoes, and did not take the "stitch in time" that "saves nine." There were worse neglects, too.

Since this fatal disease of novel-reading had come upon her she did not read her Bible scarcely at all. On Sunday afternoons she held it a while and gazed out of the window, then went hurriedly through a chapter without knowing a word that was in it. As if the Bible would do one any more good than the geography unless its words were understood and treasured up.

It was the same with prayer. She forgot it entirely, or she murmured a sentence or two while she was running down stairs in the morning or after she was in bed at night. It was mere form, and not true praying at all.

Mr. Wakefield had been sadly perplexed about Margaret. He felt sure, from what he saw and heard, that all was not well with her. She seemed to avoid him, and whenever he had an opportunity to speak with her she said as little as possible, and got away as soon as she could. What evil influence could be at work upon her? Not her step-mother's. He felt sure that if Mrs. Moore but knew how, she would be glad to help the girl. One evening as he walked homeward he was thinking about Margaret, and wondering what he could do to help her. As he came near Mr. Andrews' house somebody came out of their gate and ran down the street just in front of him. As she passed the lamp-post, and the light fell full upon her, he saw that it was Margaret. As she tuned in at her own gate a book slipped from under her arm and fell to the ground, but she did not know it. She hurried up the steps and closed the door after her. Mr. Wakefield picked up the book, slipped it inside his coat, and went up to his own room; then he lighted the gas and sat down to see what sort of a book it was which would surely help or hinder this young Christian. He read enough to satisfy him that he had found the clue to Margaret's difficulties. What soul could thrive on such mental food? "Satan is at the bottom of it!" he said, half-aloud, flinging the book from him. He sat a long time with his face between his hands, thinking.

The next evening, after tea, Mr. Wakefield lingered in the sitting-room and asked Margaret to try some of the pieces in the new Sabbath-school hymn-book. Margaret's cabinet organ had been her mother's, and was now a source of much pleasure to herself. She had learned to play sacred music well, so she and the minister often sang together. Johnnie sang a few minutes and then ran off. When they were left alone, Mr. Wakefield stepped into the hall and came back with the book he had picked up the night before.

"Margaret," he said, "can you imagine to whom this belongs? I picked it up on the street last night."

Now Margaret had been greatly troubled about the book all day; she knew Hester would be angry with her if it were lost, so it was with a sense of relief that she read the title, "Disinherited."

"Oh! I'm so glad you found it," she exclaimed, then stopped and blushed. She had a feeling that perhaps Mr. Wakefield would not quite approve of this sort of reading, and she had not meant to let him know that she ever read such books.

She felt very uncomfortable, and stood with her eyes on the carpet, waiting for him to lecture her severely, but he did nothing of the kind. When she looked up, his face and his tones were kind as he asked,—

"Do you love to read, Margaret?"

"Better than anything," promptly answered Margaret.

"Do you like books of this sort — novels?" he continued.

She studied the pattern of the carpet a moment, and twisted one of her curls, then said, almost defiantly, —

"Yes, sir; I do."

Mr. Wakefield forgot that he had meant to be very calm and gentle, and he said almost fiercely, as he walked back and forth,—

"O you poor child, I wish I could have saved you from this. Margaret, do you know what a horrible thing this novel-reading is; how the thirst for it is like the thirst for liquor? It drives out the love of Christ from the heart. It ruins souls! But there! I did not mean to frighten you," he said, as the tears gathered in Margaret's eyes. "Sit down and let us talk the matter over calmly. Let me tell you how near I came to being ruined by that trap of Satan's myself.

Just here the door-bell was heard, and Johnnie brought in Deacon Grey who had called to see the minister, while Margaret slipped out of the other door.

She flew, rather than ran, upstairs. She tip-toed softly through the hall, for she did not wish any one to see her just then. As she went by a door which stood ajar, she heard her own name, and unconsciously paused. Her step-mother's voice was saying: —

"We've got to make some different arrangements. Margaret gets worse every day. I've tried to be patient, but some days she acts like a little fury. Amelia says she sits up nights to read novels. I talked to her about it, and she just the same as told me it was not my affair. I thought it was all nonsense, her joining the church. What do such children know about it? I guess you had better send her to your aunt's if she wants her. We can get along somehow."

Then her father's voice groaned out, —

"I'm sure I don't know what is going to become of her."

Margaret waited to hear no more. She turned to go into her own room, but Amelia was there. Growing desperate, she went back into the dark hall and softly opening the door that led up garret, groped her way up the narrow stairs. She must he alone somewhere. It was a long, wide garret stretching over the whole house. This was the old homestead of the Moore family, and "take it up garret," had been said of all the lame furniture and not- wanted articles for a whole generation. It was a cheerful place by daylight; a capital place for a romp; but to-night it looked "pokerish." The tall chimneys reared themselves like grim giants at each end; old hats and coats hung from the rafters, and the moon, looking in at the gable window, made dancing shadows on the floor, of the long, bare branches of the elm-tree.

Margaret had never been up garret in the dark before. She would have been afraid if she had not been in such a tumult. She flung herself upon an old chest by the window, and cried out her mortification and anger in long, deep sobs. The moon beamed down in a kindly way, and the eye of God looked upon her in love and pity, but the poor child did not know it.

CHAPTER 14: NOTHING SATISFIES

POOR Margaret! I hope you have sympathy for the sad-hearted child, asleep on the old chest, with the moonlight streaming in and falling upon the pale, tear-stained face. We may not blame her too severely; no doubt you, who have followed this story of the Moore family thus far, hoped that Margaret's faith might be the "little leaven that should leaven the whole lump;" that her earnest, consistent life would lead others to come to Christ. But, alas! she seemed to be making a wretched failure of her Christian life. Was she mistaken? Was it, as her step-mother said, all wrong for her to join the church? Was there reason in the question she had asked: "What do such children know about it?" Let the great multitude of Christians who have come to Christ in their childhood, answer. Let Christ him self answer, in those sweet and precious words spoken of the little ones of Judea, "Suffer little children to come unto Me."

If Mr. and Mrs. Moore could only have taken in this invitation for their children, and then could have taken home to their own hearts the admonitions of the apostle in regard to their own duty, how much easier might the Christian way have been made for Margaret's feet. It had never occurred to Mr. Moore that the sentence, "bring them up in the nurture and admonition of the Lord," was addressed to him; or that the commendation of Abraham might be made his own, "For I know him that he will command his household after him, that they shall keep the way of the Lord;" nor had he thought of the warning, "Fathers, provoke not your children that they be not discouraged;" or that other in the words of Christ, "Whosoever shall offend one of these little ones." Knowing nothing of the service of Christ themselves, how could they help this young disciple?

It was late when Margaret awoke. The house was very quiet; the moonbeams still played with the branches of the tall tree at the gable of the house, and made curious and ever-changing shadows upon the floor of the long, low room. Margaret had not been missed, except by Amelia, who, not finding her in their room, said to herself, —

"She's off again with that Hester Andrews! I don't care if she does get locked out; maybe her father will realize how she is going on, if he has to let her in."

As soon as the girl recovered from her surprise at finding herself in this unusual place, she slipped off her shoes and crept softly down the stairs, moving about her room very quietly so as not to waken Aunt Amelia, who, weary with a hard day's work, was sleeping heavily.

Margaret found the old garret such a quiet retreat that after that first almost accidental visit, she went there whenever she could steal away. And one day she gained a victory in that very spot. She might in some future struggle be again vanquished, but for that time she was the conqueror. It was two or three days after her first visit; things went wrong in the kitchen; she thought Aunt Amelia more aggravating than usual. It was Monday, and the work was heavy, and perhaps the tired young woman at the helm was impatient; anyway, as soon as Margaret could escape from the hated dish-pan, she just peeped into the sick-room to find that the invalid was sleeping, and, leaving the doors ajar, that she might hear the faintest tap of the bell, she stole up the narrow and steep stairway, and seating herself upon the old chest prepared to "have it out" in a good cry. Pretty soon, glancing down behind the chest, she caught sight of the book which had caused her such mortification and sorrow. She had not been able to look Mr. Wakefield in the face since that evening when he restored the book to her with earnest, and, to her, terrible words; as she fished it up from the dust and cobwebs — for no matter how neat the housekeeping, dust and cobwebs belong to garrets— "You ugly thing!" she said, "to go slipping away from me, and to fall right down in the minister's way. Just as if he did not think meanly enough of me without this. O, dear I thought it would be grand to have the minister board here, but I wish he had never come. He never could know half how mean and hateful I am, if he did not live here. If this old book belonged to me I would burn it up, but it must go back to Hester, and of course it will slip out again, and Mr. Wakefield will find it and have a chance to give me another lecture. O, dear! What a dreadful thing he said: something about ruining souls. He said novel-reading would drive out the love of Christ, and I am afraid it is true. I wonder if I ought to give it up? Hester said this was an awful nice book, and that she was sure I would like it; but I wish I could make up my mind not to read it."

Just here there came to Margaret a thought of the sermon she had listened to only yesterday. Mr. Wakefield had chosen for his theme the peril of choosing wrong. In making the sermon practical he had spoken of the daily necessity laid upon all of choosing between right and wrong, and had tried to show some of the dangers attending a wrong choice. He had even said, "Sometimes it seems a very small matter; it may be only a question of where you will spend the next hour, yet where you will spend eternity, may hang upon your choice: or, it may be only how you will spend the evening; whether you will read this book or that; yet your peace of mind, your Christian development, may rest with your choice." These words came to Margaret now as she debated. Inclination and conscience were each clamoring for a hearing.

Once she took up the book and was about to open it, saying, "I will only read this one more, and then I'll stop!" It was strange, but the girl seemed to hear a voice saying, "Stop now; it will sting you." And she threw the book from her as though she already felt the sting. It was only the tinkle of her step-mother's bell that she heard, but, as she stood up to go downstairs, she said, with a firm voice and set lips, "I'm done with them. I'll read no more of those books." Then she ran downstairs, and for the next hour was busy attending to the wants of the invalid, who had awakened in great pain, but who noticed, even in the midst of her suffering, that her attendant was more tender and thoughtful than she had been for a long time. But that book lying on the floor where Margaret had thrown it, was to make more trouble. Aunt Amelia had noticed Margaret's absences from the inhabited parts of the house; nowadays she never found her in their own room. At first she supposed the child was with Hester Andrews, but finding that this was not the case, she determined to learn where she kept herself, and what she did. One day she had occasion to go to the garret, and, finding the book which Margaret had thrown from her in that hour of decision, she straightway concluded that "Mag went up there to read novels," so resolved to lay the case before her brother-in-law.

"The child goes around as if she were in a dream," she said. "I haven't seen any novels around lately, and 1 thought she wasn't reading them as much; but it appears she is only getting sly about it."

"Are you sure this is Margaret's book?" asked Mr. Moore.

"It has Hester Andrews' name in it," was the reply, "and Mag spends half her time hidden away somewhere. I have no doubt she stays up there reading this sort of stuff."

"I thought she was doing better lately; Sophia seems to get along very well with her."

"Well, all I have to say is, if Sophia were in this kitchen some days she would see! Why, Mag don't know what she is about half the time."

Mr. Moore sighed. Would these conflicting elements in his household never reconcile themselves and let them have peace? He must have a talk with Margaret; accordingly, he undertook a task for which he was not well fitted, and, as a matter of course, chose an unfortunate time. Margaret was more tired than usual. All that day she had been having a hard fight with her ill-humor, and, towards night, feeling that she must get away by herself, had her hand upon the garret door, when her father, coming into the room, said, "Margaret, I don't want you to go to the garret any more unless you are sent for something."

Margaret stood aghast. Of late the only hours of quiet were those spent in the garret, where she could hug her sorrows, cry out her grief, and fight out her battles. Besides, it was the spot which she had chosen for her Bible-reading, and the prayer which followed it. The nearest approach to happiness she had known in a long time, was made in the old garret, where she seemed to be finding her way back to Jesus; and was this refuge to be taken from her? She managed to stammer out, "Why not?"

"Because I prefer that you should stay below. There is plenty of room down-stairs, and it seems to me more fitting that you should make one of the family. O, Margaret! why will you be so sly about things? Though it is no wonder you wish to hide your books and your doings."

This to her! She had always prided herself upon her frankness and openness. How often had she been told that she was very out-spoken? And how often had she declared that she was not deceitful? Now, to be told by her own father that she was sly! She was pale with anger, and her voice trembled as she said, "Father, I do not know why you think I am sly, and I have not tried to hide any books — that is, not lately. I have never read any books in the garret — except the Bible."

"O, Margaret! How, then, did this come there?"

"Why? who? what?" A flush spread over the girl's face, and she hesitated, but collecting herself, she said, while the color again went out of her face, "I carried it there, but I did not read it. I know where you got it; Aunt Amelia has been trying to spy out something. She might be satisfied with taking my room from me, without taking the only place I have to go." And now Margaret, unable to keep back the tears any longer, burst into a perfect passion of sobbing, saying, between the spasms, "I can't stand it! Every pleasure I have in the world is taken away." If she could only have kept her temper in check, and talked calmly with her father, he might have withdrawn that prohibition; yet, as he never sought a place of prayer, never felt the want of a place where he might enter in and "shut the door," how could he be expected to understand the longing of the girl's heart for a chance to be alone with herself and God?

There had been a time when Mr. Moore would have stopped to pet and comfort the sobbing child, but he had been so tried with his family affairs, and felt so discouraged and so vexed with Margaret, that he walked away, leaving her sitting on the floor, where she had dropped all in a heap, in her fit of crying.

It suited her to play the martyr for the next few days. She attended to her duties quite faithfully, but wore a face long enough to give every member of the family a chill. She adhered to her resolution to read no more novels, but she went about dreaming — making herself the heroine of a romance.

During those hours spent in the garret, she had unwittingly stumbled upon a secret, one which concerned her, and gave her great joy in anticipation. One day she had been seized with the spirit of investigation, and chose an old secretary for the subject of her experiment. She remembered that this piece of furniture used to stand in her mother's room, and that when the new mother came, it had been removed to make way for her furniture. Mr. Moore said, "Sometime we will have this freshened up for Margaret;" and this gave it additional interest to the girl.

"It is a queer old thing!" she said, opening the doors and peering into the pigeon holes. "I wonder if it has any secret drawers. They always have them in books. I mean to see if I can find out." And she proceeded to pull out drawers and thump at panels, and finally was delighted to discover the object of her search: A little hidden receptacle; and in it, to her astonishment, she found a sealed letter addressed " To my daughter, Margaret, to be given to her when she is fourteen years old." She stood as if transfixed. It seemed to her as though she had heard a voice from another world. "When she is fourteen!" she read. Then, "And I am only thirteen and a half!" She put back the letter, slipped the sliding-panel back into place, shut the doors, and turned the key in the rusty lock, all the while wondering if anybody beside herself knew of the letter. This was the secret upon which she was building her romance. Again and again she said to herself, "Oh ! I wish I knew what my own dear mamma will say to me in that letter — when I am fourteen!" Meantime, into the pain and unrest of the long nights, there came to Mrs. Moore a strange visitor; she recognized an unwonted presence; and, stirred by new thoughts, she remembered how, away back, when she was not much older than Margaret, this same visitor had knocked at the door of her heart. She recalled how she had been minded to open unto Him, and how, absorbed with the ambitions of school-life, she had closed the half-open door and devoted herself to the cultivation of her mind, turning away from the truest culture; she reviewed her school-life, and the years of her work as a teacher. She had been proud of her success. During this year she had sometimes wondered if she had not made a mistake in laying down that work to take the place of wife and mother in this disorderly family; she had often wondered why she, who had been so successful in the schoolroom, had so failed in this new sphere. But, in this time of looking back, there came to her a questioning doubt of her success. Had it been a success in its truest sense? Had she not, after all, been working upon a lower plane when she ought to have sought a higher? If her pupils had gone no farther than she had led them, when they, too, were laid upon beds of pain, would they be, even as she was now, seeking in sorrow for a place of rest? tossed upon a sea of doubt and perplexity? Was there no harbor, no safe anchorage for her troubled heart?

Though she did not yet put it into words, even in her inmost heart Mrs. Moore was reaching out after Christ, with a feeling which, if expressed, would have been "Lord, save, or I perish!" Did Jesus ever hear that cry and turn away?

One morning her sister Emma came with a carriage. Mother was not quite so well as usual, and wanted to see Amelia; could she be spared for a few hours to ride out and stay to dinner? It seemed, at first, as though Amelia could not be spared. Mr. Moore had gone out of town for the day, and Margaret would be left alone as housekeeper and nurse. But Mr. Wakefield was within hearing, and came to the rescue.

"I think Miss Barrows might go," he said; "I am sure Margaret and I can keep house, and take care of Mrs. Moore, too. Just give me a bowl of bread and milk, or, rather, let me help myself; and, Miss Barrows, you surely can set out a luncheon for the boys when they come from school?"

"But," objected Miss Barrows, "some one must go down to the doctor's office at two o'clock for the medicine, and the boys hate to be kept from school."

"All right! We can manage that. I will go; or, if Mrs. Moore is sleeping, Margaret can go and I will watch."

So it was arranged, and Miss Barrows departed. The boys were quite satisfied with the dainties which she had left for them as a compensation for a cold dinner, and Mr. Wakefield seemed to enjoy his bread and milk and ginger snaps. Mrs. Moore was having a more comfortable day than usual, and her step-daughter was attentive and quiet. At two o'clock Mr. Wakefield appeared at the door of the invalid's room, and asked, "How would your mother enjoy a little reading? If she wishes, I will read to her while you go down to the office, or I will go if she prefers to have you stay with her."

Mrs. Moore, hearing this, said, "Margaret can go; I can stay alone; Mr. Wakefield need not trouble to read to me."

But Mr. Wakefield said, "It would be a pleasure to read, if Mrs. Moore would like to listen;" and so it was settled. This was one of the rare days when the invalid was able to be lifted from the wearisome bed to the great invalid's chair, which a kind neighbor had sent in for her use, and Amelia had established her there just before she left. Lying back among the pillows, with a crimson shawl touching her pale cheek, she smiled faintly as the minister softly drew a chair to the opposite side of the stove near the window, and opened a new magazine. Margaret looking in, on her way down town, thought: — "How queer! I supposed he would read the Bible!" Though why she should suppose so, when she, herself a Christian, had never offered to read a chapter to her mother, it might be difficult to say. Probably because Mr. Wakefield was a minister she expected it of him. People do expect things of the minister which they excuse themselves from doing.

"I am glad to see a Harper," said Mrs. Moore; "I used to read it always until lately."

In a low, quiet voice, Mr. Wakefield read, at first some of the lighter articles; bits from the Easy Chair, and Drawer. As he finished a tender little poem, he looked up and noticed that tears were stealing from beneath the closed eyelids of his listener. He shut the book and waited. Presently she said "That was very sweet; it seems as if it might have been a bit out of my own long-ago! Things are more prosaic nowadays," she added with a wan smile.

"Yes; things do seem more so, as we grow older, yet not less satisfactory, I think."

"Nothing satisfies."

"Nothing?" he repeated questioningly; and she replied with a sudden emphasis, " Nothing !"

"Listen to this," said the minister.

"'Then he cried unto the Lord in their trouble and he delivered them out of their distresses.'

"'For he satisfieth the longing soul, and filleth the hungry soul with goodness.'

"'They shall be abundantly satisfied with the fatness of Thy house, and Thou shalt make them drink of the river of Thy pleasures.'

"Mrs. Moore, there is a fountain that satisfies. If you would only come and drink."

CHAPTER 15: AN UNEXPECTED MEETING

MR. MOORE had been called away unexpectedly, and in a direction in which he had not been for years.

It is strange how little a thing may change all the future of a person's life, and the lives of those who, by circumstance, are linked to him!

How often one's whole history seems to depend upon what the thoughtless call "a mere accident."

Just one of these unexpected events appears in the history of this family.

We have seen at what cross purposes the different members worked, and how unfortunately they were situated, surrounded as they were by friends with more words than wisdom; people not meaning to be bad, but lacking in charity; and, having suffered prejudice to blind them, they enjoyed the luxury of using their tongues, to the sorrow both of those whom they loved and those whom they disliked. But "God reigns, let the earth rejoice;" and let all his dear people rejoice, while they remember that "All things work together for good to them that love God." To receive a telegram was not an event so unusual as to frighten the Moore household particularly.

The feeble mother might have been startled a little, had she seen the message delivered; but such things were not opened in her presence; all she learned, after her breakfast, served in her room long after the family had finished theirs, was, that a telegram had called "father" to Potterville to see a man who could not, for want of time, come to him. Potterville was a large town, boasting several railroads, two of which were trunk lines. On one of these lines, crossing that which ran near Mr. Moore's home, was coming a man whom he had not seen since he was a boy, and whose very existence he had almost forgotten.

When Mr. Moore read the name signed to the message, he could not recall it, nor imagine who could be so anxious to see him. As he repeated the name, it began to have a familiar sound, and revive some far-away memory.

He rubbed his forehead; and thought hard; then a little smile crept over his face, and he said to himself: "I wonder, I do wonder if it can be Macy! From what region has he dropped down, if it is he? Well, I'll go and see,, for if he is like himself, or as I used to know him, I would rather shake hands with him than with the President."

So, with a hasty change of linen, he hurried to the "East-bound train." This reached Potterville an hour and a half earlier than the fast mail on which his friend was expected. The time dragged slowly, and he found himself growing very nervous. Naturally his mind went roaming back over the many years which had passed since he and his boy-friend bade each other good-by under a chestnut-tree, pledging mutual friendship for all time. How wonderfully memory unrolled its record, producing with startling vividness the succeeding scenes in their turn. Since that long ago, how much of life he had lived! He had won and married a playmate of his childhood, had become the father of a family, had buried the mother of his children, and, after trying to be to them both father and mother, conscious of his failure had sought for them another mother; and now — "There's the whistle!" he said aloud, as he suddenly awoke from his dream of the past, and, with a brain strangely confused, rushed out in as much haste as though the train were about leaving, and he was afraid of missing it.

He had made up his mind that he knew just how his friend would look —if this should prove to be the one he hoped to see. Of course he could remember that only real friend of his boyhood, tried and true; whom he had selected as his one confident of all the boys in school. Even his hair was unlike that of any other boy; it was long and straight, and very black; and his face was so smooth, and his eyes so full of frolic! Yet they could be piercing eyes sometimes; and always they were clear as water, and capable of tenderness unspeakable. Oh! there would be no need of an introduction; he would know that boy anywhere.

So, with eager expectancy, he watched the passengers; he had chosen a position where he could keep a lookout along the four cars which made up the passenger portion of the train.

But though he looked sharply, and was sure he saw every one who got off, yet he could testify that no boy answering to the description, was among them. He would not have believed that he could be so disappointed! How much he had hoped to see his old chum! "How foolish I was," he said to himself, "to have built up such a castle in the air out of a telegram from a stranger!"

"Pardon me, sir, but I was expecting to meet an old friend here, to whom I had sent a message, and, as he has not come, I thought I would like to inquire about him. May I ask if you live in this neighborhood? My friend lives in the next large town west of here; or he did the last I heard of him."

All this time Mr. Moore had stood staring at the stranger who was talking to him; one of the few who had stepped off the cars. "His name," continued the gentleman, "is Thomas Moore; and I " —

"This isn't Macy Sylvester," broke in Mr. Moore, "the boy I knew thirty years ago? That can't be! "

Well, that used to be my name, but it has been so long since I have heard it in full, I could not at first think whether there was not some mistake. Then this must be Thomas— my old friend who plighted vows of friendship with me over a divided chestnut."

"But you have been growing so old," said Mr. Moore, half-dazed. "Your hair used to be as black as a raven's wing, and now it is almost white; and you wear a gray moustache!"

"See here, my boy," his friend replied, "have you had no looking-glass for the last ten years, that you should think it so strange that I have changed a little? What has become of all those auburn curls you used to wear? Why are there so many wrinkles on your face, and what about your gray hairs—or the want of them?" he added, with a genial laugh, as Mr. Moore just then lifted his hat for a moment, thereby revealing a bald spot on the top of his head.

"O, yes! I have been growing old, I know; but some way I thought you would look just as you used to. Excuse my queer actions. I'm half-dazed. But now suppose we shake hands just as we said we would; if you have not forgotten how that was, you will prove yourself to be the friend of the divided chestnut."

Then came the grasp: first, of both left hands, followed by both right hands outside of these, then three shakes, each pronouncing one word to a shake, "Firm — friends — for" — and then each whispered — "ever."

It was queer enough for two gray-headed men to go through a programme prepared for them when both faces were young and fresh. Of course they both laughed heartily, and "the ice being broken " there was no more restraint.

"Now," said the man with the moustache, "that boyhood nonsense was all right for boys, and it is all right for us to be boys, in imagination, again, especially when it proves our identity; but, since we are men, and our gray hairs admonish us that time is flying, if you can trust me enough to do so, please tell me briefly your story.

"What about your family and your business? I don't want to be inquisitive, but, as a friend, I would like to know just how the Lord has led you all these years."

For a moment Mr. Moore was tempted to reply that he didn't think the Lord had had much to do with leading him of late, but something in the clear eyes and earnest countenance before him restrained him.

Without very much detail, he told the story: of his children, of the loss of his first wife, the sickness of the one now living, and how it took the most careful management to make the two ends meet.

Mr. Sylvester listened eagerly, his face speaking plainly of the interest he felt, rejoicing if the story was joyful, and being shadowed when scenes of sickness, suffering, and death, were described, through it all watching to see if his old friend gave evidence of an acquaintance with the "Friend that sticketh closer than a brother."

When the story was completed, it was easy to see a shade of disappointment pass over the listener's face.

"And all this burden you have been carrying alone!" he exclaimed. "So much trouble, and no Comforter! How hard it must have been."

Evidently his friend did not comprehend his meaning.

"O, no!" he replied; "we had some good neighbors, for whose kindness I ought to feel very grateful; but they little understood what I felt, and though I never said so before, there have been many days when it seemed to me I would have given almost anything for some dear, tried friend who could understand how I was situated, and with whom I could have talked freely. You know what I mean: I wanted someone as true and sympathetic as you would have been — and are yet, for that matter," he added, as he saw the tears in his old friend's eyes.

It was interesting to notice how this grave, middle-aged man was being affected through the memories of boyhood, as they were brought back to him by this friend of long ago.

That old, often-repaired fence of reserve, which he had been so long strengthening around his heart, was ready to fall before this little breeze from the South-land of Love.

Yesterday he would not have believed himself capable of such "weakness" as he had come to estimate such talk of one's trouble. "The way to be a man, is to be a Stoic, and take things as they come, troubling no one else with your affairs." He had often said this to himself, and here he was, doing the very thing he had condemned, and feeling the better for it! His poor, hungry heart had been near starvation, and now seemed about to assert itself. Why, he had hardly dared to let his youngest boy put his arms about his neck, since the mother went away, lest he should break down before him; be had hardly ever kissed the soft cheeks of the boy, for fear of losing self-control. Had he but known it, much that ailed his invalid wife was that ugly fence which kept her outside.

A few tender words now and then would have been better medicine than all the quinine and bitters she had ever taken.

That she did not know what she needed, is no proof that mine is not the right prescription. If the invalid knows what is the matter, and what to take, why send for the doctor? My young readers must pardon this bit of moral application, for the sake of the older ones. If you choose, you may pass over this part, and leave it for those who need it. There are such, for I have seen them.

Well, we will go back to these friends. As Mr. Moore finished that last sentence, and saw the tears in the eyes which looked so kindly on him, he felt surprised and thankful to be able to claim such a friend. Not less glad was the friend, for he felt that here was an opportunity for a word which he prayed might be helpful.

"Had you no friend such as you describe?"

"Not one, near me; you were somewhere, I suppose, or you wouldn't be here now. But my dear mother was gone, and who had I?"

"But, Thomas, have you not heard of the Friend who 'sticketh closer than a brother?' Has he not said, 'I am with you always,' and has he not promised that, 'As one whom his mother comforteth, so will I comfort you?' Always near, stronger than a brother, more loving and tender than even a mother, is this divine Comforter; and you have not known him! Long ago, but a few years after we parted, you and I, I found this Friend; I needed him so much! When my poor heart seemed breaking at the loss of my dear father and mother, both at a stroke, I cried unto their God, and He heard me. Since then I — But there is not time to tell you of my long experience," he broke off hastily, as the train gave a warning whistle. " This I can truly say: I am glad I found Christ; and all those years no burden has been so great, no sorrow so heavy, — and I have had sorrows, — that I could not carry it with his help."

Never before had Mr. Moore been spoken to on this subject with such intense earnestness. He looked his friend in the face, and read the sincerity of the man in his pure, clear countenance, and his tenderness in the tearful eyes, and tremulous voice.

"He knows what he is talking about, and feels it, too; his is the genuine kind of religion; I would like that kind for myself. It is business with him; off the same piece with Aunt Cornelia's, or made of the same kind of stuff; both are 'all wool.' The only difference is, one is for a coat, the other for a dress."

How fast thought can travel! It took but a moment for this to pass through Mr. Moore's mind. He was almost ready for Mr. Sylvester's next sentence.

"Thomas, my dear old friend, why not now do what you have so long neglected? Why carry such heavy burdens, when your mother's God stands ready to carry them for you?

"Once you and I said, you remember, that we would be friends forever, and shook hands over it. Now let me, who am speaking for my. Master, act for Him in this, so far as I can; and you give me your hand, just as though He were here, and my hand were His; and I will shake hands for Him, and you make the pledge, and the covenant shall be ratified. Will you? Say quickly, for this is my train. Come, here is my hand; in 'His name,' give Him yours." Was it too sudden? Had he not known all about this matter for years and years, and thought of it often?

"I must go," said Mr. Sylvester, "good-by!" extending his hand again; this time it was taken and pressed most heartily. "Is this for good-by or for the covenant?" he asked.

"For both," was the firm reply; "the one for eternity."

"Good ! And good-by! I will write you from Leeds in about three weeks, I trust, when I want you to meet me here again on important business; still, it is not so important as this which we have transacted to-day.

"God bless you, dear friend!"

And he was gone.

CHAPTER 16: A RECONCILIATION

I HOPE you have not been so interested all this time in Margaret Moore and her affairs as to forget Johnnie— poor, warm-hearted, quick-tempered Johnnie! who could get into more trouble in one day, I do believe, than any other boy who ever lived; who was always sorry afterwards, although he generally forgot to say so; and who went to bed, each night, with the determination to be an angel the next day, and forgot it before he was dressed in the morning.

One day, in his roving through the house in search of amusement, he brought up in the garret. It was a place to which he seldom went, nothing being there, so far as he knew, which could be turned to account in the way of fun. But the day was cold and windy, and Johnnie was coughing hard, and had been ordered to stay in the house. What could a boy do in the house all day? He knew that Margaret had been unhappy for several weeks over the fact that she was forbidden the garret; in fact, he knew that she had cried about it. He had lain awake a whole night, he thought, and heard her sob; although, to be strictly true, it was only a half-hour. Now what in the world could there be in the garret to make a girl cry because she couldn't go there? reasoned Johnnie. Something must be hidden up there which Margaret wanted. He didn't believe it was a book, though Aunt Amelia said that Margaret "pored over novels every chance she could get." What would hinder her from keeping a book in her drawer, which had a lock and key? She could surely get a chance to peep at it once in a while, much easier than she could if it were in the garret. No, Johnnie had no faith in the book theory. The more he thought about it, the more sure he felt that she and that Hester Andrews, who was up to all sorts of mischief, had some great secret hidden in the garret; something which ought to be found out, just as likely as not. Who could tell what a girl like Hester Andrews might lead their Margaret into? Johnnie resolved to discover the secret, and felt virtuous and happy over the resolution. Behold him now, moving with noiseless step over the creaky floor, peering into every nook and corner of the great dim garret; starting at every sound of his own making, turning actually pale when, by a sudden movement, he loosened an old flowered satchel, such as our grandmothers used to carry, from the nail on which it was hanging, and it fell to the floor with a thud. Johnnie never knew before that things could make so much noise.

"Pshaw!" he said, straightening himself up, "who cares if she does hear me? I guess it's my father's own garret, and I've a right in it. He never told me to keep out."

Nevertheless, for some reason, Johnnie felt queer. Could it be because he was in search of a secret? Where could it be hidden? If he only knew something of its shape, and size, it would be so much easier to find. After a patient hour spent in poking over old boxes and bundles, finding nothing more astonishing than is usually found in an old garret, he was beginning to get discouraged, and almost decided to give up the search, when his eye lighted on the old desk.

O ho! here was a thought. The secret was hidden in some of its drawers as likely as not. Why hadn't he rummaged there before it began to grow dark ? So saying, he opened and shut drawer after drawer in eager haste.

Margaret's key had turned, it is true, when she thought she locked the desk, but the rusty lock had not. He came presently on the very paneled drawer which had been discovered by Margaret a few weeks before. In her haste she had not closed it quite securely, and Johnnie found it with less trouble than she had taken. His round eyes opened wide at the sight; who would have thought of there being another drawer in the old thing! Ah-ha! There was a letter, tucked into the very farthest corner, as though someone wanted to hide it. Here was the secret, without doubt; now he would know why Margaret wanted to get up garret so badly. She and Hester Andrews had planned to run away, perhaps, or do some other dreadful thing; and they wrote to each other about it, and the letters were kept in the secret drawer. He pounced on the package, then suddenly paused with a look of perplexity on his round face. After all, ought he to read this letter?

It did not belong to him, and certainly he had not been expected to read it, or it would not have been put in a secret drawer. But then, what if it was something that father ought to know about? Perhaps it was his duty to read it, in order to save Margaret from danger.

No, Johnnie, your great truthful eyes will not let you see wrong for right. Even should this be something which your father ought to know, your duty would be to take it to him, with the seal unbroken, and let him decide what should be done. Still in doubt, he took it in his hand, and read, with eyes which grew larger momently, the words on the envelope: — "For my dear daughter Margaret. To be given to her on her fourteenth birthday."

How Johnnie's heart beat! He understood, instantly; mother's hand had written those words; not the mother who was down-stairs, but the mother who had been gone away for so many years that Johnnie hardly ever thought of her now. Yet he remembered her, oh! very well indeed. Had she not held him in her arms times when he was tired, or sleepy, or unhappy from any cause? Hadn't she kissed his red cheeks always when she washed them! Could not he, once in a while, on lonely nights, when he could not get to sleep, think how her voice sounded when she leaned over him and said, "Mother's little boy?" Johnnie's breath came quicker and quicker. His chin quivered, and, if it had not been for an interruption, which came just then, I think he would have cried.

The interruption was his Aunt Amelia's voice at the foot of the stairs, short, sharp, and decisive: "Johnnie Moore, you come down here this instant, as fast as you can march! What business have you slipping off to the garret as quick as my back is turned? I'll tell your father of you, see if I don't." And as Johnnie, startled by her voice, dropped the panel of the secret drawer with a bang, and shoved it hastily into place, he heard her add, in no gentle tone: "I never did see such young ones as there are in this house! Always up to something. I don't wonder Sophia is sick."

By this time Johnnie was half-way down stairs. He intended to get to his own room as soon as possible, and get rid of that dreadful lump in his throat; but the door of his mother's room was ajar, and, as he slipped by, she called his name: "Would he hand her the glass of water that stood on the little table near the window?"

Her voice sounded gentler than usual, or else the boy imagined it. He brought her the glass, and stood silently by while she drank it; but, instead of giving it back to him, she laid her hand gently on the brown one, which hung listlessly at his side, and said: "Poor Johnnie! has this been a long, lonesome day?" And Johnnie, the brave, sturdy boy, who hated "fusses" and loved fun and mischief almost better than he did anything else in the world, dropped down in a little heap on the floor in front of his step-mother, and burst into tears; it was of no use; the lump in his throat must have its way.

Now, in order to understand what followed, I shall have to go back a little and tell you some things which had happened to Mrs. Moore. Do you remember the afternoon when her pastor came to read to her, and closed the reading with a few earnest words about the Lord Jesus, and his willingness to give help and comfort to all who need? That had not been the only talk they had had together. Poor Mrs. Moore, lying wearily on her bed, with plenty of time to think, was ready to own that if anybody in the world needed help and comfort, she did. Long ago, when she was a little girl younger than Margaret, she had thought for a few days that she was a Christian; but in a very short time she filled her heart with other things, and forgot all about Jesus. Of course it was harder for her to get back to the place where she could understand and feel his love, than it would have been if she had not neglected and insulted Him these many years. But He is so patient and forgiving and wonderful in his love, that all the time He stood ready to receive her, — was calling her, indeed; and the hardness of the way was all in her own heart. At last she had come to understand that there was a place for her close beside the loving Lord, and had gone to Him for rest. It was on this very day, that in going over her life, trying to find out her mistakes, she had resolved to be more patient with those children for whom the Lord Jesus had called her to care; to try to treat them in every respect as she would wish she had when He asked her for her account. She always had tried to do what she thought was her duty by them; but the trouble was, she had never understood that He had called her to give not only care, but love. Johnnie had come nearer to her heart, however, than had either of the others; and now, when she saw the tears rolling down his cheeks, she felt a great throb of pity for him. This made her voice very gentle as she said: "What is it, Johnnie? Do you feel sick tonight? Is your cold so very bad?"

"No, ma'am," said Johnnie, struggling with his sobs, "it isn't that; I don't know what is the matter; only it is lonesome, and father has not come home, and Margaret has got a letter from mother; and I want one, and she didn't write any for me; and, oh! dear me, I wish she could, but she can't."

And Johnnie rocked himself back and forth, in utter abandonment to grief. Mrs. Moore was very much startled. What did all this mean? "Margaret had a letter from mother!" What mother? Surely not the one who had been gone away for years!

Mrs. Moore bent forward hastily, and felt the pulse that was bounding in Johnnie's brown, and not over-clean, hand. No fever there. Johnnie mast know what he meant, if he could stop crying long enough to tell. By and by he did manage to mumble out, in answer to many questions, something like a connected account of his afternoon's exploit. The new mother felt almost as Margaret had when she first discovered the letter. A message from Heaven for the little girl the mother had been obliged to leave. How solemn it seemed! What would she, who knew she was going away from her darling, have to say to her? She would want her to be sure and come to her in Heaven. This the new mother decided. "And perhaps, oh! perhaps," she said to herself, "it will depend on what I do for her whether she will ever go there or not!"

"Johnnie," said Mrs. Moore at last, "I would not cry, poor little boy!

I am sorry for you, but it will only make you feel worse to cry."

"If she had only written me a letter," sobbed Johnnie, "I should have liked it so much; and I'd have done just as she said; and now she never can!"

"She didn't have time; but I can tell you what she would have said: she would have wanted you to be a good boy, and get ready to meet her in Heaven. Johnnie, suppose you and I begin now, and try to do that last; then when we see her, I will tell her what a good boy you were, and she will be glad. And, Johnnie, I will try to be a mother to you as well as I can. Will you try to love me, and help me?"

She was bending toward him, her cheeks flushed a pretty pink, and her eyes, though they were filled with tears, yet seemed to be smiling. But honest Johnnie, who always spoke his thoughts, whether they were wise or foolish, said, with eyes so full of surprise that they stopped the tears, "Why, I couldn't love you; they never love step-mothers!"

Oh! cruel world, that puts its heedless, meddling thoughts into the hearts and mouths of childhood! Such a thought as this never started in Johnnie's own brain. The pink flush deepened to crimson on the step-mother's face, but she answered quickly: —

"Oh! yes, they do; I knew a grand man once who said when his step-mother died that it seemed to him for a while as though he could not live without her. I don't suppose you can love me like that, but don't you know, Johnnie, that I am the mother whom God sent you, in the place of the one He took away? Don't you suppose He expected you to love me a little?"

Johnnie's tears were quite gone now. He was so much astonished that he did not take his great blue eyes from his mother's face. He had never heard her say anything like that before. Instead of answering the question, he asked another, his face very eager, "Do you love me?"

"Yes," said Mrs. Moore, returning the earnest gaze, without flinching, "I do love you, Johnnie, and want to help you." She hesitated a moment, then went on steadily: "It has not been very pleasant in our home, because — well, Johnnie, you know you haven't tried very hard to make me love you, and I have felt sometimes as though none of you cared whether I loved you or not; but very lately I began to love the Lord Jesus Christ, and it is going to make everything very different."

She had not intended to say all this; indeed, when she called Johnnie, she had not meant to say anything of her new hopes and plans. Her object had been simply to begin, by having a friendly talk with the boy. But his tears, and his pitiful wail for a "letter from mother," had touched her heart as nothing about him had ever done before; and to-night she felt that she did love, and long to help, the poor lonesome child. Johnnie was watching her with steadfast, critical gaze, saying nothing. At last he drew a long, relieved breath, as though satisfied with the result of his investigations, and said aloud in emphatic tones, "Then I will."

Just what he meant was apparent to no one but himself; but if you had seen into his heart just then, you would have known that it expressed determination to "stand by" this mother from this time forth. If she really loved him, and he found that, somehow, he could not help thinking she did, that settled the matter. Johnnie was not much given to tears, nor did he spend a great deal of time in reflection. Great things had happened to him to-night; things that would make a difference with all his future life. He dimly realized it, but he did not want to talk about it any more; so he looked about him, eagerly, for an excuse to get away, and finally decided that his mother needed some fresh water, and hurried from the room. Mrs. Moore gave a long sigh as the door closed after him. How much of a beginning had she made in the new life which she meant to live? How much of the heart-story she had told him, did the boy understand? It is almost a pity she could not have peeped into the sturdy little heart as its owner stumped down the stairs. She would have seen something like this: —

"I don't care what Mag and West say, nor what any of 'em say, I'm going to stand by her. She's a great deal better than I thought they ever could be ; and she said she loved me, and I believe her, and I mean to love her myself ; so there!"

Now it happened that this was the evening of the very day on which Mr. Moore had gone to Potterville to meet his old friend. At the foot of the stairs Johnnie met him as he entered the front door. "How are you, my boy?" he said, and bent down and kissed the hard red cheek, the "boy" being so much astonished thereat that he forgot to return the kiss. It is a mournful fact that this father had not kissed his youngest child before in many many weeks. As soon as he could lay aside his wraps and bundles, Mr. Moore went at once to see how his wife had borne the long day after him. How much of a beginning had she made in the new life which she meant to live? How much of the heart-story she had told him, did the boy understand? It is almost a pity she could not have peeped into the sturdy little heart as its owner stumped down the stairs. She would have seen something like this: —

"I don't care what Mag and West say, nor what any of 'em say, I'm going to stand by her. She's a great deal better than I thought they ever could be ; and she said she loved me, and I believe her, and I mean to love her myself ; so there!"

Now it happened that this was the evening of the very day on which Mr. Moore had gone to Potterville to meet his old friend. At the foot of the stairs Johnnie met him as he entered the front door. "How are you, my boy?" he said, and bent down and kissed the hard red cheek, the "boy" being so much astonished thereat that he forgot to return the kiss. It is a mournful fact that this father had not kissed his youngest child before in many many weeks. As soon as he could lay aside his wraps and bundles, Mr. Moore went at once to see how his wife had borne the long day.

And from there Amelia called to him to come and eat the dinner that she had kept warm, as the family had taken dinner and supper together earlier in the day. While swallowing his last cup of tea, he heard the dull thud of a shutter as it banged back and forth in the wind. "Where is that, I wonder?" he asked, and Amelia answered : "Oh! I suppose it is in the garret; Johnnie slipped up there when my back was turned, and I suppose he opened the doors and windows and did all the mischief he could think of before I missed him. I meant to go up and see what he had managed to do, but I have been so driven from one thing to another all day, I couldn't. I haven't had a minute." And Mr. Moore, looking at her tired face, which seemed to be growing old too fast, wondered if she knew anything about the " burden bearer " of whom he had been hearing this day. "Did you find the man you went to see?" asked Amelia, suddenly. "Who was it, anyway?"

"It was my dear old friend," Mr. Moore said, "the best friend I ever had." Then he pushed back his plate and said: " I will go up and close that shutter; the noise will trouble Sophia. How has she been to-day?"

"Oh ! I don't know; about as usual, I guess. Johnnie was in there a long time this afternoon. When I called him from the garret he slipped in there, and I saw when he came down that he had been crying, so I suppose he got into some scrape and worried her. He is too full of mischief to live, anyway; I never saw such a boy." It was Mr. Moore's turn to sigh; already the home burdens were pressing heavily, after his few hours of rest. He went with very slow steps up the stairs to the old garret. Once there, he looked around him curiously. He was quite as much a stranger in this part of the house as was Johnnie. But all about him, set neatly in rows, or hanging from the beams, were familiar boxes, trunks, and bundles; pieces of all the years seemed peeping out at him from this neat store-room. The scene fitted in with the day's experience. Had he not been back into the past? Just behind the wide old chimney a rope was stretched, and an old-fashioned curtain hung from it. He remembered the quaint, gay calico; that curtain used to be his mother's. With gentle hand he lifted it and looked behind it. Who had made a secret chamber here, and for what purpose?

An old chair, having but three legs, a bit of wood doing duty for the fourth, stood near the window, and on it lay a book. The floor had been swept clean, and a strip of carpet was spread before the chair.

With a curious choking in his throat, Mr. Moore bent down, and took the worn little book in his hand. He recognized it instantly— his wife's old Bible. Her name was on the flyleaf, and below it the words:

"For Margaret, from her mother." It all flashed over him in an instant; here was where Margaret came to read her Bible, and to pray. She had told him that she read no book in the garret but her Bible, and he had forbidden her to come here! The tears which had been very ready all day, fell on the Bible now, but I am glad to tell you that the next thing this poor troubled father did was to get on his knees in the little closet Margaret had made, and I think the angels who wait to carry good news from earth to Heaven, must have hurried home just then to tell a joyful story; for, with his head bowed on the little old Bible, Mr. Moore gave himself to the Lord Jesus Christ, to be His servant forever.

CHAPTER 17: NEW THINGS TO THINK OF

WHEN Mr. Moore at last came down the garret stairs it was late. Amelia had kept up a clatter in the kitchen as long as she could consistently make herself believe she was doing any work hoping Mr. Moore would come back and administer a thorough whipping to Master Johnnie. Not that she hated him, or wished to revenge some of the numerous tricks he had played on her, but she was very tired that night. It had been a particularly trying day for her, and the sight of Mr. Moore's worn face at the tea-table roused a feeling of indignation in her against all boys in general, and Johnnie Moore in particular.

To think that her sister's life should be so full of trouble all because of those children! It was her opinion that Sophia would be very happy with her husband, even though he was rather poor, if it wasn't for those "young ones," as she called them.

But at last the work was done. The dishes had been washed, carefully wiped, and set in martial array, exactly at the right angle; the floor brushed free from every imaginary speck of dust or crumb. The clock was wound, the sponge set; even the stove had received an extra polish, and stood sleepy and black, ready to guard the still, dark kitchen during the night; the windows were fastened, and the door, and if there had been a cat, Amelia would have put him out for the night; but no cat was allowed around the premises. There positively was not another thing for Amelia to do. She stood a moment looking at the clock, then she took her lamp, tried the back door once more to be sure she had locked it, and went up to her sister's room.

It was time she helped Sophia to bed. Probably she was all tired out by this time if she had had a combat with that Johnnie! She hastened her steps, expecting to find her sister very cross at having been left so long alone. But no, Mrs. Moore sat quietly looking into the fire, a trifle sad-looking, to be sure, but without the habitual worried wrinkles she had been won't to wear.

She raised her head as Amelia entered, and asked where Mr. Moore was.

"He's gone up garret to close a rattling shutter," replied Amelia, "and to see what last piece of mischief that scamp of a Johnnie has been up to," she would like to have added, but she caught the words before they escaped her. There was no need to worry this sick sister; there were enough other things that could not be kept from her.

It was a pity that she had not spoken out this time, for she might have heard that about Johnnie which would have softened her heart toward him. She was surprised when, in answer to her offer of help, her sister said quietly: —

"No, Amelia, I think I'll wait a little while. I'm not very tired."

There was a something in her sister's words and face which astonished Amelia more than the fact that she wanted to sit up longer. She couldn't quite determine just what sort of a look it was, but it was something new, such as had never been on Sophia's face before.

She took up her light once more and went to her own room. Margaret had gone to bed, and Amelia observed, with a sniff, that the bedclothes were all awry. She had been crying, too, for there were traces of tears still on her face, and the deep-drawn breaths every now and then had the shiver of a sob in them. This made Amelia sniff again. She was sure she never cried when she was such a great girl as Margaret. She put down the lamp on the corner of the bureau, and went to find a pair of stockings to darn. The ones she found had not very large holes in them, and there was no immediate necessity for darning them that night, when she was so tired, but she must have something to do, and she did not feel like going to bed until Mr. Moore came down. She began to feel uneasy about his staying in the garret so long, for what could a man in his right mind find to do in a dark, dusty garret, unless there had been some terrible mischief done there that he was trying to right? But Amelia worked on, finishing that pair of stockings and another one before he came. She remembered the tired look on his face, and began to think that perhaps he might have been taken sick, and she ought to go and see, when she heard his step on the stair. She was somewhat surprised when she saw, by the light of the lamp in his hand, how utterly untroubled was his face. He went to his own room, and she shut her door with a sharp bang that made Margaret stir in her sleep, and went about her preparations for the night, trying vainly to conjure up a reason for her brother-in-law's long stay in the garret, as people will about things that are no concern of theirs.

Mr. Moore was surprised to find his wife sitting up yet. He saw, too, the changed expression of her face, which Amelia had noted — the hardness all gone out.

They never knew which began it, nor how it started, but they had a long talk then and a good many explanations. Somehow the light which came from the little worn Bible in the garret shone in Mr. Moore's face and filled his heart, and he could not help telling his wife all about it. They told each other how they had found the Lord Jesus Christ, and each was so pleased and surprised to find that the other understood.

Margaret would scarcely have believed her senses if she could have heard her step-mother telling her father that she knew she had not done all she could have done, and that it was mostly her fault that there had been so much trouble. He comforted her, and told her they had neither of them done right; that they would start out all new again and see what they could do, in the strength of their new Helper.

Then Mrs. Moore told her husband of her visit from Johnnie, and the talk they had had. The story touched him as nothing had done since his wife died, and his eyes filled with tears.

Mr. Moore was called away very early next morning to attend to some urgent business. He took his cup of coffee and a bite of bread standing by the kitchen table, and then was off. He did not come back to dinner, so he had no chance to tell Margaret that she was free now to go to the garret as often as she would.

Margaret was cross. In fact she was a good deal more than cross. Amelia had been very domineering all day, and then, when she went upstairs her step-mother spoke kindly to her, and she had answered her crossly. Of course that had made her feel all the crosser.

She stood by the window looking out on the world. The dull gray sky, the slushy streets, and bare, shivering branches, made but a desolate picture. She had about decided that there was no use in trying to be good any more. She couldn't be, and what was the use of trying to be what she couldn't? She had been a martyr long enough, and she would just have a good time now, and do as she pleased. She told herself that her heart was as black as a thundercloud, and as hard as — she had not quite decided what, when she saw Johnnie running up the fast darkening street, holding a little package in his hand, and shouting wildly to her.

A package for her? What could it be? From the post-office, too! Who could have sent it? Her heart beat high, and she forgot all about the blackness and hardness of it.

Her fingers trembled as she cut the string and opened the paper wrappings.

A little olive-green book! — Margaret loved olive-green — with sprigs of gold all over it, and red edges. "Ethics of the Dust," she read. "What a queer title! What does it mean, I wonder?" she said aloud.

But there was nobody in the room to answer her, for Johnnie, seeing it was "nothing but a book, and no pictures in it at that!" had gone back to his snow-balling on Beech Street.

She turned to the fly-leaf. There was her own name, "Margaret Moore, from her friend, Elmer Newton."

She turned over the pages, reading a little, reveling in the story of the "Crystal Orders," "Crystal Quarrels," "Crystal Sorrows," and "Crystal Rest."

There were paragraphs marked here and there, but it was growing dark, so she lit the lamp, and sat down by the large dining-table. Here was a marked paragraph that looked very inviting: —

"Look up at your own room window; you can just see it from where you sit. I am glad that it is left open as it ought to, in so fine a day. But do you see what a black spot it looks in the sun-lighted wall?"

Lucilla. — "Yes, it looks as black as ink."

"Yet you know it is a very bright room when you are inside of it; quite as bright as there is any occasion for it to be, that its little lady may see to keep it tidy. Well, it is very probable, also, that if you look into your heart from the sun's point of view, it might appear a very black hole, indeed; nay, the sun may sometimes think good to tell you that it looks so to Him; but He will come into it, and make it very cheerful for you, for all that, if you don't put the shutters up. And the one question for you, remember, is not 'dark or light?' but, 'tidy or untidy?' Look well to your sweeping and garnishing; and be sure it is only the banished spirit, or some of the seven wickeder ones at his back, who will still whisper to you that it is all black."

Margaret was astonished that she should so have found an answer to her own thoughts. She read it over again. How should she go to work to tidy up her heart for Jesus to come in? But her quick brain answered the question: "Put out all the ugly, dirty things in it. Ugly thoughts and words and feelings." She turned the pages uneasily. Ah! Here was another marked paragraph!

"God is a kind Father. He sets us all in the places where he wishes us to be employed; and that employment is truly 'our Father's business.' He chooses work for every creature which will be delightful to them, if they do it simply and humbly. He gives us always strength enough and sense enough for what He wants us to do; if we either tire ourselves or puzzle ourselves, it is our own fault. And we may always be sure, whatever we are doing, that we can not be pleasing Him if we are not happy ourselves. Now, away with you, children; and be as happy as you can. And when you can not, at least don't plume yourselves upon pouting."

Margaret began to feel as if John Ruskin had written those words just for her. But was it true? Would her work be always delightful to her if she did it simply and humbly? Wiping the dishes for Aunt Amelia, for instance, and mending Johnnie's stockings, could those ever be delightful tasks ?

A sudden resolve came over her. She would try it. She bowed her head on the little green-and-gold book, and prayed, "Dear Jesus, if Thou wilt give me the strength and sense, I will try to be simple and humble." Then she heard the upstairs door close, and she knew that Aunt Amelia was coming down to get supper, so she put the new treasure in a safe place, and went straight to the work He had chosen for her.

"Yes," Margaret decided, "there is a sense of pleasure, even at first, in having Aunt Amelia say, when she came in and saw the table-cloth already on the table: 'Well, I declare! Beginning to set the table without being told! What's come over you?"

She had to go back once, and straighten the knives and forks, for she remembered that she was doing it for Him, and that it must be done as perfectly as He gave her the sense with which to do it.

There didn't seem to be nearly so many dishes to-night, and somehow, they wiped faster than usual. Was it because she was doing it for Him? she wondered.

She found that it required some patience to mend those long-neglected stockings as well as she could, but she decided, when it was done, that it had been delightful work, and well worth the patience when, the next morning, Johnnie said : —

"I say, Mag, what splendid big darns you put in my stockings. I didn't know you could do it so good. They're most as good as new ones now."

One other surprise Margaret had that night.

Her father called her to him as she was going into her own room, and told her she was at liberty to go to the garret now as often as she chose. He paused a moment, and seemed embarrassed, and then went on : —

"Margaret, I am sorry I was so hasty with you. I have found out that what you said was all true. I am glad you are trying to be a good girl, and I hope you will have a better father hereafter." It was all he could say, for you must remember that he was not accustomed to speak to his children on such subjects. He would have liked to have had Margaret know that he had found his Saviour, but he did not know exactly how to tell her.

Margaret went to her room with many things to think of, and wonder about, that night.

CHAPTER 18: THE TRUE REASON

"IT seems to me," said Amelia, as she sat down a plate of cold chicken with a little more emphasis than seemed necessary, "that you have too much to do nowadays. This is the third time this month that you have had to get up to go on the early train on some sort of business. And we have to light up the house, and wake up Sophia, and you come back at night as tired as a dog."

"It is quite an honor," said Mr. Moore, as he pushed back his chair, and proceeded to put his napkin in the ring, "to be sent on such important errands. It is true that since I have been promoted I have more to do, but I get a much larger salary, you remember. But I am sorry that it makes so much trouble. A bite of any kind would do for me."

"It isn't that," said Amelia grimly. "It doesn't make a particle of difference in this house now how much folks have to do for other people; the spirit of unselfishness seems to have entered into you all, and it is a pity if I can't have a little. I don't mind the trouble." "It is the spirit of Christ," said Mr. Moore, rising as he spoke, and he added kindly, "I wish you had Him for a friend, Amelia."

You have heard nothing about Mr. Moore's promotion? I know it, but you must remember that we never engaged to tell you everything that happened to this family. If we did, we should never get this story finished. Still, you ought to be told a little about it.

You remember Mr. Sylvester, of course, and the hint he gave that he wanted to see Mr. Moore in Pottersville in a few weeks' time on important business? Well, they met again; and the business proved to be connected with the firm for which Mr. Moore had worked for years. Mr. Sylvester had recently become a partner in the business, had greatly enlarged its operations, and, in casting about for the right man to take a responsible place in it, had remembered his old friend, and so managed matters, that he was called to fill the place. So without moving from his home, or changing his place of business, Mr. Moore suddenly found himself lifted to a good position, and receiving an excellent salary; so much for old friends.

"You are going to the city?" said the minister, as he met Mr. Moore in the hall, "would it be too much trouble for you to hand this note to Secretary Lawrence, at the Y. M. C. A. Rooms? If you have any extra time, you would find it very pleasant to stop in at the noon prayer meeting."

"Thank you," said Mr. Moore, as he stopped to put the letter in his pocket. "No, it will not be too much trouble. Good-morning!"

And in less than fifteen minutes he was in a car of the early train, being whirled along toward New York. Here he had plenty of time for thought, and thought was more pleasant to him than it had been for some time. The Moores' skies were much less cloudy than they had been for years. Mr. Moore had given the true reason. The spirit of Christ had entered the home, and had made a difference in the most trivial matters of everyday life. Not that everything always went all right; not that Margaret's temper had been completely subdued; not that Johnnie's mischief had vanished; not that Mrs. Moore was perfect, but after any trouble there was sorrow — and sunshine. For sunshine can never be perfectly bright unless there is sorrow for sin.

It had been but a few weeks since Aunt Cornelia had come to the front again. This was the letter she had written: —

Mr dear Nephew:

Since my plans for Margaret have been (undoubtedly wisely) overturned, I have been anxious to do something for another of your children. Although Margaret cannot be spared from her mother, I think Weston could. Our schools are considered excellent, and if he will not be lonesome with only an old woman, I wish he could come and help make the winter less dreary for me. There are plenty of books, and plenty of fun in coasting and skating during the winter, and some pleasant, good boys. I think it would be a good chance for him, and shall be glad to see him here if you all think best. I will pay his traveling (and of course all other) expenses.

Remember me kindly to Sophia, Margaret, and Johnnie. I hope to see Weston very soon.

Your loving aunt,
Cornelia.

After much talk in the Moore family, it was decided that Weston should accept the invitation, and start East immediately. It is true that he did not look forward to the winter with Aunt Cornelia with all the pleasure that Margaret had, and it is also true that she was at first not entirely reconciled to his going in her stead. Many times during his preparation for departure, did she rush up to the garret to gain strength by a word of prayer, or a glance into the Bible, or the book Elmer had sent her. But she would invariably return cheery and ready to help. So she bade Weston good-by at the door with a hearty sisterly kiss, and returned to her home-life. She did not then realize that in trying to do faithfully and patiently her everyday duties, she would be doing as good service as in battling with the great world outside, or in that small portion of it embracing Aunt Cornelia's home, and Weston's school.

But to return to Mr. Moore. He left the train in the Grand Central Depot, and hurried out into the crowded streets. What a scene of tumult it was! A sea of life, with multitudes of human beings surging in its waves, all seeming to be in a hurry, all having their separate joys and sorrows, temptations and aids. Carts and carriages of all kinds blocked the street; here and there a policeman was engaged in helping a frightened woman with a baby carriage to escape from prancing horses or drunken drivers. Policemen are at a premium in New York. Mr. Moore pushed his way along through the crowd, and across the street as fast as circumstances—meaning people and vehicles— would permit, until he finally saw ahead the sign of his New York firm. Here he found a dingy, dusty office, and several glum-looking men, sitting behind desks covered with ledgers and bank-books and day-books of all kinds, dating back to prehistoric ages, smelling musty, and covered with dust. The glum-looking men looked at the new-comer glumly, and regarded him severely throughout the whole conversation, but afterward praised him to his employers for his energy and quickness of thought.

The business transacted, Mr. Moore started in search of the Y. M. C. A. Rooms. There he found the Mr. Lawrence to whom he was to deliver Mr. Wakefield's letter, and was promptly invited to remain to the "noon prayer meeting."

"What a strange time for religious service!" said Mr. Moore, unused to city ways.

"I know it seems so," said Mr. Lawrence, "but many clerks, workingmen, and all sorts of persons who have a half-hour's leisure at noon, come to the prayer meetings at this hour, and we do good work here. Will you come to the platform with me?" And without more words, Mr. Moore found himself mounted on an elevation at one end of a well-filled room, before many men of all ages and classes of society. He was at first rather embarrassed, never having been in such a position before, but soon interested himself in the faces of the audience. There was a young man in one of the front seats who particularly attracted his attention. He had a handsome, but rather hardened face, which bore a look of almost despair on it. He was poorly dressed, although there seemed to be about him an air of refinement. For some reason, he seemed strangely familiar to the visitor on the platform.

Mr. Lawrence read the story of the Prodigal Son, and made a few very earnest remarks upon it. "Our Father is always willing to receive wanderers," were his closing words, "no matter how far away they have strayed. Will not some one accept the invitation, and come to Him now?"

As soon as the closing prayer was concluded, Mr. Lawrence turned to introduce Mr. Moore to the president of the association, but while they were talking the young man the visitor had noticed came up; there were tears in his eyes. "I have made up my mind to come home," he said softly.

"Thank the Lord!" said Mr. Lawrence, as he turned to speak with him. After a few moments' talk he asked the young man if he would like to sign one of the Y. M. C. A. pledges, a simply-worded promise to "Try to do whatever was the will of the Lord Jesus Christ, and to endeavor throughout one's whole life to lead a Christian life." The young man turned to the writing-table, and, at the bottom of one of the pledge cards, signed his name in bold, round characters, "Jacob Z. Williams."

Mr. Moore, who had been looking on with interest, started suddenly. "May I inquire what your middle name is?" he asked abruptly.

The young man smiled. "Zabed," he said. "It is a queer old-fashioned one, but was my — father's," and a shadow passed over his face.

What was the matter with Mr. Moore? Just this: He remembered very distinctly a summer's day, a little country depot, a primitive ox-team, an old withered man, with an old tobacco pipe. He heard the words again: "If you ever see my Jake, and he needs a lift, why, just you remember the steers; that's all. I dunno where that boy is, nor how he's goin' to git home."

Uncle Zabed Williams!

"I think," said Mr. Moore, addressing the young man, "that I know your father — that is, if you are Jake.'"

Young Williams turned quickly. "Is it possible?" he asked. And then followed many questions. Was his father living? Was he well? Did he live in the same old place? Would he be willing to receive back his wandering son? None of which questions, save the last, Mr. Moore was able to answer. Of that one, he felt sure; but it had been a long time since he had seen " Uncle Zab," and he might not be living now.

"I will arise," said the young man, "and go to my father. And I will say unto him, Father, I have sinned against heaven and against thee, and am no more worthy to be called thy son." And on the evening train

Mr. Moore and Jacob Williams started out together.

The young prodigal gave his newly-found friend some of his history. "My father was always good to me," he said, "but I became dissatisfied with the drudgery of country and farm life, and finally got all the money I could from him, and went to the city. It was not long before I found that I would better have stayed at home, and I lost all my money, and tried hard to earn more. I wrote to father, and borrowed some from him. Again and again this happened, and I finally resolved never to go back till I could support myself and pay father for what I had borrowed. The time has not come yet. But when I decided to go to my Heavenly Father, and heard so providentially of my earthly one, I resolved to go home. I hope he will receive me back — and, indeed, that he is there to receive me. I don't deserve anything so good."

"I have no doubt," said Mr. Moore, "that you will find him safe and sound, and will be a help to him all the rest of his life. Here we are at my place. Salemville is a few miles beyond. Good-by!" And he was off.

At his door were Margaret and Johnnie waiting to meet him, and he kissed them both tenderly. This was a little thing, one that thousands of children never think of at all, but the Moore children were just getting used to being kissed — very often. It was a little sign of the coming pleasantness of their life.

After supper, when Margaret had finished her work, and Amelia had gone to bed to nurse a headache, the whole family gathered in Mrs. Moore's room.

"I have had a remarkable experience to-day," said Mr. Moore, and he told them the story of "Jake," the prodigal son.

It was about this time that a young man was walking up a winding country road through the little village of Salemville. Once and again he stopped to look about him at the familiar scenery on every hand. The moon was shining, and lighted up the fields and farmhouses with its beautiful silver light. Did it not seem to smile down on the returned wanderer, he thought, as once more he came home?

Just as the Moore family were about to start for bed, Mr. Moore said, "Let us all kneel down and pray — for Jake, and for ourselves." And his wife never offered a more thankful prayer in her life than when her husband set up the family altar in their home. For after that it became their habit to gather for prayer before Johnnie went to bed, and to have a blessing asked at the table. Margaret was at first surprised, then delighted. This was what her father had meant by those few words when he told her she might go to the garret. And the first chance she had to go there again, she was on her knees by the old chest, thanking God that her father had learned to love Him.

It was when the Moore family were all in bed that night, when Johnnie was snoring loudly, and Aunt Amelia was still awake with her headache, that a few miles away a young man was kneeling by the side of a bed, with the moonlight resting on the face of an old man, whose white hair was pushed back from his forehead, and who was listening to some words from the younger. "He is always ready, father, and willing to forgive, just as you were willing to forgive me, and receive me back; I know, for I have found Him. The blood of Jesus Christ His Son cleanseth us from all sin. Will you not accept His salvation?"

And the old man answered, "Aye, if He'll have me."

Not many minutes later, while the moonlight still streamed in upon his face, the eyes were closed, the tongue and heart were still, but about all there was a look of peace. Such peace as only Christ can give.

A few days later Mr. Moore received a letter bearing the postmark of Salemville. He opened it quickly. It was, as he supposed, from Jacob Williams.

Dear Friend: —

Because of your kindness to me a few days ago, I take the first opportunity of thanking you again, and telling you of my father. Only yesterday we laid him to rest in the cemetery on the hill. He was injured by an accident in a sleigh, and died the night I came. So I arrived just in time. It gives me more joy than I can tell you to say that he fully forgave me for all the wrong I have done — yes, welcomed me joyfully back, and at the eleventh hour accepted my Saviour. If it were not for the wasted years of my life, and the wrong I did him, I should have reason to be happy that I was able to comfort his last hours. Yet as I looked at his gray hairs and deeply furrowed face, now still and cold, I felt that I had whitened his hair, had furrowed his face, and had killed him! How much of my life would I take back, if it were possible!

I do not know what I shall do now. I have nothing to support myself with, although I have an ordinary education, and must look up a place. I shall be here, however, for some weeks. If you have time I should be very happy to have a word from you once in a while, as I have you to thank for being at my father's bedside in his last hours, to point the way of salvation to him, and to receive his forgiveness.

Yours respectfully,
Jacob Z. Williams.

It was but the next day that Mr. Moore was stopped on the street by a friend of his, on his way to the office.

"Moore," said the gentleman, "I don't suppose you know of any young fellow who would be a help to us at the store? We want one who is well enough educated to keep accounts, and write business letters, and so forth, but who will be willing to do errands and help in the lading."

"I'm not sure," said Mr. Moore, "but I know just the one." And he showed him young Williams' letter. The store for which the gentleman was inquiring was a new one, with good men at its head, and Mr. Moore felt that it would be a good place for his young friend, if he chose to take it.

The end of it was that in a few weeks Mr. Williams was established in the new store, and had obtained a neat, comfortable room in a neighbor's house, taking board at Mr. Moore's, which he paid for by bringing in wood, and building the fires in the morning, and "helping generally," as Mr. Moore said. For Amelia was not strong enough to do these things, and Mr. Moore was too busy. And so the young man became almost a member of the family, and won the affection of all by his quiet readiness to help, and his pleasant manner.

A few weeks after he had come, Amelia left, for her mother needed her. Mrs. Moore was almost well again, and Margaret felt sure she could manage the work. "I think you will get along all right," said Amelia, as she bade good-by to her sister, "for a new spirit seems to have entered this household, that makes everything go right. As nearly as I can make out, it comes from the garret."

"It comes from higher than the garret," said Mrs. Moore.

CHAPTER 19: A REVELATION

IN two days more Margaret would be fourteen; then that letter would be here. What a revelation it would be. It would be almost the voice of her dear own mother as she spoke on her dying bed. But what was in it? Would it give her joy or pain? And why was she not permitted to read it long ago? Why when she was fourteen? And what if there were commands or requests in it which it would not be pleasant to obey?

No wonder, as Margaret was so absorbed in thinking of the possibilities of the letter, that Mr. and Mrs. Moore noticed daily absent-mindedness in the daughter; that sometimes the dishes were actually placed on the back-stairs instead of the pantry-shelves, and that the potatoes were occasionally sought for in the attic rather than in the cellar. Margaret's mind was hourly busied with the letter.

As the time drew near to go to the hiding-place of the letter and break the seal and read, her heart and flesh fairly failed, but she had been growing in faith during the last weeks, and she resolved, by the help of God, to carry out her mother's wishes, however much self-denial it might require.

While she sat in her rocking-chair by the window thinking it over, and softly humming to herself, —

" Jesus, I my cross have taken,
All to leave and follow Thee,"

there came a ring at the front door. Before she could hurry below the caller had been let in and was inquiring for her.

"I am after Maggie," said the familiar voice of Mattie Randall to Mrs. Moore. "Mamma is going to give me a birthday party to-morrow evening. A good many are invited. We're going to have games and refreshments — icecream and everything — just a splendid time, and of course Maggie must come. You'll let her, won't you, Mrs. Moore?

Oh! here she comes. O Maggie, what do you think?" — and the excited girl ran over the particulars of her party, patting in many new points of interest not mentioned to Mrs. Moore.

"I am engaged for to-morrow evening," was Margaret's calm answer.

"Engaged!" said Mattie contemptuously. "What engagement can you possibly have that need keep you from my party? That's all nonsense. You'll come, won't you? Be sure to be there by eight o'clock."

"I can't be in two places at once," Margaret said quietly. "I told you I had an engagement."

"With whom, and for what?" asked the rude girl.

"With Margaret Moore, and for — myself."

Mrs. Moore was silent. The other questioner with a toss of the head answered, "Indeed! But perhaps you will explain."

"Margaret Moore is going to keep her own birthday."

"You! What! Alone? You can't get anyone to it, I'm sure. They're all promised to mine."

"I can keep it alone if no one cares to come to help me," was Margaret's quiet answer, but a smile came and went as she thought within her heart, "My own mother will be there, and my Master."

"And so you really are not going to accept my invitation? You'll be the first to refuse."

"How can I, Mattie, with my previous engagement?"

At this the girl proudly wheeled and bowing a cold "Very well," left.

Mrs. Moore looked at Margaret as if she thought she had lost her senses, and wondered if there were not some deep scheme at work in the young girl's head.

Somehow Margaret could not trust herself to a conversation with her mother; her heart was too full of the things just before her.

Really, Mattie Randall's party had no attractions for her. She had thought it all over, and decided not to read the letter until the evening of her birthday, when all should be quiet in the house, and she could have the time to herself without fear of interruption and she would go to the garret and sit by her mother's Bible, and in her mother's chair to read it. And the day wore away.

Miss Mattie was more than nettled at Margaret's calm refusal. She was maddened.

"I'll pay her for refusing to come to my party. I'll see about her birthday. Her birthday, indeed! As if that was of any account.

"They say she's getting to be very good nowadays. I suppose she thinks my party's too worldly an affair for her saintship since she's joined the church. The little hypocrite! Her Aunt Amelia told my cousin Jule that she kept dime novels up in the garret and went up there to read them, and told her father she went up to read her Bible. Her aunt said she shouldn't wonder a bit if she ran away or did some other dreadful thing, her head was so crammed full of adventures and things. As likely as not this is the very night she's planned to go. I shouldn't wonder a bit. She wouldn't have stayed away from my party for nothing and missed all the fun.

"What if I should write a note to Mr. Moore and warn him to look out for her! Wouldn't that be a good joke on her, though? I guess she'd find out it wasn't quite so much fun to have a party all by herself. Besides, I should not wonder a bit if she were intending to run away, and if she is, of course I ought to tell her father."

Quieting thus her conscience, she turned into the post-office and penned in a disguised hand these few words, and dropped the letter addressed to Mr. Moore, into the letter-box: —

Your Margaret means mischief to-night. I am not permitted to tell all I know of her plans to leave home, but as a friend I advise you to watch.   A   Friend.

Some hours after Mr. Moore took the note from the office, but, being busied with another matter, he slipped it into his pocket, at the same moment letting it slip out of his mind.

And the evening of the birthdays came on. Mattie's home across the square was brilliant as mid-day. Throngs of the village girls and boys were pressing in. In the course of the evening some one whispered to her neighbor, "I 'wonder why Margaret Moore is not here? Was she slighted? Queer, isn't it?"

But the whisper had somehow crossed the room and reached the quick ear of Mattie Randall, who was prepared to tell her confidential friends what "they say" about Maggie, and to unfold her own opinions. It was "a splendid way to pay her off, the hateful little thing!" she told herself.

And the listeners listened and opened their eyes, and exclaimed: "What! Margaret Moore?" "She?" "I never heard of such a thing!" "Who do they say she's going with?" "The little hypocrite! "

Then the music began, and there was a rustle of feet and dresses and the dancing had begun.

Refreshments were passed, with sparkling wine in tiny glasses. Some did not touch it, but many drank, and for the first time, and were excited by it.

Two boys in the corner had just been talking with Miss Mattie about Margaret Moore. One said to the other: "Let's go and see. Maybe the fun is going on now."

Accordingly they slipped out at a side door, and stole across the park towards Margaret's home.

It was long past midnight. The lights in the neighboring houses were all out, and, save in Mattie's house, a painful stillness reigned.

Only through the lattice of Margaret's garret refuge they thought they discovered a glimmer of light.

In the early evening, when Margaret had finished her usual after-tea duties, and found herself alone, her mother's letter in her hand, and she about to open and read, she suddenly stopped.

"What was that? Who is calling me?"

She spoke below a whisper, but it was only the merry voices of the party-goers, one saying to the other, as they passed below her window, "This is Margaret Moore's house. I wonder if she's going to Mattie Randall's party?"

"Guess not, if all they say about her is true," from another.

"What do they say?"

"Too much of a saint. Don't ever do anything so wicked as to go to parties nowadays."

"I don't believe a word of it," said the first. "You don't catch Margaret Moore letting go a party such as Mattie'll give to-night for religion." "Yes," from another, "I'd like to see the girl who'll do that."

"You don't know Margaret Moore or you wouldn't say so. I wish I were half as good as she is." This from still another.

And Margaret from her attic window heard now a full sentence, then but a broken expression. She knew they were discussing her, and that among the passers-by but one seemed to utter a word in her behalf. And, holding her letter before the dim light, she finally stammered out: —

"What would my dead mother say of me? Which side would she be on?"

She was about to open the precious epistle, her heart fluttering and fingers shaking, but at that moment there came a sharp gust of wind, and her light went out.

Feeling around for a match and not finding one, she softly stole down to her room, but the door creaked loudly, and fearing lest she might awaken her parents, she stood almost breathless for a moment, and then, moving quietly with the utmost care, was soon back in the garret, the lamp relighted and ready to read:—

My darling Margaret: —

[At those words, so strange to her and tender, her eyes filled as she pressed the letter to her heart, sobbing. "Oh! if some one had said that to me long ago," she thought.]

Your mother must say a few words to you before she goes to her heavenly home. When you are fourteen years old, my precious daughter, you will be old enough to understand and do the things I ask of you. And first of all, my dear child, see to it that you are heart and soul for Jesus. Could I live my life over again, I should wish to walk daily and hourly with the Lord Jesus, breathing in and breathing out

His blessed spirit, especially at home, and endeavoring to let my companions feel that my heart and treasure are in Heaven. Dear, dear one, your mother pleads with you not to follow after the vain things of this fading world, but to keep the world under your feet, and make all your companions know that you are the child of a King. Promise me this, Margaret, dear, before you read further —

["I promise," murmured the little girl solemnly.]

And promise me again that you will be a dutiful and loving daughter, trying to make your father happy, and that you will try to be a patient and beautiful sister, and be very choice of your companions. Darling one, on my dying bed I write these warning words, and I look up to the Saviour near me praying: "Oh! save my child from the first false step. Keep her in the hour of temptation, and when the time comes bring my dear one safe and pure to glory." So, darling, you will promise your mother this, too, to choose none but true Christians for your intimate friends?—

["Yes, darling mother, I promise."]

Dropping upon her knees, she made the promises again before the Lord, asking help and strength, and so kneeling, she fell asleep.

The two listeners below, hearing nothing, their curiosity aroused by the stories of the evening, made up their minds to find out what was going on in that garret. Creeping stealthily around to the other side of the house, they discovered a ladder; as quickly it was brought and leaned against the house by the low kitchen, from whose roof they hoped to be able to reach the garret window by the use of the ladder which they would pull up after them.

One of them began to mount, and was very near the roof, when a round of the ladder gave way, and he was hurled violently to the ground, crashing through the shrubbery, and groaning with fright and pain.

The noise aroused Mr. Moore, who suddenly sprang from his sleep, and quickly threw up the window. The street-lamps were still flashing, and gave light sufficient to discern the outlines of things, revealing to Mr. Moore's excited gaze the ladder, while at its foot was a dark figure struggling to disentangle itself from the thick bushes and escape.

"Whose there?" loudly called the father, but no answer came. For a moment he waited and gazed. Nothing now was to be heard but the sound of rapidly retreating footsteps.

The father concluded that the invaders, whoever they were, would not return that night, but thought it would be safe to remove the ladder.

He threw his coat about him, fumbling meantime in its pockets for matches, and as he did so his hand touched the envelope so hastily put there the day before. As soon as he had a light, he tore it open and read. His face turned ashy pale, and without a word he tossed the note to Mrs. Moore, and rushed to Margaret's room. Without waiting for a word from the daughter, he pushed the door ajar and called "Margaret, Margaret, are you here?"

No one was there. He now was sure the room was vacant and his child gone.

Stunned, bewildered, he passed his hand across his forehead, lest he might be still dreaming. Then turning suddenly, he rushed back to his wife, repeating at every step, "Gone ! gone! gone! Wife, she's gone; get up quickly, I must pursue them. Quick, wife, oh! quick." And the poor father, hardly knowing what he did in his haste to find his boots, overturned a table with a loud noise that seemed to ring through the house.

Then came a knock at the door, and the familiar voice of Margaret spoke: —

"Why, papa, what is it? I was frightened out of my sleep. Are you sick? Is mamma? How she breathes!"

In a moment she was at her mother's bedside bathing her face and fanning fresh air upon the gasping mother, while Mr. Moore, looking first at one and then at the other, was too beside himself to render any aid to Margaret in her brave effort to arouse her mother, but at length Mrs. Moore opened her eyes.

CHAPTER 20: UNEXPECTED COMPANY

ALTHOUGH Mrs. Moore's eyes were open, she was really quite unable to see through all the peculiar circumstances. Neither was Mr. Moore much less bewildered than she.

What did it mean? Here stood the girl who was supposed but a few minutes before either to have run away or been stolen! It could not all be a dream, for there was that letter of warning which someone had kindly sent them, and the ladder still stood where it did when some one fell from it. Margaret certainly was not in her room when her father looked there for her. All these circumstances were clear, and all pointed as straight as the links of logic could. Many a poor fellow has been hung on evidence not so clear as was before them. But there stood Margaret — a little excited, it is true — why should she not be ? — but with a face as shining as — well, as any good, pure girl's face is, especially when it is illumined by the indwelling Spirit.

For a few minutes nothing was said, beyond Margaret's murmured "Poor mamma!" for she thought that all the trouble of the night grew out of the fact that her mother was suddenly taken ill again; and she supposed the low "Thank God!" that came from the father's trembling lips, meant that his wife was better.

But really his mind was busy with this mystery. How could he doubt the child, or how believe her? Something must be said; how should he begin?

Margaret's face was resolute enough, but he could see no lines in it that looked like deception. Still, it was very late, and she was not in her room, and there was a ladder, and some one — just then he caught sight of the corner of a piece of paper, hidden in Margaret's dress; it was her precious letter which she had slipped in there for safe keeping. In a flash there occurred to her father a way to open this terrible subject without charging her directly with having done wrong. She could not object to his reading any letter which it was proper for her to receive; and if this letter should have something in it which would explain the other, the way to speak would be only too clear. Acting upon the impulse of the moment, he spoke with more sternness of voice than he had meant to use: "Margaret, give me the letter which you have hidden in your dress."

For a moment Margaret, having forgotten that her letter was with her, and a corner of it in sight, did not know what he meant, and stood looking at him startled and bewildered. This seemed to the father like hesitancy, and an attempt to keep from him a letter which she was ashamed to have him see. He therefore repeated his direction with more sternness than before, and on the instant, Margaret remembered her treasure. Fortunately she had no wish to conceal anything, though she certainly would not have chosen such a time for showing her mother's letter; and it seemed very strange to her that her father should call for it just then and there. She would have waited for a quiet Sunday evening, if she could have had her way; but there was, of course, no excuse to offer for not obeying at once. Her cheeks flushed a little as she passed the precious paper into his hands, and then busied herself about something for her mother.

Mr. Moore, with a stern face and an anxious heart, adjusted his glasses, and walked over to where the lamp was standing, on a little shelf near the grate. He did not notice the address on the envelope, but drew out the letter slowly, as one who would like to put off unwelcome facts as long as possible; he dreaded to read what he felt he must know.

What was the matter now? Mrs. Moore, from her position on the bed, was anxiously watching his movements; she understood something of what he feared, and she too dreaded the explanation which this letter might give. When she saw her husband's face change suddenly, and then saw the tears roll down his cheeks, she felt that their worst fears must in some bewildering way be realized. It was her eager, anxious "O, father! what is the matter?" which brought him suddenly back to the bedside. But what he did was to put his arms around Margaret and kiss her with a peculiar tenderness; then he handed her back the letter. "It is not for me, daughter; certainly I must not read it unless you want me to."

Poor bewildered Margaret! Is it any wonder that she lost her self-control and sobbed almost hysterically? She had been through strange and exciting experiences all day. The strain upon her in anticipating what that letter from her own dear mother would say, had been very great to one of her peculiar temperament; and now had followed this sudden illness, and these mysterious scenes, her father's sternness over, she knew not what, and then his kisses, and his tears. What did it all mean?

"What is the matter?" said Mrs. Moore in great excitement. "Is something wrong? won't you explain?"

And Mr. Moore in answer laid a caressing hand on his daughter's bowed head. "Nothing is wrong here," he said; "I am sure of so much; I do not understand about the noise outside, but it will be time enough for that in the morning. We have very much to be thankful for. Margaret, how very selfish it was in us all to forget your birthday."

"O, father!" murmured Margaret from the pillow where her face was buried, "won't you take the letter? I want you to read it; you must want to read every word she said."

And she handed back to him the precious letter, consecrated by being the last words her own dear mother had ever written.

As he read it, the slow tears followed one another down his cheeks. I suppose it would be difficult to describe the exact feelings of these three people while this scene was taking place. Especially was Mrs. Moore bewildered. Her husband had been too much absorbed with Margaret and her letter, to realize what a strain all this was to the so lately recovered wife; but he suddenly roused himself, and looked over at her pale questioning face.

"Shall I read it aloud, Margaret?" he asked; "I think this mother would like to hear it." There was a little struggle in Margaret's heart; it was so unlike what she would have chosen — she had meant to show it to them both, but not together. She wanted each of them to read it alone, at some quiet time; to her it was such a sacred, confidential letter, that she shrank even from any talk about it. But had not she promised to try to give up her own way?

"If you think best, father," was her low-toned answer, and the tender words were read aloud.

She need not have been afraid of the "talk," for there was very little said. "It is a precious letter," murmured the living mother, breaking at last the silence which fell, after the reading ceased: "A dear, precious letter; I am glad for you, Margaret; and it will help us all, I think."

And her father, deeply moved, kissed her again and again, as he gave it back, and said: "It sounds like her, my daughter; I know you will treasure it always; may God help us all to help each other. And now it is very late; you ought to be sleeping. Would you like me to go up-stairs with you?"

"O no!" said Margaret, wonderingly; she knew nothing about the ladder and the noise. "I am not at all afraid; but I don't feel much like sleeping."

And then Mrs. Moore made her wish known: "Before you go, won't you both kneel down here by the bed, and ask God to help us all to live better lives?"

That was a family worship which Margaret never forgot. To her great surprise, it was her step-mother's voice that led the prayer. How earnestly she thanked God for leading those three to a knowledge of Himself; how earnestly she prayed for Weston and Johnnie! and for their daughter Margaret on her fourteenth birthday. How humble and tender her voice was when she asked for wisdom and grace to be to them all that she ought to be, and could be, and to live among them as one who remembered that their own dear mother was gone to Heaven, and was waiting for them there.

Mr. Moore's voice spoke a solemn "Amen," at the close, but Margaret could only cry. But she bent down, before she went away, and kissed her mother, smiling on her through her tears. She did not feel like sleeping, you remember, yet in a very few minutes from that time, she had forgotten all the strange experiences of the day and night, in a sound, healthful sleep.

Rest was not, however, so easy for Mr. Moore; in the first place he thought it wise to light a lantern, and make a tour of the grounds, and take down that ladder. His search was rewarded; near the ladder he found a jack-knife with initials engraved on it; and an envelope addressed, containing an invitation to the party across the way. The name on the envelope and the initials on the knife corresponded.

The handwriting of the person who sent the anonymous letter had evidently been disguised, yet, on comparing the two, it was quite plainly to be seen that the one who sent the invitation, and the one who addressed the letter without name, were the same persons.

Mr. Moore knew the young man whose name was on the jack-knife; he decided not to make the matter public in any way, but to see if he could get an influence over the boy, and try to help him.

A few days after all these things happened, it chanced that Mr. Moore had an opportunity of speaking with the boy in question, when no one else was near. Drawing from his pocket the stray knife, he said: "I believe I have something here which belongs to you; I ought to beg your pardon for keeping it as long as I have; but there has been no favorable opportunity for returning it."

The boy turned a very red face toward him, but took the knife in silence; before he had thought of anything to say, Mr. Moore drew from another pocket the envelope, with its card of invitation, and passed it to him, saying simply: "This lay very near the knife. And here, by the way, is another envelope, the hand writing of which reminds me very much of the other. What do you think about it?" The scheme worked perfectly. The boy, glad to have something suggested to him to say, studied the envelope for a moment, then said, "It looks to me like the same."

"Do you think you could be sure of it?" asked Mr. Moore.

"Why, yes," with a slight hesitancy; then, after a moment more of careful studying, "Yes, sir, I'm sure it is; no one else makes a W like that."

"So I think," said Mr. Moore. "And now, young man, you see there are some things I know, but there are others about which I am not quite so clear. In my opinion, this letter and a certain ladder are closely related. I can imagine certain things, but in regard to some of them I would like an explanation, and I think I have a right to demand it. I do not propose to be hard on you; if I am not mistaken, you are already ashamed of your share in this entertainment, and I don't believe you will practice acrobatics by night again; but I think you may be able to give me a little help in preventing other and more serious troubles which are likely to result, if people foster the habit of writing words to which they are ashamed to sign their names."

The young fellow was caught; was, indeed, to a certain extent, confided in. He was shown the mysterious letter, which at first had given Mr. Moore so much anxiety, and then he frankly told all he knew, which was enough to convince Mr. Moore that a high-tempered and weakbrained girl was the source of all this trouble.

He gave the boy permission to tell her the whole story, and warn her against such folly in the future.

It was quite late when Margaret came downstairs the morning after her exciting night. Not because she had been slow in getting the consent of herself to rise, or had been leisurely about her toilet when she was at last awake. The truth was, she overslept, and father and mother had been careful not to have her disturbed.

The family were seated at the breakfast table when she entered the room. Under her plate lay a letter.

"From Aunt Cornelia!" she exclaimed eagerly, and produced from it a lovely rose whose perfume filled the room. The letter was being slipped into her pocket for a more quiet hour, but her father said: "How is that? Aren't you going to read it? I'm afraid Aunt Cornelia wouldn't feel complimented if she should see her letter put aside for breakfast."

"Do read it, quick!" said Johnnie, "or let me; I'm hungrier for a letter from Aunt Cornelia and West than I am for buckwheat cakes."

Poor Margaret was discovering that people are not all alike; instead of having the lovely, quiet time she had planned for with that precious letter, she must read it to the family at once. That is, the Margaret who was trying to be unselfish about little things must do so.

It was a very short letter, but it came near spoiling her breakfast, and Johnnie's, too. Just a few lines, to say that they should expect a nice warm supper waiting for them that very evening; for, contrary to her expectations, she had found that she and Weston could spend the short vacation with them.

Johnnie went off into such ecstasies of delight over this news, that he almost overturned the table in his glee. It seemed to him so long, so "dreadful long" since Weston went away; and now to think he and Aunt Cornelia were both coming, this very day!

But there was a postscript to the letter. Aunt Cornelia said she was coming in the hope that, now their mother was so much better, Margaret could be spared to go back with her for a nice long visit. This sobered Johnnie for several minutes; poor noisy, roguish, warmhearted Johnnie! He sat with his fork poised in air, and a doleful look on his face, as he said he "wished aunties didn't have to live such a long way from home; and he wished folks didn't have to go to school at all." Then he drew a long sigh, and passed his plate for some more of the warmed potatoes.

Fortunately, with Johnnie, sorrowful feelings did not last long; his busy young brain was soon at work over plans for the day; what he would have to do to get ready for Weston; how many new things there were to show him, and what nice treat they could have for supper. To each and all of these matters Johnnie attended.

There was a bossy calf Weston had never seen; so smooth and sleek that she had been named Deer. Then both his and Weston's hens had indulged in a family of chickens, and though Weston had not been there to watch his, it had two the most. What fun it would be to tell him about it! and, "Couldn't they have chicken and biscuits in gravy for supper?" It was decided by the elder ones of the family to have only a lunch at dinner time, and put off their regular dinner until the travelers came.

Over this Johnnie looked grave for a minute, then finally burst forth with his difficulty: "But s'posing they shouldn't come to-day, after all; folks don't, sometimes; then wouldn't we have any dinner at all, to-day?"

When the laugh which this raised was over, he went with his father to catch some chickens which were not of any account, because they belonged to Mr. Moore, and not to Johnnie and Weston.

That was a busy day for the entire Moore family. Of course the spare room must be swept and dusted, and the bed made up afresh, and everything put in beautiful order; not forgetting the flowers which Aunt Cornelia loved, and to which Margaret attended; as she did indeed to many other things. Just as matters were in fairly good order, Johnnie came "marching home" not in soldier array, but with his arms full of vines and mosses, and other woodsy treasures, with which he insisted the room must be trimmed. Margaret was tired, but good-natured, and setting to work again, made a bower of beauty out of Johnnie's supplies.

Long before train time, the horse was harnessed, and Johnnie, with his arms around the fine fellow's neck, gave him some information.

"Now, Ned, you must do your best to-night, 'cause they don't know you; West doesn't even know we've got you; but he'll like you first-rate; I promise you that." And Ned bowed his head a great many times, and said as plainly as a horse could: "That's all right; I'm ready to do my part; don't you be afraid."

And when that long-waited-for train finally whistled, and the travelers for whom Mr. Moore and Johnnie were watching, stepped out on the platform, behold there were three of them!

Now, in order to explain, I shall have to take you back a few weeks and introduce you to a poor organ grinder, who was taken sick in the city where Aunt Cornelia lived. He had been fond of setting up his organ under Aunt Cornelia's window, and many a good dinner had come to him from the kitchen. Once she came out herself and asked about his cough, and gave him some medicine, and asked where he lived.

Some days afterwards, when she found he did not come again, she resolved to look him up, and found him very sick and weak. After that the poor organ grinder had such care and comfort as only a thoughtful woman can give. As he grew weaker, and became conscious that he was going to die, he seemed troubled about something. He knew so little of the English language, that it was hard to understand him, or be sure that he understood what was said to him. But Aunt Cornelia could not help feeling that the most important thing he certainly understood. He would often speak the "Name that is above every name," clasping his hands as he did so, and looking upward with such a peaceful expression, that she could not believe the troubled look was for himself.

One day he made them understand that he must have his old coat, and from it he drew a little book, and handed it to Aunt Cornelia. There was much writing in it that she could not read, but at last, after puzzling over it a long time, she found the address of a New York firm, and read it to him. His face grew bright, and with much effort he succeeded in making her understand that the old organ must be sent back to that address. Then he pointed to the trained Newfoundland dog who had been his one faithful companion in this land of strangers. What was to be done with Pedro? The wise old fellow looked sadly from one to the other, and seemed to understand all that was going on, which was more than Aunt Cornelia did for a long time. At last, however, it dawned upon her that the organ grinder wanted to give Pedro to her. After that, the troubled look passed away. For the few remaining hours of the old man's life, he seemed perfectly at rest. Do you think that Aunt Cornelia left the worn-out old body to be buried in the Potter's Field, at public expense? Not she! To be sure she might have done so without wronging any person. But had she not been made the Italian's heir and executor? She had inherited all his estate — that faithful dog — and she felt in honor bound to see that his body had a respectable Christian burial. So she paid for a grave in the cemetery, and followed the body there, next to Pedro, the chief, and indeed the only mourner.

As for Pedro, he adopted her at once; needing not even an invitation to follow her home, and establish himself as the protector.

Now, the Moores, as a family, had not been in the habit of indulging in pets of any kind. Things were changing with them, however, even in this respect, as Johnnie's calf and Margaret's canary could have told you; but the idea of having a dog had not occurred, as yet, even to Johnnie ; or if it had, he thought it too wild a wish to be mentioned; yet if you had taken him aside some day, and asked him confidentially what he really would like better than anything else in the world, he would have answered, "A great big Newfoundland dog." This, by some mysterious process, Aunt Cornelia discovered; and it will account for that unexpected passenger who came on four feet.

It was a very happy company that gathered around the Moore dinner table; there was much talking and laughing, but one boy made the most of his remarks to his beloved Pedro, who stood by his side with his great head in Johnnie's lap.

CHAPTER 21: LITTLE INTERFERENCES

IT was while Mrs. Moore and Margaret were clearing the table and washing the dishes that Aunt Cornelia asked her nephew, "How is Frances? She has not written to me for a long while." "I think she is well; I have seen very little of her lately; while Sophia was sick my duty was here every spare moment I could get; and since I have been doing extra work for the firm it has been pretty busy times with me. Frances was in the office the other day --well, come to think of it, it must have been six weeks or more ago. I meet Irving on the street now and then."

"But, Thomas, do you mean to tell me that during the time Sophia was sick Frances never came to see her or you?"

"Oh! we did not expect it; you know Frances never comes here."

"But in case of a protracted illness, it might have been reasonably expected."

Mr. Moore sighed, and Aunt Cornelia, dropping that subject said, "Sophia looks well." "Yes, I think so."

"Even better than before she was sick; she looks rested. And, Thomas, I think you are looking very well indeed; your work seems to agree with you, though Sophia says you have been working very hard."

"Yes, the work is hard and plenty of it. But now that Sophia is well, I have less home care." Just then Margaret passed through the room and Mrs. Merwin remarked: "Margaret has changed wonderfully. She has grown tall and she looks fairly radiant; not much like the forlorn child she was last summer."

Mr. Moore came over and sat beside Aunt Cornelia, who, looking at him closely, said, "Thomas, what have you done with your wrinkles? I thought the last time I was here that you were growing old fast. But you are all smoothed out."

Mr. Moore laughed — a little happy laugh. "Well, Auntie, you seem to have taken in the fact that things here have changed somewhat.

We have passed through some pretty stormy times, but we seem to have come out into fair weather and smooth sailing. The truth is, Sophia and I have begun life all over again. If we look rested, it is because we have learned where to lay our burdens."

"Thomas, do you mean that you and Sophia have become Christians?"

"I mean just that."

"Praise the Lord!" said Aunt Cornelia fervently.

"I should have written to you," continued Mr. Moore, "but it was all so new that I did not seem to know how to tell it; it has never been an easy thing for me to put my thoughts on paper."

"But, Thomas, you can tell it. How did you reach the decision?"

"The Lord hedged me in. There was a time when, for a few months, I could see no way out of our troubles. They multiplied until they seemed sevenfold, and our prospects of happiness as a family looked dark indeed. Then, in strange and unexpected ways, the claims of Christ were presented again and again. The question what I would do with Jesus, followed me until I was constrained to yield, and then, to my surprise, I found that Sophia had already heard the Saviour's call and had responded with a surrender of herself." "Wonderful!" said Aunt Cornelia. "Do you know that all the early part of the winter I was so anxious for you two people; it seemed to me that you were likely to make shipwreck of your lives, just at this point; and I asked the Lord to take the guidance of you and your affairs. Then later there came to me a restfulness about you all. I could not quite understand it, but I believe now it was the blessed Lord himself who took the burden off my heart." After a little more talk, Aunt Cornelia asked, "Thomas, does Frances know about this?" "No; as I told you, I have scarcely seen Frances; and I do not know how I could speak to her of this matter while she feels so unreconciled to Sophia."

"It might make a difference — it ought to. I must go up there to-morrow; perhaps you would like to have me tell her."

The last dish had by this time been washed and dried, and Mrs. Moore now joined them, Margaret delaying to fill the tea-kettle, saying:

"Mother, you can hang up your apron for to night; I will stir up the batter-cakes before I go to bed. Aunt Cornelia shall see what nice ones I can make."

Meantime Weston had been introduced to the new bossy calf, had been to consult with Johnnie about a kennel for Pedro, and had also been down to the office for the last mail, and soon they were all gathered in the sitting-room, Margaret beside Aunt Cornelia, whose hand was laid caressingly upon the young girl's shoulder.

"Is it decided that I am to take Margaret home with me for a long visit?" she asked, looking at Mrs. Moore.

"I do not know — that is, we have not come to any spoken

decision. So far as I am concerned, I am willing; she is a great help to me" —Margaret's cheeks flushed and her heart gave a bound at this word of commendation — "but I can get along; and she has had a hard winter, I guess," looking fondly at the girl who with her cheeks aflame was almost ready to declare that she would not be hired to leave home. Mr. Moore said he had been too busy to consider the question; and anyway it would be as her mother thought best. He was afraid Sophia would overdo, but they would talk it over and decide in a day or two.

"Don't worry, Margaret," said Mrs. Moore; "I think the decision will be favorable."

Conversation ran on cheerily until presently Mrs. Moore, noticing Mrs. Merwin's tired looks, said, —

"Thomas, I think your aunt is tired enough for bed; would it not be better to have prayers at once, so she can get some rest?"

Mr. Moore gave a little start of embarrassment; it was the first time they had entertained company since the establishment of the family altar; he had not found it difficult to pray with his wife and children, but he had not thought how it would be to lift up his voice in prayer in the presence of others. And strangely enough at just that moment Aunt Cornelia seemed to him the person of all others before whom he could not pray. He had not hesitated to speak to her of his new-found love and joy, yet prayer seemed another sort of confession for which he was not ready. He knew so little of the forms of prayer. He did not know that Margaret, when she heard him pray, had said to herself, "Father talks right out of his heart."

Once Mr. Wakefield had suggested that they would like to hear his voice in the prayer-meeting, and Mr. Moore replied, "Yes, I want to be heard there, but I am not quite ready. It is all so new; I must learn to pray in secret, and with my family: as the Lord gives me strength and utterance, I have promised him to use his gifts." And once or twice, of late, he had felt almost as if he must use his voice in public. Here was a new and unthought-of situation. And there sat Weston! the boy who had never heard his father's voice in prayer. He would be so taken by surprise. If he had only been written to about this changed home! But though these thoughts passed through Mr. Moore's mind in a whirl, while Margaret stepped to the door to call Johnnie, who had gone to see if Pedro was settled for the night, there was no apparent hesitation upon his part.

It was in a clear firm voice that he repeated the verse: "'Lord, if I have found grace in thy sight, show me now thy way, that I may know thee,'" and added: "This has been my prayer all day; I think I have a growing desire to know the ways of the Lord."

Mrs. Moore said: "My verse for to-day was 'Only fear the Lord and serve him in truth with all your heart, for consider how great things he hath done for you.' And I have been considering the great things he hath done for me; it seems to me if I keep on considering until the end of life, I shall never have done."

Then Margaret gave her verse which had been her help for the day, but Johnnie had been much too busy to think of verses, and frankly said so. Mrs. Merwin, catching the thought of the hour, said with great fervor, —

"'Oh! sing unto the Lord a new song, for he hath done marvelous things.' To-night as never before I sing a ' new song.'"

Then Mr. Moore prayed, and I think he forgot all his fears. If he remembered Aunt Cornelia, it was to thank God for her prayers, for her influence and helpfulness; if he remembered Weston, it was to ask God to let the Holy Spirit touch his heart and bring him into harmony with Christ and his loving plans. Weston Moore never forgot that prayer; and yet he gave no sign that his heart was touched; he slipped away and soon was heard whistling a merry tune. Margaret went out to the kitchen to stir the cakes while Mrs. Moore showed Aunt Cornelia to her room. As Margaret slowly stirred the batter, sifting in the flour with care, Weston came and stood beside her, still whistling; soon, however, he stopped to say: —

"Say, Mag, what's struck this family? How did we get to be such a company of saints, anyway? I thought you were doing that for the whole of us!" Margaret was silent; she did not know how to reply to this flippant speech, and Weston, seeing she did not speak, went on,—

"I suppose folks think it was your good example after you joined the church that turned the rest of them; but you see, Mag, everybody didn't live with you." And Weston laughed in his old teasing way; if he expected Margaret to fly into a passion, as of old, he was mistaken. She only said, in a tone of distress, "O, Weston!"

"O, Margie ! I don't mean anything. But you know you didn't always keep up your reputation for saintship, and I just wanted to tease you a little. But now I am really wondering how all the rest of this goodness got into the family! Was it Mr. Wakefield?"

"Weston, I think it was just the Lord himself came and spoke to father and mother." Then, after a moment, "Weston, I know well enough, without your telling me, that I made an awful failure trying to live a Christian life. But I did mean it, though I did not know how to live it. If you would only" —

"Don't, Mag, don't preach," interrupted Weston, seeing the conversation was likely to take a more earnest tone than he had meant to have it; "you were not meant for an exhorter — isn't that what they call them? But I promise you one thing; I won't tease you any more."

"Oh! I don't think I would mind it now; at least, not so much."

The boy went on eagerly, without seeming to notice her words: "I tell you, Mag, father is a man to be proud of! I must say I admire him in this new departure. Still I should think life here would be rather poky. I am glad I am going back to Aunt Cornelia's. There are some tip-top fellows there."

Margaret had finished her work, and brushing the flour from her apron said, "It is just lovely here now! Mother is perfectly splendid. Johnnie is just as fond of her as he can be." "Well, she does seem nicer, that's a fact! I didn't know she could be so bright and lively as she was at the supper-table. She laughed and talked just like — well, like anybody."

"She is nice!" was Margaret's emphatic reply, as she turned to bolt the outside doors before putting out the light. As she went to say good-night to her father and mother, she heard Mr. Moore saying,—

"I saw Duncan to-night coming up, and he says his wife and Elmer are coming next Tuesday." Then turning to Margaret, he added, "So you will have your friend back again, but they will stay only a few weeks. They are all going to their cottage for the summer. I think we must let you go home with Aunt Cornelia, but we shall miss you sadly. Someway it seems as if we had just begun to live for one another." When they were alone Mr. Moore said, "I have been thinking that if Margaret went away, we might manage a pleasant surprise for her. Suppose we were to take the room down-stairs for ours, and give her the one we occupy now, and put in some new furniture; not a great deal, of course, just now, but I think I can afford a new carpet. Then I was up garret looking at that old desk. It can be repaired and redressed, and there is nothing Margaret would like so well, for the sake of the associations."

"I am glad you have suggested the plan. I had been wishing to do something to make a change in her room."

"And I think it will be much better for you to be down-stairs; going up and down so much is not good for you."

It was pleasant to know that her comfort was thought of as well as the daughter's pleasure; Mrs. Moore fell asleep with a light heart, though the body was weary with the excitements of the last twenty-four hours.

Meantime, Margaret lay thinking about Weston, and going to Aunt Cornelia's, and her letter, and Elmer Newton. Her thoughts were in a tangle. Should she show her letter to Weston? Surely not when he was in such a reckless mood as he appeared to be in that night. Yet someway it seemed as if he ought to share it. Perhaps he would receive it as a message for him as well as for her. She would watch his moods and take advantage of a quieter one. Then there came another thought: If she went away, she would miss seeing the Duncans. Her father had said they would miss her dreadfully; she was half a mind not to go at all, and unable to decide anything she fell asleep.

Aunt Cornelia did not go to see her niece the next day as she planned. She said as she came to breakfast: —

"I believe I took cold yesterday; the coach was overheated, and when we changed at the junction, we had to stand in the wind, waiting for the train to draw up, until I was quite chilled." Through the day she grew worse, and a physician was called who prescribed for a severe cold, which he said might settle upon the lungs unless great care was taken. He ordered his patient to bed, and charged the family not to let the temperature of the room run below a certain point. It was the next day that she said, —

"'Thomas, I wish you would send word to Frances that I am here, and unable to go to see her, and that I would like to have her come and see me."

"I'll go myself," was her nephew's prompt reply.

"What an age since you were here!" exclaimed Mrs. Irving.

"Yes; but you know we have had sickness at our house nearly all winter."

"I did hear that your wife was an invalid, and I was so sorry; poor fellow! it must be hard to have a sick wife; I supposed you had married a strong woman; that was my one consolation. Your expenses must have been enormous."

"Somewhat heavy, yet less than they m;ght have been, but tor the kindness of our friends. Sophia's sister came to stay for several months, and Margaret made a very good little helper." "Poor Mag! she must be about worn out. Mrs. Munsey told me that the child looked dreadfully. I have not seen her at church but once or twice in all winter."

"Then I am afraid you were not there to see, for Margaret has missed very few Sabbaths."

"Oh! well, never mind. Let her come and spend a few weeks with me and get rested."

"Thank you; but she is quite well, and very happy at home. She will probably go home with Aunt Cornelia for a few weeks. I came up to tell you that Auntie is here, and that she would like to have you come and see her."

"Aunt Cornelia at your house! Why does she not come here?"

"Because the doctor has forbidden her. She planned to visit you yesterday— she only came night before last — but she was obliged to call Dr. Woods, and he says she must on no account go out for several days. At present she is sick in bed."

"But, Thomas, can't we have her brought up here in a close carriage? I am sure if she is sick a niece is the proper person to take care of her, rather than a stranger. Don't you think she can be moved? I will go myself and see Dr. Woods about it."

"That is hardly necessary or wise. You will do better to consult Aunt Cornelia first. If she wishes to be moved up here, perhaps it could be managed, but she has good care; and you can spend all the time you wish with her unmolested by any members of my family. You can come as Aunt Cornelia's guest, if you do not choose to have it otherwise. Of course it would gratify me to have you come as the guest of the family, but that must rest with you."

"I would like to see Auntie," said Mrs. Irving thoughtfully, "but really, Thomas, you must see that I cannot go down to your house to visit her."

"Excuse me, Frances, but I do not see anything to hinder. As I have told you, you will be welcome whenever you choose to come; I wish you would not be so absurd. The truth is, I do not feel like coming here, so long as you are not willing to receive my wife. Sophia has always urged my visiting you, saying she did not wish to separate us. But I think, Frances, you will acknowledge that I owe it to a faithful wife and mother not to visit where she is not received."

"I knew it would come," said Mrs. Irving, in a pathetic tone; "I knew the time would come when I should be given up. O, Thomas! we have been so devoted to each other always, and now to think that a stranger should come between us;" and she shed a few becoming tears, while Mr. Moore sat looking at her with a perplexed air; at last he said, "Frances, this is very foolish; there is no one to come between us. Sophia would gladly receive you and forget all your neglect of her; I assure you, there will never be a word said about it" —

What a mistake he was making! Mrs. Irving's policy was never to get angry, but she was nearer that state of mind than she often allowed herself to be. She interrupted her brother.

"Word said about it! about what? You seem to convey the idea that I have given cause for something to be said. So careful as I have been, too! Knowing that with my dislike of step-mothers I should be sure to offend, I have kept entirely aloof. I am sure, Thomas, I have been a faithful sister. I have said very little about the unhappy state of affairs at your house, though I have tried to show my sympathy, by planning treats for the children, because I knew how unhappy they were at home. I have never said much to you, because I know that when a man has made a mistake, he does not want to be told of it continually, but, Thomas, you know you have my sympathy."

"Really, Frances, I do not need sympathy."

"I know; I ought not to have spoken even in this guarded way. That is another peculiarity of men; they do not like to be pitied. But about Margaret. I have been talking it over with Mr. Irving, and we would like to have her come and spend a year or so, with us. I will provide for her in every respect, and it will be a relief both to Margaret and to — your wife."

Mr. Moore was in danger of losing patience entirely, but he controlled himself. He remembered too that his sister was not entirely to blame. He had made a mistake away back in those troublous days when he had silently accepted her sympathy. How should she know that things were different? He had meant to tell her this evening, but the conversation was not helping him along in that direction.

"I am in earnest," continued Mrs. Irving. "A girl of Margaret's age needs care, and training; and this I could give her, as well as other advantages."

"Thank you; but it seems to me that Margaret's parents are the proper persons to give this care and training of which you speak. Frances, you forget that you are speaking of or rather that you are ignoring my wife and my children's mother."

"Oh! it is very nice and proper of you to put it that way, but of course I understand how it is. And I wish you would let me help you bear the burden."

Once more Mr. Moore made an effort to say what he felt must be said. "Frances, listen to me! I acknowledge there was a time when my wife and the children did not get along quite smoothly; I suppose people must always learn to adapt themselves to new situations and circumstances. But in our case a new element has come into the family life, to help us along; we have come out of our trials with a rich blessing. You will understand me perhaps when I tell you that Sophia and I expect to unite with the church next Sabbath. Now, it occurs to me that as members of the same church, and as Christians, there might with propriety be different relations established between our families."

"Oh! that does not follow. I do not call upon half the people who belong to our church."

He had not told her as he had meant to; right along with the telling he had given her a rebuke. Not a word had he spoken of the joy and peace that reigned in his heart, of his love for her, and his longing for her real sympathy. His heart was very sore over the course of this sister who might have been such a help and comfort. But he did not know how to say more; some way he could not reach her, so he only added, rising to go, "Shall I send up the carriage for you in the morning?"

"No, you need not send; if I make up my mind to go, I'll walk down, but I think I'll wait; Aunt Cornelia may be able to come up before she goes home. I should like to have her moved up here, but of course if she prefers your house and a stranger's care, it is all right."

Mrs. Irving was vexed — she could not have told at what; could she, a professedly Christian woman, be displeased because another woman was about to profess her faith in Christ? That thrust of her brother's about the proper relations to be sustained between Christians, rankled; heretofore she had excused herself by saying that her brother's wife was not of her sphere, and that they would probably find very little in common; but here was a new phase of affairs, and it might be that as a Christian woman Mrs. Moore would be in advance. She had a vague notion that this despised sister-in-law might be recognized as a power in the church, and she did not like the thought of hearing Mrs. Moore quoted and referred to.

However, all she said as she sat alone where her brother had left her was,—

"A carriage, indeed!"

Mrs. Merwin looked in vain for her niece. Towards evening of the next day she said: — "Weston, do you not think it would be proper for you to go and call on your Aunt Frances? I shall not be able to go, but you might do the calling for both of us."

"Yes," said Mrs. Moore quickly, "Margaret has not been there lately, I think; suppose you take her up this evening."

Mrs. Irving greeted her young visitors warmly. "How in the world is it, Margie, that I have this honor of a visit from you? Mrs. Moore has kept you pretty close lately. Did you steal away?" This last with a little laugh which, however, had an ill-natured ring.

"O, no! it was mother herself that proposed it," said Margaret brightly.

"Oh! I suppose she wanted you out of the way so she could say what she pleased to Aunt Cornelia. By the way, how is Auntie?"

"She is better to-day; the doctor says she will be all right in a few days."

"Humph! I thought it was only a plan to keep her from coming here, or a ruse to get me there, so Mrs. Moore could say I had called. But, never mind, you and I will have a good time. What shall I order for a treat? Margie, I have been talking to your father about your coming to stay a long time with me — a year or two; what do you think of that? "

"I don't know what you mean," stammered Margaret. "Why should I live here?"

"For two or three reasons: in the first place as my niece, or rather as my adopted daughter, you would have every advantage; my piano stands unopened month after month, and I would have you take lessons of Rameur. Then up here you would be introduced to the best families — the Hunters, the Camerons, and all the people on the hill. And besides, I want you. Wouldn't it be nice to live where you were wanted?"

"Of course. But I am wanted and needed, too, at home."

"Are you?"

That was all she said, but a suspicion was planted in Margaret's heart, to rankle.

CHAPTER 22: A DECISION

MARGARET had not yet said to herself in so many words: "I'm going home with Aunt Cornelia to spend the whole summer, yet she went about all the next day with little waves of gladness breaking over her which rippled into snatches of song. She held secret counsels with herself as to her wardrobe, whether her blue gingham was not too short and too narrow to be allowed to go along, and decided that her pink muslin would do nicely if it were let down two inches. She looked over her bureau drawers and knew that she ought to go straightway and put some needed stitches in here and there, but somehow she could not settle to it. She flitted about when she had leisure, in doors and out, too happy to put herself down to sober work. There was one drawback to entire content, though—Johnnie had gone a-fishing.

Margaret always dreaded to have him go. It is true nothing had ever happened to him yet when he went, but she always felt ill at ease until he was safely home. She asked her father not to let him go, but he had answered:—

"That won't do, Margaret; a boy can't be brought up in a bandbox. He must learn to take care of himself. I shall tell him to be careful."

As it drew near night, Margaret began her customary watching; watching always brought him. While she set the table for tea her ears were keenly alive to any sound of Johnnie's whoop when he should appear at the kitchen door with a sorry little string of very young fish. She put on the plates, then went to the window and looked down the street, then came the cups and saucers, and another searching of the street. By the time the table was ready she had made many journeys to the window, but no boy with a fishpole had turned the corner and come towards home, strain her eyes as she might. At supper when her father asked, "Where is Johnnie?" she could scarcely steady her voice to say, "He hasn't got home yet from fishing."

And then she saw her father glance uneasily at the clock. Johnnie had never been so late before. Oh! if something had happened to him. It was a good supper, but somehow Margaret's throat seemed closed up. She could scarcely swallow. If Johnnie should not come before dark then surely something was wrong. It was growing dusk now. As soon as she well could she left the table, and seizing her hat and sacque from the hall rack ran swiftly down the street toward the river. Black River was well named. Its waters were dark, and it flowed swiftly between high banks, rolling and tumbling into foam over its rocky bed. It always made Margaret shudder to look at it. It seemed so fierce and wild. It looked positively angry to-night with a high wind rising, and a black cloud flying along the sky. Margaret stopped when she reached the bank and looked down into the dark rushing water. What if Johnnie had slipped off that rock and was lying at the bottom now, dead!

She went on as fast as she could go toward the mill near which was a group of men and boys. They were bending over somebody who lay on the ground. Margaret gave one bound and reached the spot. Yes, it was Johnnie! He had fallen from the slippery beam into the water just as Jacob Williams was going into the mill to do a business errand for his employer. Quick as a flash the young man's coat came off and he dashed in after Johnnie, getting firm hold of the boy as he was about to sink the second time. Just as Margaret got there, her father and the doctor came driving down the street at full speed. She tried to push her way through to Johnnie, but the doctor ordered every one to stand back. Choosing one or two strong men to help him, he worked fast and hard. In a short time Johnnie opened his eyes and moaned.

"All right!" the doctor said, "We shall save him."

And the cheery "All right!" was passed through the crowd. The minutes had seemed like hours, though, to the sister, standing by watching, holding her lips shut close lest she should scream, clinching her trembling hands tight together, trying to fight down a strange sensation, which made her feel like sinking down in a heap on the ground.

They brought blankets, and Johnnie, wrapped up and resting in his father's arms, was driven toward home.

"Where's my fish pole?" he asked in a weak voice as he started.

It was dark now, and Margaret ran by a shorter way so fast that she got home before the carriage reached there. She found her mother at the gate watching for her, almost as excited as herself, for the messenger had come with the news just after Margaret had left the house.

"He's safe," she cried, and the tears ran over her face as Mrs. Moore put her arms about her and held her close in silence for an instant. Then they both turned away to make everything ready in Johnnie's room.

It was a very limp little boy who was laid on his bed. Margaret cried again when she saw his white face with wet curls straggling about his forehead.

"I am drowned at last, Mag," he whispered, roguish as ever, when she bent over him after the others had gone out, and he was made comfortable. "You always said I would be drowned."

"Hush, Johnnie," Margaret said, giving him a long kiss. "You almost died. Oh! what would I have done without you?"

"I guess I would 'a' drowned, sure," Johnnie murmured, as he closed his eyes wearily, "if somebody hadn't pulled me out. Was it Jake Williams? I saw him looking at me just as I went," and at the remembrance of that moment Johnnie shuddered.

"Say, Mag," he said, half-opening his eyes again, "when I was in the water I knew I wasn't a good boy. I was afraid. I want to be good."

"Dear Johnnie," said his sister, kissing him again, "I'll ask God to make you good, and you will too, won't you? You can just whisper now, 'Dear Jesus, take me, and make me good.' Then you must go right to sleep."

It was more than a week after this. Johnnie was himself again and, boylike, had apparently almost forgotten that he ever came near losing his life. Aunt Cornelia was well, too, and had gone to spend a few days with Aunt Frances. An early tea that night left Margaret time to come out on the porch and watch the sunset after the dishes were washed.

"Isn't it strange how things you've longed for come around if you just wait for them?"

she said as she sat down on the upper step. She was speaking partly to herself and partly to Johnnie, who was sitting on the bottom step with jack-knife, sticks, twine, and bits of cloth and paper scattered about him, making a very long tail to his kite.

"Yes; and things come sometimes when you don't wait for 'em and don't want 'em," said Johnnie, whose face was still swollen from an attack of toothache. He squinted one eye as he spoke, taking sight at his kite string to see if it was exactly in the middle. He looked so comical with his puffy cheek and puckered eye, that Margaret laughed.

"It isn't any fun to have the toothache, Miss Moore," said Johnnie. "Perhaps you'd like to try it. You'd look funny enough with your face swelled up. Your little nose would be turned up more'n it is now. I can just seem to see you." And Johnnie laughed.

Margaret felt a little annoyed at once. Her nose did turn up just the slightest bit, and she did not like to have it spoken of. Johnnie had not teased her badly in a long time. She had made more of a companion of him lately than she used to do, and since that dreadful day he fell into the river she had felt very tenderly toward him. They must not fall back into their old habits of quarreling, not for anything. With a good tug at herself she conquered, and after a minute laughed too, and said: —

"I guess I would look funny, but don't let's talk about toothache. What do you say to my going off to Massachusetts? That's what I meant by things happening that had been waited and longed for. Here's Aunt Cornelia all ready to take me, and father says I can go." Johnnie did not answer at once. He was thinking of something else for a moment.

"Mag is different," he was saying to himself. "She'd have got as mad as a hen once if I'd said her nose turned up."

"I know something," he said at last, "that we're going to have if you go off this summer, and that's a hired girl. I hope she'll have red hair, and be cross as sixty. Then won't I have fun! I'll tease her — some."

"O, Johnnie!" said Margaret, "I thought you were going to be a good boy."

"I am," said Johnnie. "It isn't wicked to tease folks who are nothing to you."

"It is," said Margaret. "It's unkind and hateful and rude. You won't tease anybody any more, will you, Johnnie?"

"Not to hurt 'em," said Johnnie. "I won't put any bent pins in chairs, nor trip 'em up."

"What makes you think we are to have a girl?" said Margaret.

"Why, I heard father tell mother she should. He said it would be too hard for her if you went away, and she said No, she would get along. She wouldn't have a girl till the debt was all paid up — what debt?"

"Oh! something about a mortgage on the house," Margaret said vaguely.

"Why, father gets a bigger salary now, doesn't he?"

"Yes; but it takes a great deal of money to pay mortgages. He pays a little every year. He said it would take two years more to get it all paid."

"Well, father said that would be all right," went on Johnnie, "and she must have a girl. Shall you stay all summer, Mag? It'll be an awful deaf and dumb house if you do."

Margaret looked down at her youngest brother, his tangled curly head bent over his work and his swollen cheek gave him a forlorn look, as if he needed somebody to pet him and look after him. She rested her chin on her hand and went off into deep thought. Ought she not, after all, to leave home this summer? Was every pleasure held out to her to be hedged around by a great big "ought not"? She wished somebody would say: "You must go home with Aunt Cornelia; it is your duty, and you must do it." How plain and easy the way would be made. It was so hard to have to decide things for one's self, and Conscience was so troublesome, always putting in "ifs" and " buts " and "oughts," even after things were decided.

It was only a minute that such petulant thought held sway. Then she leaned her head back against the post, and with her eyes fixed on the clear light of that golden strip of sky, tried to see things just as they were. She had been reading that day the definition of the term "pro and con." She would gather up the pros and cons on this subject. It stood like this: —

Pros: I want to go; father said I could; Aunt Cornelia wants me to; I shall have a lovely time; I have worked hard and I deserve to go; it will help me to be good to be with Aunt Cornelia; and it will be — (Margaret hesitated for a word) — improving in every way for me. Now for the—

Cons : They can't spare me at home; it will cost a good deal to keep a girl; Johnnie will be lonesome —

There were a great many cons concerning Johnnie. She was intent on them for a few minutes. Johnnie was always getting into scrapes. He had seemed to like to be with her of late. She had great influence over him. Perhaps if she went away, and there was no school to keep him out of mischief, he would get to going with that bad Andrews boy again, and by the time she got home he would be gone to ruin, or perhaps he would be lonesome and go fishing all the time and be drowned. Just then there came looming up before her one of the most delightful "pros." There was Aunt Cornelia's pretty home four miles out of the city: there would be rides to the city; shopping in grand stores; visits to art galleries.

How delightful to exchange dishwashing and sweeping for all these pleasant things, with leisure to do what she pleased for a whole summer. And then, with another thought of Johnnie, lonesome, tempted, straggling, came the final and decisive "con." It would please Jesus better if she did not go. It was as clear as that sunset sky. She felt as sure of it as if lie had whispered in her ear, "Don't go, dear child!" There was no more debating. She leaned her head back again, strangely peaceful and happy.

Johnnie meantime had finished his kite and gone out on the street to give it a fly, while Mrs. Moore had come to the door and stood looking out, unperceived by Margaret. She noticed the happy expression on the face turned up to the fading clouds. It was a true earnest face, and Mrs. Moore thought so as she watched it. "How different Margaret was. She was really growing lovely." The heart of the step-mother warmed toward the daughter and following an impulse, she did what was unusual for her; she stepped out and laid her hand softly on Margaret's head, which a ray of sunshine was turning into gold.

"Are you thinking about going away? Is that what makes you look so happy?" she asked.

Margaret started and looked up, surprised. The look which met hers was actually a loving one. The tears sprang into her eyes, and she reached for her mother's other hand and held it close without speaking.

"I am glad you are going for one reason," Mrs. Moore went on; "you will have a great deal of pleasure and a change, and you deserve it, but on another account, I'm sorry. We are just beginning to understand each other and have some good times at home."

"Mother," said Margaret, speaking that name out full and round, which she had once said she would never give to her step-mother, "I don't deserve anything. I was a cross, hateful girl, and I wonder how you ever had any patience with me."

"I didn't always, you know," Mrs. Moore said. "I meant to do everything exactly right when I came here, but I didn't know how to manage. I guess I might have done better if I had had more patience and known how — and — one thing more, Margaret, if I had been a Christian woman. I wanted a chance to tell you this, and to have you know that I feel almost as if you were my very own daughter.

I am as proud of you as I can be. But let us talk some business now. What dress can you wear for the journey?"

"The dress I have on will do," said Margaret. Her mother looked at her in surprise. It was a pale pink print. "For my journeys to the post-office and on errands, I mean; I have made up my mind not to go this summer, mother."

"You poor child! why not? It will be too bad to have you disappointed again."

While they talked it over, the sunset changed into twilight, and when Mr. Moore came in for the night he was filled with surprise and delight at sight of his wife and daughter sitting on the steps with their arms about each other. At last there was peace and quiet happiness in his home. His heart swelled with gratitude.

"You won't think I am ungrateful, will you?" Margaret said next day, when she told Aunt Cornelia that she had decided not to go home with her.

"No, indeed, dear child," Aunt Cornelia said, kissing her. "I am glad you are willing to give up your own pleasure for Johnnie's sake. I dare say he needs you. A temperament like his should have much help and guarding. He is intense and impulsive. There is material in him for a grand man or for a very bad one. The self-denial you practice now will be rewarded. A boy with a good sister has as fair again a chance of turning out a good man as one who has none. So hold fast to Johnnie, dear; you'll not be sorry. You need not think I give you up easily, though. It is a great disappointment to me, but sometime, somehow, it will all come around right for me to have you."

The morning Aunt Cornelia started for home she slipped a small envelope into Margaret's hand, saying: "My dear, this is the money I was going to spend for your journey to and from my house. I am going to give it to you to do with just as you please. I think you can be trusted to use it wisely."

Margaret was delighted. She had never had much money to use as she pleased. She was glad, too, that Aunt Cornelia trusted her. She devoted it to as many as twenty-five different objects before one day had passed. It was astonishing how much twenty-five dollars accomplished in imagination. She bought herself a silk dress, then a new coat for her father, then a handsome suit for Johnnie. There were times when it was all spent in books, and again every member of the family was to have a nice present; then a handsome chair for the parlor; some new curtains; a new carpet for her room; sometimes it was devoted entirely to the poor. Between the great variety of ways and wishes, it seemed doubtful whether it would ever be spent at all.

CHAPTER 23: A HAPPY BIRTHDAY

I HAVE to go out in the country a couple of miles," said Mr. Moore, one pleasant morning to his wife. "Don't you want to go along?"

"No; I can't go, she said;" "I must see to my bread. Take Margaret."

A drive was a rare enough pleasure to make Margaret drop her duster and fly up-stairs to smooth her hair in great glee.

The road wound along amid green fields and orchards. The air was fragrant with apple blossoms, and birds were singing and building nests.

"How nice it must be to live in the country," Margaret said, as she watched a girl about her own age reach up from the porch where she stood to the overhanging branches of an old apple-tree, break off a spray of blossoms and fasten them in her belt.

"But you would be lonely in the country, and soon grow tired of it, wouldn't you?" her father said.

"O, no! I'm sure I shouldn't. Who would ever be tired of a great green yard and watching the birds and having room enough to see the sunset?"

Margaret had never been out of the place where she was born. It was a large manufacturing town with narrow streets, and for the most part small lots. The houses stood very near the street and very near neighboring houses, so the country looked to Margaret like another world, wide and free and glad.

They stopped at last before a large farmhouse. Mr. Stoddard, the man Mr. Moore had come to see, was hoeing corn near by. He came across the field and leaned on the fence while he talked. Just opposite was a cottage with vines running over the porch. It was a pretty place, standing on a rise of ground, shaded by a large elm-tree.

There were lilacs in bloom, and green grass was everywhere. Margaret wondered why the place had such a shut-up look, but just then she heard Mr. Stoddard tell her father that his son's wife had died a few weeks before. "The boy couldn't bear to stay around here," he said, "so he's gone to Texas, and there's his house just as he left it. I'm sure I don't know what to do with it. He said to rent it if I could to some nice small family who would take care of Mary's things, but it isn't so easy to find a nice family that wants to come out so far unless they have some farming business."

While he talked, Margaret's thoughts were busy. A bright idea came into her head. What if they could rent that house and come out there for two or three months! It almost took her breath away. She wanted to ask what the rent would be, but she felt too shy. She wanted to whisper to her father to ask, but she couldn't get a chance, and then, her father might think she was crazy to think of such a thing. Before she knew it the business was finished, and her father was turning the horse and saying, " Good-morning! "

"Father," Margaret ventured as they drove along, "can I do exactly what I please with the money Aunt Cornelia gave me?"

"That is what she said. Of course she didn't expect you to do anything very foolish with it."

"Would it be very foolish if I were to try to hire that pretty cottage for three months, and we all go out there and live?"

Margaret pulled her hat farther over her face after making that daring proposition, and cast sidewise glances at her father. Encouraged by his silence, because he did not ridicule the idea at once, she went on eagerly to plead her cause.

"You know mother was brought up on a farm, and she will like it, and it'll do her good, and it will be such a nice, safe place for Johnnie through vacation. He can't fall in the river, nor play with Tom Andrews, and I should like it above all things. It would be almost as good as going to Aunt Cornelia's. Johnnie and I could go berrying and fishing together and have plenty of fun. Then it would be so nice to walk on all that soft grass and have plenty of air to breathe and room to see off."

"I don't know but it would be a good plan," Mr. Moore said at last, when Margaret paused to take breath.

"Do you?" said Margaret, clapping her hands in delight. "I was so afraid you would not think so. O, father! if we could only turn about and go and see what the rent will be. It seems as if I couldn't wait another day."

Mr. Moore glanced at his watch, and, as he had time, he was anxious to please his girl who, during the last few months, had so often given up her own pleasure for others. The horse's head was turned again toward the farm.

"You must prepare for disappointment, Margaret," he said on the way. "It's likely the rent of such a place will be beyond the reach of our pocket books even for a short time."

"We came back to ask if you would rent your son's place for the summer, and what you would ask," Mr. Moore said, as the farmer came up to the fence again.

"It depends some on who wants it," Mr. Stoddard said, as he took off his hat and wiped the perspiration from his forehead.

"What if I should want it? There are but four in my family at present."

"All right; you can have it. I'll be glad to have you out here."

"Perhaps I can't afford to come when you tell me the rent," Mr. Moore said.

Mr. Stoddard held fast to a tuft of gray beard on his chin, and thought a moment.

Summer visitors had not yet invaded that region, or he would never have named the price he did.

"Why, about twenty-five dollars, I reckon." he said at last.

Margaret's eyes danced. It was all she could do to keep from giving a little scream of delight.

"All right," said Mr. Moore, "I'll take it." He was about to say, "I'll consult my wife and let you know," then he suddenly concluded to surprise her.

"Don't the young lady want to go in and take a look around?" the farmer asked.

The young lady was only too willing. They went first into the vegetable garden, where beets, onions, beans, peas and com were growing finely. In the front yard were rose bushes and flower beds. And how neat the little house was, with its matting-covered floors, home-made rugs, and cheap white curtains. Everything was in beautiful order, as if the young wife had stepped out for a minute, and had not gone the long journey from which there is no returning.

"There couldn't be anything better for us if it had been made on purpose," Margaret told her father as she stood in the pretty little chamber which she thought would probably be hers.

Not long afterward, one day after dinner, Mr. Moore told his wife he should need Margaret's help for a few hours. She was accustomed to do little jobs of writing for him in the office when he was overrun with work, so Mrs. Moore thought nothing of it.

Margaret made an errand into the pantry just then, for in spite of herself her face would break into smiles.

Her father and she had a fine plan for that day. They visited the grocery and bakery and fruit stores and laid in a supply of things for a nice tea. Then they picked up Johnnie and drove to the cottage they had hired. Margaret made a fire in the kitchen stove and filled the small teakettle. Then she proceeded to set the table with a table cloth she had smuggled from home.

Meantime Mr. Moore had gone back to town to ask his wife to take a ride.

"But I don't know anybody here," she protested, when they drove up to the cottage and he asked her to go in.

"Never mind if you don't; I know them, and they are nice folks," her husband said, lifting her out.

Her astonished looks when she saw Margaret and Johnnie, made great fun for them.

"Why! what are you all doing here?" she asked. "Have you set up housekeeping, Margaret?"

"Let us have tea now," Mr. Moore said, "explanations will be in order afterward."

All had a keen appetite and pronounced the supper capital. After it was dispatched, Mr. and Mrs. Moore went out and sat on the porch.

"You're company now, you know," Margaret said.

While she and Johnnie cleared off the table, Mr. Moore told his wife all about Margaret's plan, and asked her if she would like to spend the summer there.

"Yes, indeed I should," she said, leaning back in the rocking-chair. "I haven't felt so rested in a long time. It seems like my old home. What a perfect treasure Margaret is growing into. She will make us all ashamed with her unselfish spirit. I never knew anyone to change as she has."

Just then Johnnie's voice was heard shouting, "Say, Mag, there's a place between two big trees for a swing, and there's a trout brook over in the orchard, and there's going to be lots of snow apples."

Happy Johnnie, and happy Margaret!

After the grounds had been thoroughly explored, and Margaret had called her mother to go up-stairs and see the pleasant little chambers, they locked up the house and went back to town.

The next morning found them full of cheerful bustle, preparing to leave their house for the summer, and packing what was to be taken to the farm.

"We're as big as anybody," Johnnie remarked, as he stuffed his fishing suit, his box for bait, and second-best shoes into an old satchel. "We're going out of town for the summer."

They went the very next day and took possession of their new home, for Margaret had said: —

"Don't let's waste a single minute of that grass and sweet air."

"It will be nothing but fun to do the work here," she told her mother when they were arranging the dishes in the pantry. "Everything is so convenient. See this nice little china closet opening into the dining-room and kitchen, too, and how white the work-table is, and what bright tins! I shall be afraid to touch anything, it is all so new and pretty. It makes me think of a book I was reading where some girls had good times housekeeping. They kept everything so nice everywhere that one of them said, 'Pretty soon it would be hard to tell whether they dined in the kitchen, or kitched in the dining-room.'"

"Mother," said Margaret, "let us take turns doing the work. "One week you cook and I will sweep and wash dishes, and the next week you take my place and let me learn your part. I should like to get breakfast and dinner with these nice little pots and kettles."

"Well, that will suit me nicely," her mother said, "but won't it be too hard for you to learn bread-making when you are the cook?"

"O, no! I will watch just how you do it for two or three weeks; then I'll be all right."

Mrs. Moore smiled to think that Margaret supposed she could learn the whole art of baking in so short a time.

"I suppose you never will have a better opportunity," she said, "for we hope to keep you in school steadily next year, but it will take more time and patience than you think."

"Well, I'll play I go to Cooking School this summer. Alice Austin went, and she feels very grand because she can make bread."

Margaret enjoyed the novelty of the new place and the new tools to work with so much, that housework was not the drudgery it had been at home. She began to put spirit and zeal into her work when it was her week to cook. It was pleasant to be up the first one in the morning, when everything was fresh and cool and dripping with dew ; when the world looked all made over new. She always ran first to see if a new rose had opened on the vine at the end of the porch, or if a bud had started on the sweet peas. She had not much time for that, though; the breakfast must be early for her father's sake. Her table was always set the night before, so while the tea-kettle boiled she went down cellar— such a cool, sweet, airy cellar as it was, with a stone floor, and clean as a parlor — and brought milk and butter and berries. Then the coffee must be made, the steak broiled, or the eggs cooked, and the brown bread and white bread cut — breakfast was all ready, on the table, neatly arranged, and all in good time.

There was a wide back porch, with morning-glories and scarlet beans running about it. Here Margaret loved to sit and shell peas, or pick over berries, singing at her work, so unlike the scowling Margaret of other days that, as her mother passed to and fro on the way to the pantry, she could but linger sometimes, screened by a door, to watch and enjoy the picture. It was pleasant, too, when the work was all done, and Margaret sat on the front piazza with her mother, sewing, or went on long tramps with Johnnie in search of berries or wintergreens. There was not an hour in the day when the little home was not enjoyed. Even when it rained and was cool and damp there was a new pleasure, for there was a bit of a fireplace in the sitting-room, and they kindled a little fire and drew around it with books and work. Johnnie made kites and tops, and sometimes Margaret read a story book aloud. They even made the discovery in these days that their new mother knew how to tell stories, capital ones, too, because they were about real boys and girls. Whenever she began, "When I was teaching in Groton, there was a boy," or "When I was a girl," then her listeners were all attention. They began to think they had a jewel of a mother. They might have made that discovery long ago if they had allowed themselves to see her good qualities as distinctly as her poor ones.

And yet, there was no denying that Mrs. Moore was changed. Her manner was gentler, and her voice softer. She had lost that severe, set look, and, as Johnnie confided to Margaret, "looked sort o' loving out of her eyes, and didn't scold any more."

"Next week's my birthday," Johnnie announced one day as he lay on the grass looking up at the sky. "I wish I could have a party."

"A party!" laughed Margaret.

"Yes; I think I might. I never had anybody to tea in all my life."

"How many would you like to invite?" Mrs. Moore asked.

"Oh! two or three."

"Well, you may have such a party as that. Our table will just about hold three more.

Get pencil and paper and make out your list. That's the way girls do when they have company."

"Oh! I don't need any pencil. I've got 'em in my head."

"Well, who's first?"

"Jake Williams, of course. A fellow ought to be thankful his birthday, if he never is again."

"That's one," said Margaret, counting on her fingers. "Who's next?"

"Mr. Plunkett."

Mr. Plunkett was a round little old man, with a shining face, bald head, and big silver spectacles astride of his nose. He was in a humble position, eking out his living by doing odd jobs, such as mending clocks and pumps, besides being sexton of the church. He was the friend of all the boys in town, and by being called often to deal with refractory locks or pumps at Mr. Moore's, he and Johnnie had become quite intimate. Nobody could get up a bow and arrow like Mr. Plunkett. His jack-knife was sharp, and he was perfectly willing to lend it. Moreover, in any emergency, he always stood ready to lend a helping hand to his favorites, and Johnnie was a special one.

He knew a great many stories, too, of Indians, wild horses, and sea serpents. Margaret hesitated before bending down her third finger, saying in surprise and unbelief, —

"You don't want him!"

"Course I do. He's the nicest man in this town."

"Suppose we let Johnnie choose his company, and what he will have for supper, then when our birthday comes we will do the same," said Mrs. Moore.

At this Johnnie gave a gleeful whoop and turned a somersault.

"All right; we will. Who comes next?" said Margaret.

"Miss Hamilton."

"O, Johnnie! what a queer mixture," and Margaret went off into a long fit of laughter.

Miss Hamilton was Johnnie's teacher in Sabbath-school, a rich man's daughter. So delicate and dainty she seemed in her silk gown, white feathers and light gloves, that Margaret imagined she would scorn to come to a country tea with Mr. Plunkett and Jake Williams as guests.

"What's the matter now? I'm sure she's nice enough," Johnnie said stoutly, "and I want her," and then Margaret laughed again while Mrs. Moore said: —

"Well, now let's make out a bill of fare. What are you going to have for supper?"

Johnnie reflected.

"New potatoes and green peas, and chicken, and strawberry shortcake," he said at last.

"That will be a very nice supper," Mrs. Moore answered.

"O, mother!" protested Margaret, "do you think so? It'll seem so — countrified — and — what will Miss Hamilton think?"

"She'll think she's hungry and wants a good supper," said Johnnie, "and no nonsense."

"It would be nicer," went on Margaret, "to have just biscuits and cold tongue, and strawberries and cake. Don't you think so mother?"

"No," Mrs. Moore answered; "I think, with Johnnie, that when people come out into the country they are hungry, and like fresh vegetables and something a little more substantial than a usual tea. You know I was brought up in the country, and we had a good many visitors."

"All right," Margaret assented. "How would it do to have the table set out doors under the elm?"

"Can't we?" said Johnnie, bringing himself to a sitting posture in his eagerness.

"Why, yes, I guess so," Mrs. Moore said slowly. "I can pass the things out the pantry window to Margaret."

"Oh! goody, good," ejaculated Johnnie, standing on his head a second or two.

"There's another thing," he said, sitting up again, "I'm going to give presents to my company."

"What kind of presents?" asked Margaret. "You'll see," Johnnie said, looking wise. After tea, when Mr. Moore sat on the porch reading his newspaper, Johnnie came out to Margaret, with a box in his hand. His father had brought it out to him from home. It was the box which contained his treasures which had been gathered through the years.

"See here, Mag," he said, "I'll tell you my secrets if you want to know."

So, in a loud whisper, he unfolded his plans. Producing a curious top, which was wound up by a key, and would spin a long time, he said:

"This is for Mr. Plunkett, 'cause he likes machinery and things. I'm going to give my glass swan to Miss Hamilton — can't you tie a little blue ribbon round its neck?—My gold dollar I'm going to give to Jake Williams, 'cause it's the preciousest thing I've got."

Margaret thought, "What a dear little fellow you are, Johnnie," but she didn't say it.

"And how do you s'pose I'm going to fix 'em to have fun?" he asked. "I'm going to take three big oranges and cut 'em in two, then what I dig out I'll eat, an' I'll put the presents inside, and pin them together. Won't they be astonished when they open 'em?"

"I should think they would," said Margaret.

Mr. Moore was not so deep in his paper but that he heard all that went on, and he had hard work to keep a smile from twisting his mouth.

The day came at last. Johnnie almost thought it never would. It was as pleasant a summer day, too, as ever a boy had for his birthday.

Something wonderful had happened that morning. Mr. Moore, before he started to town, called Johnnie and gave him a little package. It held fifty gold dollars, which were to be given to Jacob Williams!

"Why, father, isn't it too much?" Johnnie said, so astonished he could scarcely speak.

"No," he said; "my boy's life is worth a great deal more than fifty dollars. I wish I could make it five hundred."

Such a time as Johnnie had stuffing those dollars into that orange!

Everything was ready now. The house was made into a bower of beauty with flowers and ferns. The birthday cake was made, though Johnnie hadn't spoken for one; the table was set, the chickens were stewing, and Miss Hamilton, fair and lovely in a fresh muslin, had arrived. She was charmed with everything, and went off with Johnnie to the brook and the orchard, and she went to see the little chickens, and played croquet, and swung, and was, as her admiring pupil said, "just as nice as she could be."

At tea time came Mr. Plunkett and Jake Williams, both feeling, it must be confessed, somewhat like cats in a strange garret. They soon were put at their ease, though, for they felt at home with Mr. Moore; and Miss Hamilton was bright and social.

It was the "squarest meal" Mr. Plunkett had enjoyed for many a day. Even Miss Hamilton said there never was such a good birthday supper before, never.

The oranges were the last course, of course. They were on the side table with a pile of small plates beside them. Johnnie passed them. He knew which orange belonged to whom. Then began his fun, when Mr. Plunkett looked over his great spectacles at the top he found in his orange; when Jacob Williams' yellow dollars came tumbling out on his plate, and Miss Hamilton exclaimed over her pretty swan. She set it swimming in a bowl of water, while Johnnie wound up the top and sent it spinning over the table, and Jacob Williams was still digging for gold in the depths of his orange.

CHAPTER 24: A WONDERFUL DAY

JOHNNIE had gone into town to get the windmill Mr. Plunket had promised him, and Margaret, her morning work all done, was lying in the hammock looking up into the green boughs, now watching the busy white clouds hurry across the blue sky, now looking at two robins who were debating in a neighboring bush whether they should build in the old elm or the apple-tree.

She thought of the party, how well it had gone off and how happy Johnnie seemed to be. She remembered how bright and merry he looked as he rode away. He had tossed his cap in the air while he was waiting for his father to come, and told Margaret he was having "just bangdelicious times this summer." She was glad he enjoyed it all, and glad she had given up her pleasure, and then a little thought came stealing in, an evil little thought, that she was a very good girl to give up so much for her brother's sake, and that it was too bad she couldn't have some fun herself; that she ought to have a reward for being so good. Just here she recognized from whom the thought came, and stopped her swinging.

"Margaret Moore, I'm ashamed of you!" she said half aloud, then turning she buried her face, covered with her hands, deep in the meshes of the hammock and lifted her heart up for help.

"Dear Jesus," she prayed, "take that thought away out of my heart and make me pure. Forgive me and help me never to feel that way again."

When she lifted her head again the ugly thought was gone, and in its place was sunshine and peace. So she lay back and rocked, touching now a heel, now a toe to the soft turf, to keep up the motion. The bees and the birds made a hum and a buzz and a twitter all about her, and now and then a heart-sick apple found it couldn't hold on to the branch any longer and dropped with a dull thud to the ground. The sights and sounds and smells were all very restful; so was the hammock, and

Margaret's eyelids went drooping, drooping, and she would have been asleep in a minute more, but along the hard country road there came a soft echo of tiny feet a-dancing; nearer and nearer they came, until they stopped right in front of the gate. Margaret's eyes opened very suddenly, up came her head, her feet were planted firmly on the ground, and she rested one arm on the edge of the hammock as she leaned forward to see what it might be.

There by the grassy roadside, stamping and shaking themselves, stood two very shaggy Indian ponies, hitched to the dearest little basket phaeton that ever was made. Some one was getting out — a young man. Who could it be? Some one to see her father, perhaps, or a stranger to inquire the way to Bonamy's Rocks, or some one who had made a mistake and thought somebody else lived there. She sat quite still until the stranger had tied the ponies to a maple-tree, opened the gate and come part way up the walk, then she began to think that she must get up and meet him, for mother was in the back yard and would never hear him, but before she had made up her mind he called out: —

"So this is where you have hidden yourself, little wood nymph, is it ? Why didn't you let us know what had become of you? Here I've been in town a whole day and a half and only just discovered you."

The voice was familiar, and the face, too, but he was so tall. It wasn't — it couldn't be — was it Elmer Newton?

The astonishment showed so plainly in her face that the young man couldn't but laugh, and with that old familiar laugh came recognition to Margaret. She sprang up and went to meet him, saying, "O, Elmer!" then stopped and hesitated. It didn't sound right to call such a very grown-up man by his first name, and she tried again. "Mr. Newton, I mean," she said stiffly, trying to pucker her face into a dignified expression, which so amused the young fellow that he laughed again.

"I'm very glad to see you," she managed to say, more than ever embarrassed by his laugh.

"Now, Margaret," said he reproachfully, "are you going to put on airs and go to calling me mister? First you had forgotten me, and now you are going to treat me in this way. It is too bad!"

"But, but"—said Margaret, laughing a little now, herself, although her face was still rather red — "you are so — so" — she stopped again, not sure whether to say "so grown-up," or what.

"So what?" said he, laughing again.

"So tall," finished Margaret in desperation. And then they both laughed together, long and loud, and Mrs. Moore came through the hall to the front door to see what was the matter. She came out to welcome him, and Margaret had a chance to study him a little and find the old Elmer in the new one.

Mrs. Moore led the way to the house and sent Margaret after a glass of cold milk for her friend; presently Margaret took him all about the orchard, and to the trout brook, and showed him the birds' nests, and the violets and ferns that grew in shady nooks, and when they went back to the house Elmer said: —

"Now get your hat, Margaret, and come and try my team; you haven't seen them yet; they are beauties."

Margaret had forgotten all about the ponies, so taken up was she with studying this new, old friend; now she hurried to get her hat, and was soon admiring the beautiful little creatures. They seemed to like her immediately, for they rubbed their noses against her hand, and offered to kiss her, which made her shout with delight almost as loudly as Johnnie would have done had he been there.

"Come," said Elmer, smiling over her ecstasies, "hurry and get in, or we shall not have time for much riding before dinner time."

They were soon skimming over the smooth road that wound white and inviting ahead of them, and Margaret felt as if she were flying. The little ponies seemed to think it good fun to race ahead, and draw that cunning little carriage after them, and made no effort at all, but went hurrying on as if each were trying to get ahead of the other.

On they flew, past odd old country farmhouses, with barns a great deal nicer than themselves, past a field full of buttercups and daisies, with here and there an old cow having a good time amongst it all, past sleepy sheep, and frisky lambs, past greedy hens and chickens, and a very important rooster strutting about, and Margaret saw all these things, but didn't take any of them in. She seemed to be storing them up to think over some time when all was not quite so exciting. They came into the shade of a lovely maple grove; it looked dark and cool; the birds seemed all so happy there, and Elmer was telling her a funny story of his college life; her laugh rang out merrily on the fern-scented air, and she felt almost like one of those happy birds up in the branches. Who would have thought that all this was going to happen when that quiet morning dawned, and she had finished her work and sat down to rest and think, in the hammock? Oh! This was a wonderful day. And there was a prospect of more like it, for Elmer said that his brother-in-law was obliged to stay in town all summer, and his sister didn't want to leave him, so they had decided to take a little cottage half-way between there and town; and that he hadn't seen his sister in so long that he didn't care to go away anywhere. Margaret stole a look at him and thought to herself that he was the same bright funny interesting boy that he was when she last saw him, even if he had grown tall and handsome, and looked like a young gentleman. She didn't believe he would be so disagreeable as some young gentlemen were when they grew up. He was different from other boys.

So they grew better acquainted, and Margaret began to feel quite at her ease with him again.

Elmer had promised Mrs. Moore to bring Margaret back in time for dinner, so the ponies must needs turn around sometime, and fly the other way. Before they hardly knew it they were back at the door again, and Elmer had lifted his hat and left her standing on the front porch.

She came to herself pretty soon, and remembered that she ought to have asked him to come again, and that she hadn't been at all polite, nor remembered to thank him for the wonderful ride. She took off her hat in a sort of daze, feeling as if she were a piece of a fairy tale, and afraid she would wake up soon, and find it all a dream.

She could talk of nothing but those ponies, all day, and Johnnie told her when he came home and exhibited his windmill, that she had "ponies on the brain" and couldn't think of anything else. Nevertheless, he was very anxious himself to see the small horses.

Had Margaret heard the conversation that was carried on between her mother and Elmer while she was gone to get the glass of milk, she would not have gone around so quietly the next morning at her work, wondering how long it would be before he came again. She had scarcely finished her work, and smoothed her hair preparatory to sitting down to her sewing, before she heard the little dancing feet again, but this time there was no roll of carriage wheels behind. She peeped out the window; there were both the ponies, sure enough, but Elmer was just springing from the saddle of one, and the other had a saddle, too—such a pretty cunning one!

Elmer came up the walk with a big bundle which he tossed to Margaret, saying: —

"There, Miss Midget, my beloved sister sent that to you, as she thought it might be of service to you in getting up a costume. She said something about an alderney jacket, or something of the kind."

Margaret laughed merrily. "I guess you mean a jersey, don't you?"

With eager fingers she undid the bundle and out came many folds of a long blue riding skirt.

"Why, I believe it will just match my blue jersey," she said, and hurried away to try, for Elmer was admonishing her that it was getting late, and he wanted to take her to Crystal Lake that morning.

It didn't take long to array herself. She felt very funny coming down-stairs with such a long dress on, but she was soon seated on the smaller of the two ponies, and taking her first lessons in riding. Presently they were started, Elmer on the other pony by her side.

Crystal Lake was not such a very long ride, but it was far enough for one who had never ridden before. The morning was fresh and bright, and Margaret enjoyed every inch of the way.

Soon Elmer began to point out to her different rocks and curious-colored strata in the banks on either side of the road, and Margaret opened her eyes wide when he told her that they were made, one grain at a time, in layers, and that it took long to make such a little layer of reddish-colored earth. She had never studied geology, and knew very little about the formation of banks and rocks. When her companion found she was interested in it, he said they would stop a few minutes. He tied the ponies to a tree, while they two studied the strange markings in some of the rocks, and searched for trilobites, and finally sat down on a great bowlder while its story was being told; how it had traveled years and years ago on the top of a mountain of ice and snow, miles and miles away from that spot, and how, after long years of traveling and grinding on the rocks and hillsides as it passed, and being beaten by the rain, and frozen and cracked until there was but a comparatively small piece of it left, it had come to this warmer region, and the kind winds had melted its ice car, which began to travel slower and slower, and at last turned to water and ran down the slope, leaving the poor weary bowlder at rest on this hill by the roadside, and here they were sitting on it.

Margaret thought this was more delightful than any fairy story she had ever read, and was delighted when Elmer offered to help her during the summer if she would like to study geology. They mounted their ponies and went on, studying the rocks and hillsides as they went, Elmer opening up a whole world of wonderful things to her view, so that she had hardly time to think how delightful it was that she was on a real pony, and was really riding horseback herself, instead of standing by the roadside and watching some one else go by.

She looked at Elmer and thought what a wonderful boy he was, and how much he knew. But it was not that he knew so much. He had simply given her the benefit of what he did know in such a way that she longed for more.

It was not until they had looked at the beautiful lake as long as they wished, and had turned their ponies' heads toward home again, that Elmer said, after a pause: —

"Margaret, I've been wondering how you are getting on with serving the King. Do you find it hard work, or have you found it good? Have you kept close to Jesus all the way? How is it?"

Margaret's eyes shone. She had wanted to tell him how much she loved Jesus; how He had given her peace and joy in serving Him, and what wonderful things had come to pass in their household, but she had not known what words to use, nor how to begin; she was not used yet to talking about Jesus as familiarly as Elmer spoke of Him, but she was glad of this opportunity; she told him all about what a hard road she had traveled, and how Jesus had led her out to the light, and how her father and mother both belonged to Him, and how Johnnie was trying, and— Then she stopped. She had been going to tell how she gave up her visit to Aunt Cornelia's for Johnnie's sake, but there came the remembrance of the ugly thought that had come to her in the hammock. She shut her lips tight, and firmly resolved not to say anything about that, for it would seem like praising herself, and she had prayed that such thoughts should be taken from her heart, now it was her business to see that they were not invited there by what she said. Elmer asked about her brother Weston, promised to write him a letter, and suggested to Margaret that they two pray for him; then he softly repeated, — "Where two of you shall agree on earth as touching anything that ye shall ask of my Father, it shall be done unto you."

"Is that in the Bible? Is it truly? I never saw it. Oh! why doesn't everybody go to work and agree to pray for some one else and then every one would be Christians in a little while?" exclaimed Margaret.

"Well, why don't they?" said Elmer thoughtfully. "Why don't we do all the things we ought to do? Margaret, shall you and I claim that promise right away? We will try and always use a promise as soon as we see it, and then there will be two people acting up to their knowledge, at least:"

"I think that would be grand," said Margaret, her face all aglow with a new light.

"Do you remember what Mr. Ruskin says in the book I sent you? It reads something like this, if I remember rightly: —

"'You are always to dress beautifully, not finely, unless on occasion. Also you are to dress as many other people as you can, and to teach them how to dress, if they don't know; and to consider every ill-dressed woman or child whom you see anywhere, as a personal disgrace; and to get at them, somehow, until everybody is as beautifully dressed as birds.' Suppose we should carry that out a little farther, and say that we ought to consider every one who is ignorant, as well as ill-dressed, a personal disgrace; and that we ought to help them to dress their minds beautifully as well as their bodies; and then suppose we go a little farther still and say that everybody around us who is not a Christian, that is, who does not know and love Jesus, is a personal disgrace; at least until we have done our best to get people to dress up their souls, as well as their bodies and minds? Did you ever think of that, Margaret?"

"No; I never did," she said, her face growing pink and her eyes bright with the thought, and then she said in a self-reproachful tone, "There's the berry girl, I guess she needs all three dresses, and she has brought berries every day for two weeks, and I never thought! How much work there is to be done. Why didn't I begin before?" She almost dropped her whip, so eager was she; and Elmer, as he stooped over his saddle to catch it, smiled at the enthusiastic face and wished all the workers of the world could realize the need for haste as this young servant did; and then he smiled again at the difference one short year had made in Margaret.

CHAPTER 25: THE BERRY GIRL

A TALL awkward girl of fifteen, with a long cape sunbonnet almost hiding her freckled face, hands the color of untanned leather and a faded calico dress hanging loosely about her, stood in the kitchen door with a pail of berries she had brought for sale, just as Margaret came down-stairs one afternoon.

While Mrs. Moore attended to the buying of the berries, Margaret went to the rose vine which climbed over the porch and picked some of the finest roses, brought them in, and trimming off the dead leaves placed them in a vase of water. The girl in the sunbonnet watched the other girl intently; not a motion escaped her, not a tuck or a ruffle in the well-fitting pink gingham.

"How she kind o' springs around when she steps," the girl said to herself. She glanced down at the trim feet which were tripping about, and then at her own overgrown ones shod in stout calfskin, and declared to herself that she could "walk nice" too, if she had such soft shiny buttoned boots. But she sighed when she looked at Margaret's long glossy braids ending in wavy curls, and reflected that nothing could ever bring her frowsy stubbed locks into that shape.

Margaret hummed a tune as she went off into the front room and put her vase on the mantel.

"She's happy!" sighed the girl. "No wonder!"

Until the other day when she was riding with Elmer, Margaret had never given the berry girl a second thought, except to remark to herself that she was dreadfully "homely" and "wore horrid-looking dresses." She remembered the talk now as she came out again and busied herself picking up the rose leaves from the table and wiping off the spatters she had made, she noticed the girl's eyes fixed upon her. It was such an eager, hungry look it made Margaret feel sorry for her. Obeying an impulse as the girl came out, she pulled off one of the finest roses. Handing it to her she said, "Do you like flowers?"

A little while afterward Margaret put on her hat and sauntered down the pleasant country road. She liked to walk in the narrow grass-bordered path under the shade of the maples which lined Farmer Stoddard's fields. It was so pleasant to feel free to swing her sun hat by one string, to sing aloud with no one but the birds to hear, and join in, and to hunt for wild flowers and berries in the nooks of the fences.

As she drew near a clump of elder-berry bushes and was about to reach up for a spray of the blossoms, she heard the sound of bitter weeping. Somebody was in trouble, but there was nobody to be seen. Margaret stepped softly around the other side, and there at the foot of a large tree sat the berry girl, her pail at her feet, her sunbonnet thrown off, her arms crossed over her knees and her face buried in them, sobbing as if her heart were broken.

Margaret snapped off a twig to let her know that she was there, and the girl lifted her head in a scared way.

"What's the matter?" asked Margaret. "Has anything happened to you?"

No answer. The head went down again and all was still.

"Won't you tell me? Can't I help you?" said Margaret, in a tone so gentle that the head was lifted again, though a pair of sunburned hands came up and covered the tear-stained face.

"No. Nobody can't help me!" the girl said, in a tone that was almost fierce.

"Tell me all about it, please?" Margaret said coaxingly.

"There ain't nothin' to tell, only — I ain't nobody, nor nothin', an' never will be."

Margaret could have laughed at the odd speech and the odder figure with the shaggy head, only the distress was too real.

There was silence for a few seconds then, Margaret thinking: "Yes, she does; she needs all three dresses. Here's somebody for me to help."

"Do you live far away?" she asked, partly because she did not know what else to say.

The girl straightened up then, put on her sunbonnet and pointed down the lane toward a little old house standing in a weedy yard.

"Have you any brothers and sisters?"

"No. Me 'n Aunt Polly lives all alone. I s'pose I was a goose to cry," she jerked out after another silence, "but I couldn't help it! You've got a nice, pretty, pleasant home, you're pretty, an' your dress sets, an' your shoes shine, an' your hair shines, an' you have ribbons an' things, an' you know things lots, an' here I am!" whereupon she went off into another big sob.

"Yes," Margaret said, looking troubled. "I have a nice home, but I'm not pretty, and — I don't know much — I truly don't. I haven't been to school in a whole year."

"I never went more'n a year all put together." "Don't feel bad," ventured Margaret after another troubled pause. "Perhaps I can help you some in your studies this summer. And it's easy enough to make your shoes shine, your hair, too, for that matter. And I can show you how to take in your dresses to make them fit better."

"You could take out my freckles, too, I s'pose, and take in my big mouth," the girl said grimly.

Margaret laughed at that, but she looked serious again as she said: "Oh! those things are not of so much account as you think. My Aunt Cornelia says if a girl has a sweet spirit, intelligence and good manners, it is better than to have a beautiful face without all these." "Manners! That's what I want. Aunt Polly says I ain't got none, an' never will have," the queer girl said with such vim that Margaret laughed again in spite of herself.

Silence again, while Margaret pulled an elderberry blossom to pieces and thought, then she said: —

"Would you really like to have me teach you and help you all I can in everything?"

"To be like other folks? You just bet I would."

"Then I'll begin now," said Margaret. "You must not talk slang."

"Slang! What's slang?"

"Talk such as 'You just bet.'"

The girl opened her eyes wide at that and began to say: —

"You just bet I'll never say it again," but checked herself.

"You haven't told me your name," Margaret said as she put on her hat and arose to go.

"I don't like to. It's a nasty, mean name" — pulling off bits of grass as she spoke — "I hate it! Sallie Marier Bunce. That's what 'tis!"

"What is there so bad about that name?" Margaret said, bending over to hunt a four-leaved clover, partly to hide a smile. "I have a schoolmate by the name of Sallie, and there's a very nice family by the name of Bunce living on Clinton Street."

"Be there, now?" the girl said with a brightening face. "But Sallie Marier ain't nice together. They laughed at it when I went to school."

"Leave off Sallie, then. Maria Bunce is a good enough name for any girl. Now I must go. If you'll come up to our house and bring one of your dresses to-morrow afternoon I'll show you how to fix it. Will you come?"

"Yes, I will; you jus' b— Yes, I'll come."

As Margaret walked home her thoughts were busy. Here was this poor Sallie Maria envying her just as she had envied very rich girls, and now that she came to think about it, those very girls seemed to feel the same way towards others who were a little above them. So nobody was quite content and happy with her lot. What then was the use of wishing for more money and richer clothes if they did not bring pleasure? There would always be somebody a little higher up, do what one would. It was best to take things as they came to you and be thankful, and feel that God knew exactly what was best for one. That was what she should try to do hereafter.

After Margaret had preached herself this wholesome little sermon she went off into plans for Sallie Maria, thereby assisting her good resolution, for nobody is so content and happy as one who has forgotten herself and is doing something to help others. The wonder is that most people have gray hairs before they find it out.

Like many another energetic young person, Margaret planned work enough in those few minutes for a whole missionary society. She must teach Sallie Maria, no—Maria; she should call her by that name entirely; it would help to elevate the girl — she must teach her to make her dresses, to throw back her shoulders, hold up her head, and walk straight. She must give her lessons in arithmetic and grammar, teach her not to say "be they" and "ain't got none," and ever so many more things. Where should she begin in that? The grammar would be harder to compass than the manners. And then she must teach her the Bible. She would have long Sunday afternoons for that. How nice it would be, one scholar all to herself. She had longed for some work to do for Christ, and here it was; so much, too! She would do her very best. She would be patient; she would try to help this girl get a beautiful dress, for her mind and soul, yes, and her body.

Full of her new projects Margaret went straight to her mother with them. She had learned in the last few months it was a much better way than to try to keep her plans secret and go on without advice or help as she used to do.

"Yes," Mrs. Moore said, "it will be a good thing. I feel sorry for the poor girl every time she comes. She looks as if she had been neglected when she was little."

The next afternoon Margaret established herself in the upper hall by a window overlooking the road. The sewing machine was there and the work-basket furnished with scissors, needles, tapes, and all sorts of thread. She was impatient to begin and was glad when she saw Maria in the distance coming down the road with a bundle. Margaret greeted her warmly, saying: —

"Come right up-stairs and try your dress on, the first thing. We mustn't waste a bit of time."

It was a calico of orange and blue which Maria produced.

"Who cuts your dresses?" Margaret asked when the baggy waist was buttoned. Her tone had a tinge of despair in it, the waist was such a very bad fit.

"Aunt Polly; but she says it's a big bother."

Margaret filled her mouth with pins and proceeded to pin up shoulder seams and under-arm seams. She felt quite workmanlike, and really succeeded in making the waist fit very well. The skirt came next, and had to be let down. Margaret set Maria to ripping off the band while she sewed the waist on the machine. Both the seamstresses were so busy that there was very little time for any lesson but sewing. This was thorough, though. Many little things about the fit of the waist, sewing in the sleeves, etc., were laboriously explained to the eager listener.

"There's something I want to learn even more'n this, though," Maria said at last with a sigh.

"What's that?"

"'Rithmetic."

"How far have you been in arithmetic?"

"Oh! I can cipher pretty well. I went to reduction; but it's that other head 'rithmetic bothers me."

"Mental arithmetic," said Margaret.

"Yes, that's it." And then Maria, with her thread drawn out, her needle poised in the air, her eyes fixed, repeated slowly: "Twelve is three fourths of what number? That's one of 'em."

"That's easy enough," said Margaret. "If twelve is three fourths of a certain number, then one fourth of that number is one third of twelve which is four. If four is one fourth of that number, then four fourths will be four times four, which is sixteen. Therefore twelve is three fourths of sixteen."

"Yes, that's it," said Maria. "That old 'therefore' was in. They rattled it off just as you do, and I couldn't get head or tail to it."

"Well, I can make you understand it, I guess," said Margaret. "I'll cut up an apple and show you just how it is. But why are you so anxious to know arithmetic?"

There was silence a moment, and then Maria, with her face growing redder, said below her breath,—

"You won't tell anybody if I tell you?" "No."

"Well, some day I want to know enough to teach the school up to the Corners."

Margaret was still for a minute while she thought what a hopeless ambition it was. Then, glancing at Maria's eager face, she said: —

"Who knows but you will? They say people can get what they aim for if they work hard enough."

And Maria slowly turned over the words in her mind and treasured them up.

When the dress was done, and Maria put it on and went into Margaret's room to look in the glass, she could scarcely believe it was herself.

"I look the least mite like you — at the back of me," she said, twisting her head around to see herself the better.

Margaret secretly hoped it was "the least mite," and yet she tried to feel glad that the poor girl should have that much pleasure.

"I begin to feel's if I was somebody, with this frock on an' you a-callin' me Marier all the afternoon," she said as she gave Margaret a thankful look.

"You mustn't say 'Marier,'" said Margaret. "There's no 'er ' to Mari-a."

The owner of the name pronounced it then, satisfactorily, adding: "Aunt Polly always calls me 'Sallie Marier.' I'm a-goin' to have a new dress for meetin', when I sell twenty more quarts of berries," Maria confided to her new friend.

"Church, not meetin'," corrected Margaret. "What kind are you going to have?"

"Oh! a calico dress; pink, I guess; somethin' like that one o' yours, only brighter."

Margaret thought a moment and cast a glance at the sunburned face, which needed no bright pink to heighten its color.

"I wouldn't get pink if I were you," she said. "It will not become you so well as something else. A black-and-white check is pretty and neat-looking, and would be more—more ladylike for church."

Now if there was anything that Maria desired, it was to be like a lady, so she assented at once with a hearty "All right,"

"If I give you the money would you buy it for me when you go to town?" Maria asked, wriggling about in an embarrassed way, as if she were asking a great favor. This was an immense proof of confidence in Margaret. If there was anything that she had " lotted on," as Aunt Polly would have said, it was going to the village to pick out that new dress.

Obeying a generous impulse, Margaret said: "I'll tell you what we'll do; we'll ride into town with father some cool morning and buy it, and then walk back."

There! What had she done? Was she courageous enough to go to the stores and be seen in the streets with such an odd-looking creature? What if she should meet the Barstowe girls? She must take that back somehow or other. She happened to look at Maria just then and was ashamed of herself. Such a gladness as was on Maria's face! Her cheeks fairly glowed, and the tears were actually standing in her eyes.

"Can I ? Can I go with you?" she said.

"Of course you can," Margaret told her, while she told herself at the same time: "Great missionary you are! Afraid of the Barstowe girls!" — "And I'll help you make your dress. My patterns will fit you nicely," she said aloud.

"Oh! my! will you?" said Maria, which was her way of expressing warmest thanks.

"See here, Maria," Margaret said, as they stood at the gate, and the girl was about to start home, then she hesitated as if not quite sure of her ground. "You want me to help you in everything, you are sure?" she said.

"'Course I do."

"Well, then, you must learn to walk in the right way. You mustn't turn in your toes and stick your head out away ahead of yourself."

"How shall I do?" said Maria, looking down at her feet.

"Why, turn out your toes — so, and keep them out, then fix your eyes on something higher than your head, hold your chin in, and start."

Maria struck an attitude. She turned out her toes as directed, threw back her head, fixed her eyes on the top of a tall tree near her, grasped her chin with one hand and started. Then Margaret laughed. It was very funny, and she laughed till Maria, wondering and half-vexed at firsts joined in and laughed, too.

"This is the way," Margaret said, coming out of the gate and walking up and down on the grassy roadside; "throw your shoulders back —so; I forgot to tell you that; turn out your toes, bend your head just a little till your chin draws in; don't take hold of it; fix your eyes on something just a little higher than your head, straight before you, and off in the distance, not near by. There! that's all," and Margaret walked off with a free, graceful swing.

The pupil, looking on admiringly, vowed in her secret heart never to give up till she could walk like that. She practiced the toes and the shoulders and the chin several times, then marched off down the road, receiving an encouraging "first-rate" from Margaret. She still looked funny, though, stepping off in that stiff, precise way, and Margaret wanted to go off into another fit of laughter, but she ordered it back, and only smiled when Maria turned around, and called out, "You know you're to come to-morrow and bring your arithmetic."

Maria, intent on her pedestrian lesson, could only nod assent.

CHAPTER 26: "AUNT POLLY"

MARIA BUNCE had never before felt just as she did on her way home from her first lesson in dressmaking and language. She had never known much about a feeling called gratitude. It is wonderful how "circumstances alter cases"!

The task she had been engaged in that afternoon, and the many corrections suggested by her new teacher, would, under ordinary circumstances, have made her irritable and miserable. As it was, she thought of Margaret Moore with a feeling which might almost be called reverence.

Yet, had she but known it, there was much in her past life which might have awakened gratitude.

Poor old Aunt Polly had never, even in childhood, had occasion to fret over lessons in grammar and arithmetic. She did once go to school for a few weeks, and was under the training of a young man who had undertaken to teach her the mysteries of spelling and writing. She had learned a little, but poverty had prevented her having the advantage in after years of being with those who were educated; and she soon forgot all but the ability to read slowly and hesitatingly.

As I think of this poor wrinkled specimen of humanity to-day, I cannot help but think what she might have been. Poor soul! how she had been stunted in her growth of mind and heart, as well as in body. How changed she was from what she appeared when a little girl of twelve!

Some few kinks in the hair remained; but there were not many hairs to kink. These were no longer of a beautiful brown, but almost white, and looking as though the poor soul greatly needed a cap, and must have long ago lost her comb. Yet, as I said, I cannot help thinking what she might have been, in this life, and what the religion of Jesus Christ might make her fit for in the eternity that is to come.

You would hardly suppose that Aunt Polly ever thought of anything but what she saw or heard around her. Should you have seen her feeding her chickens, or picking wood with which to cook her scanty meal, or sitting at the window knitting away at that coarse stocking, you would never guess of what she was thinking. It was a way she had, that of closing her smarting eyes, and running back the panorama of her life, away back almost as far as she could; and then would she roll it along slowly, stopping here and there to dwell on the scene and live it over again.

Not that she saw anything which you might call very beautiful or attractive, but compared with her surroundings then, and her experiences in the days with which this story has to do, they seemed to her pleasant.

True there was much in this panorama which she did not want to look upon, and cared not how quickly it passed by.

Let us remember that Memory is a faithful painter, and that his colors are fast, and so give only such things to paint as we will like to look at in the years to come.

She, poor soul, was not always called "Aunt Polly." There was a time when she was called "Little Polly," and, would you believe it, " Pretty Polly!"

Well, it was during those years that she went for a little while to school, and learned all she ever had a chance to gain from school-life.

This little old woman has a picture of her teacher, clear and bright even to her dim sight.

"Photograph?"

O, no! when she was a little girl no one knew how to take photographs.

Aunt Polly's picture was hung where it will never fade. The Hand which hung it there will keep it always in the picture gallery of memory.

She sees the young man now. She remembers his patience with her mistakes and blunders. She thinks she can almost hear his words of encouragement, and so often has recalled his tender words as, after the hours of school, he walked part of the way home with her, and told her simply and lovingly of the Great Teacher. Once he had just knelt on that bit of moss under the old beech by the quiet road, and asked so earnestly that Jesus would always be her Teacher.

She saw him rise with, as it seemed to her, an almost shining face, and then he took her hand and said, "Just tell Him all about everything, as you would the kindest and best friend, always remembering He can hear, and will and can do what is best."

Then with a "Good-night," and "Good-by!" he turned away.

She remembered how her young heart was melted, and how she followed her teacher's form as long as she could, till it was hidden behind the woods; but even more vivid than all this was the experience of the next day.

She had resolved that she would do just as her teacher had asked her to, and had wondered what it was that made him so different from all her other acquaintances, so kind and patient and unselfish, and desirous of helping every one.

With mind filled with these thoughts, and with just a little dawn of hope breaking in upon a life which had always seemed to her so dark, she hastened as early as her work would let her, to the old schoolhouse.

She had been thinking so fast and so intently that she had not noticed the building till almost at the door. Glancing up she discovered that it was not open. She tried the door; it was locked. She looked at the windows; the shatters were closed.

Could it be so very early?

A little early—earlier than the other scholars; but not earlier than her teacher was wont to be there.

Looking again, and wondering, she saw a piece of paper tacked to the door. It proved to be a notice; and its preparation showed the teacher's thoughtfulness. Remembering that many of the pupils were small, and others very backward, and that some of those who came the greatest distance, were the least able to read writing, he printed it, so that all might read for themselves. But I do not think he imagined that this was the last kindness he would ever be able to show his pupils.

The facts were these: late at night a telegram had brought him word that his father was very ill, and that he must lose no time in getting home.

The next stage would pass through the village about three o'clock in the morning, and he prepared to take it.

In the midst of the many things he had to do, he thought of his scholars, and took time to prepare the notice, and add to it a few kind, farewell words.

These Polly carefully spelled out, together with the fact that the only one who had ever awakened in her heart a sense of genuine gratitude, and whom she really had ever felt that she cared much for, had gone!

There the poor dazed child stood for some moments, staring at the paper; and might have stood for an hour, had she not been roused by the laughter of some romping girls who were on their way to school.

Had Polly been guilty of some crime, she would not have fled more hastily. She had a feeling that she must get to some spot where no one could see her, and cry and cry.

She knew she could not remain there and keep from crying, and the thought of being seen shedding tears for the teacher, was one not to be considered for a moment.

So she ran as fast as her feet would carry her over the stone wall, and through the pasture down the hill, following the path made by the hoofs of the cows as they came and went into the woods for shade and water.

On, on, she tramped under the deep shade of the tall dark hemlock and spruce and broadarmed beech, till she came to the high rock behind which was the old spring; there she threw herself upon the ground and wept till it seemed as though her heart would break.

Her one friend was gone — the only one she ever had or ever would have! But even then there came creeping into her mind the thought of that other and greater Friend of whom her teacher had told her only the night before.

How near that Friend was! and yet she could not see Him, so knew it not.

She did not know it was His Spirit suggesting these new and better thoughts of hope and possible help. Yet to her surprise there came over her mind a feeling for which she could not account. A few minutes before she had felt as though she did not want to live; and yet she must, because she could not die, without killing herself, and that she did not dare to do; but now she felt that she could go back home and do what was wanted of her, and some way it would be all right. She did not understand it; she did not know that her best Friend had come to that spring with her— the great Burden-bearer — and was so tenderly taking the burden away.

At last she thought she would get down on her knees on that moss, as her teacher had done the day before, and tell Jesus all about her trouble; the same as she would if she could see Him. This she did; she "talked to Him," as she called it, for some time; then with a face looking a little sad, but peaceful, she started through the woods toward home.

She and the wood robin sang together as she went along, and the chickadees sang their sweetest song for her; and how could she help thanking them for it?

And how do we know but the dear Lord who sent the birds to sing their sweet songs for her, took to Himself the thanks which they could not understand?

How queer things are! Just to think that "pretty Polly" of thirteen is "Aunt Polly" seventy-three, and poor and wrinkled and old!

But does she not have something sweet to remember? Don't you wish you could look into that memory gallery and see the picture as she sees it ?

It did not seem much to do at the time; but how glad that teacher will be all down the years of eternity— if there are any years there— that he did not put off that opportunity of the little talk and prayer with Polly till some "more convenient season;" for you will remember the "more convenient season" never came.

"What a bright, sunny soul she must have been all these years," I think I hear you say; and I am sorry to have to contradict the thought and disappoint you.

The truth is, our little girl had to return to a very unlovely home — if it could be called home — and spend her years with people who cared nothing about the Sabbath, or church, or Sabbath-school, or even the Bible.

O, yes! there were Christian people not far away; some of them went to church every Sabbath, driving past the cabin which the poor people called "home."

There were ever so many little boys and girls who had seen Polly in school, and who had seen her at the store with her little basket of eggs, but, isn't it queer? not one of those bright boys or pretty girls had ever invited this little girl to come to their parties, or picnics, or even to their Sabbath-school?

Perhaps they thought she had no clothes good enough to wear to such places.

But, do you know, I cannot help thinking that they might have made it possible for Polly to have had better dresses and shoes? I am just now thinking what the Master said: "The poor ye have always with you, and when ye will, ye may do them good." Might not some of those people have helped to send a little sunshine into Polly's path?

Well, I did not mean to take so much time to tell you about Maria's old aunt, but being interested in her—I mean the aunt, as well as Maria—it seemed to me that you might like to know her story. You will think better of her now, I feel sure, and won't blame her so much for not giving Maria better instruction and neater-fitting clothes.

Oh! I could tell you more about her; how she took Maria when she was only a few hours old, and was left with neither father nor mother, and how she comforted the dying mother by promising to care for her baby.

This was no light task for one who had almost nothing, and could hope for nothing but what her hands might be able to earn.

Many and many a time had the aunt gone hungry that she might buy milk of her wealthy neighbor for the baby. And now all her poor old heart was bound up in her "Sallie Maria." For her she lived, and for her she planned, even to the keeping of that old tumble-down cabin, and the little garden spot, with its few currant bushes, rhubarb roots, and red roses, that the child might have a home when left alone in the world. But God plans for all of us better than we think.

Now, to return to Margaret and her appointment with Maria.

It was something of a cross to go to the store with one so uncouth as was this poor girl, but she had no idea of backing out of the bargain, and so they went on their shopping trip, to make the wonderful purchase.

It was hard for Maria to see why she should not take the very pinkest goods in the store; but her heart had been taken captive, so she went with it, and would have taken anything her new friend had suggested.

While weighing the weighty question as to which of the two pretty pieces should be chosen, Margaret was startled at the sound of a familiar, "Good-morning!" from her friend, Elmer Newton.

"So you are out shopping this morning," he said. "Can I be of any service in helping to decide which among so many?"

"My friend, Miss Maria Bunce, Mr. Newton." And "Mr. Newton" lifted his hat no less gracefully to this "friend" than he had to Margaret, and Maria, while she blushed to her ears at this new experience, at the same time thought that "Miss Bunce" was not such a bad-sounding name, after all.

At first this seemed to Margaret a rather embarrassing experience. She had hoped that by coming early she might avoid encountering any one for whom she would much care if she was seen with Maria; but soon, instead of regretting young Newton's presence, she was glad of it, for she began to feel that he was going to be a helper.

You will remember the plan was to ride to town with Mr. Moore, and walk back; and with this purpose in mind they presently left the store.

Margaret had hardly thought of the ponies, but there they were. As she looked at them, she called Maria's attention to their beautiful manes and tails.

"Pretty, aren't they?" said the young man; "and as good as they look, as I will soon prove to you," and he motioned both to jump in.

Of course one of the girls thanked him, and persisted that the load would prove too much for so light a carriage, but as he persisted, they were soon seated and speeding on the road to Aunt Polly's cabin.

No one could have been more courteous to any lady than was Elmer to Maria, and Margaret was glad. If it did not read, "It is more blessed to give than to receive," I could not have told which one of the trio was the happiest.

Arrived at Aunt Polly's home, both girls were dismayed to find that it was Elmer's evident intention to make a call.

You will remember that Margaret had never seen the inside of the cabin, or been introduced to its owner.

As it was, Elmer had to introduce himself.

Aunt Polly half arose from her chair as her eyes rested on the stranger, then sat down again, a look of great bewilderment on her face, and her thoughts instantly traveled back to her old memory gallery; it seemed to her that the teacher of so long ago stood before her.

She hardly heard the cordial "Good-morning, madam! I am Elmer Newton; this is my friend, Margaret Moore, and I believe you are Aunt Polly."

"You look enough like him to be his shadow," she said at last, with a long-drawn sigh. "But of course you ain't, for that was a great while ago."

Then she roused to the present, invited her visitors to "set down" and make themselves "to home," and was as pleasant as she knew how to be.

Before Elmer had been in the cabin half an hour he knew more of this poor old pilgrim's past life, of her hopes and fears for the future, and of her present needs, than was known by any of her neighbors near whom she had lived for years.

As he and Margaret finally drove away, I do not know which of the two was the more eager in making plans to bring a little sunshine into that poor home.

CHAPTER 27: EXPECTED COMPANY

ELMER'S ponies were at the depot, in front of a two-seated wagon, in which had been seated their master, and Johnnie, and Margaret. The said ponies were now tied, and all three passengers were at the edge of the railroad track, looking with eager eyes to where, up the far-stretching line of track, a faint cloud of smoke was just appearing, and a long, low whistle signified the approach of the evening express. Then they could hear its thundering voice roaring, "Coming! coming! coming!" and, with a fearful groan, as the brakes tugged at the wheels, and a dreadful hiss as the steam gasped out its dying breath, and dripped, lifeless, on the ground, the train was still, and crowds of people, with all manner of luggage, trying to occupy the same space at the same time, were pouring off and on. But the eyes of the Moore party were fixed on a figure which with difficulty wended its way to the platform, and soon was lost to sight in their embraces.

"You darling old Weston," Margaret was saying, and the sentiments of the others, varied somewhat, did not differ very materially from hers.

It was now toward the last of August, and Weston had written that he was homesick, and was going to start for home as soon as Aunt Cornelia would let him. That lady wrote that while she would miss him very much, she felt that he ought to be at home again. Weston had reported himself as "dying" to see Margaret's little house in the country, and the ponies behind which she appeared to be spending so much time, and the chickens, therefore the hitching up of the ponies on this very evening, and the drive to the train in the twilight.

Off again down the long country road, tongues flew merrily. Weston had to hear the latest news about everything from Johnnie, to whom it would have been a great grievance if the chickens and kittens had been heard from through any other medium than himself. So Margaret waited for her talk with Weston until later. He was listening, however, between Johnnie's pieces of news, to her and Elmer.

177

"Have you seen Maria to-day?" asked the latter.

"No," said Margaret, laughing. "I was surprised, too, for she went to the Sunday-school picnic yesterday, and I supposed her dress would need a good many repairs. Mine always does after a picnic. But she can do her sewing herself now, if it isn't too hard."

"She is coming on," said Elmer, and then they laughed again, but in a very pleased and contented way.

"How is Aunt Polly?" he asked presently.

"I feel quite a stranger up in your direction, since the rain has actually kept me in town for three days."

"She is better," said Margaret. "Did I tell you Mrs. Sandford let Maria off for a day and a half to go and help her? The old lady had a nice time then. Poor thing! she misses Maria very much, but she is so rejoiced over the thought of her earning money regularly, that she bears the separation very well.

"The doctor came out yesterday to see her. Wasn't it nice in him? And he was just as attentive to her as though she were a rich woman. He says she may get better for a while, but that she cannot live long. It will be very sad for Maria to lose her, won't it?

"Oh! you don't know how kind Jacob Williams is to Aunt Polly. He does all her errands, and looks after her comfort in every way he can think of. Why, I didn't tell you he had got back, did I? Don't you believe he found that his father was the very Zabed Williams to whom that money was left! Of course it is all Jacob's now. Isn't it queer to think of him as quite a rich man? Weston, did you see much of Jacob Williams while you were at Aunt Cornelia's? we were so surprised to find that he had been there."

"I should say I did," answered Weston significantly. "We had a good time together." "How do Maria and Jacob get along?" asked Elmer. "Maria will worship him, will she not, if he has been kind to Aunt Polly?"

"Oh! they are very good friends," said Margaret, laughing.

By this time the ponies had stopped at the gate, and Mr. and Mrs. Moore had come out to meet Weston. No less tender or earnest, although somewhat less vociferous, were their greetings than those of Margaret and Johnnie had been.

"I will tell you," said Margaret, coming into the yard — having left her hat in the house — one kitten on one shoulder, another making its way down her arm, "I will tell you, Weston, where you will have to sleep: up garret!"

"Well," said the new-comer, "if that is your company room, I shall be obliged to put up with it — put up, very literally, I guess. So you have a garret here as well as down town?"

"Yes; and a nice little one. Not very warm at night, you know; but in the day time you will probably not want to stay there."

"Not being either Shadrach, Meshach, or Abed-nego," put in the merry voice of Elmer, who had come up to say good-night. "Sweet dreams to all of you. I shall probably be around in the morning."

"I haven't a doubt of it," called back Mr. Moore, as the ponies trotted toward oats and beds.

It was late that evening before the family retired. In fact it was not until a marked silence warned them to look for Johnnie, and they found him in a horizontal position under the sofa, that they prepared to say good-night.

"Mother," said Margaret, as Mr. Moore playfully threatened to put out the light if they didn't go to bed immediately, "don't you think Weston is changed a little — for the better, I mean?"

"I don't know," said Mrs. Moore. "Sisters are very observing. I don't know but he is. I always thought Aunt Cornelia had a good influence over him."

A little later silence and slumber reigned in the house. Silence, save for the loud tick of the clock, the rustle of the leaves outside in the breeze of the summer night, and the occasional snore from the restless sleeper.

Not long after breakfast the next morning Margaret betook herself to the garret to put Weston's room in order, and found the proprietor gazing out of the window.

"It is a beautiful morning," he said, turning toward her. "Can you take a walk, Margie?"

"We will see," said Margaret, "after you have helped me make this bed, and have filled your pitcher. You see I am going to put you to work right away."

"All right," said Weston, whistling a bar of some nondescript tune. "Margie, it is so good to be home again!"

"I am glad you think so. You must have had a very nice time at Aunt Cornelia's."

"Fact," said Weston, "but then"—and there were some very distinct strains of "No Place like Home" in the whistling this time.

Shortly afterward they two were walking down one of Margaret's favorite country paths, green and fresh with dew. After quite a walk they came to a little brook which chattered merrily along the ground, over which, just in the shade of a spreading oak, was a pretty little bridge. Here Weston threw himself down, his feet dangling in dangerous proximity to the water, and Margaret sat on the roots of the tree, smiling at his laziness.

"It is a lovely place," he said presently.

"I am glad you think so," said Margaret. "It is my favorite spot."

"Margie," said Weston, after a moment's silence, "what do you think of Jacob Williams?"

"Think of him!" answered Margaret, in surprise. "Why, just what I always did. I think he is a nice good young man, and saved Johnnie's life. Why?"

"Oh! nothing, only I have reason to think a good deal of him. Fact is, Margie, it was he who led me to choose Jesus for my Captain."

"O, Weston!"

"Yes," he said, in answer to her delighted exclamation, "I have learned the lesson at last. I couldn't help seeing, Margie, how your religion helped you. You were so much less cross, you know. And it was the same way with mother; and father was ever so different. Then there was Aunt Cornelia, you know; a fellow couldn't help thinking, Margie. Jacob Williams stayed with us a couple of weeks; Aunt Cornelia wanted his help about the new building; and we had lots of fun. We took long walks, and he told ever so many good stories. One night he asked me if I wouldn't be a Christian; and he seemed so anxious and troubled. We got talking about things, and he told me his whole story. It's a queer one, Margie; and it astonished me to find how father was mixed up in it, and myself, too, after a fashion. That was the way he came to be good — only, of course, he didn't say he was good. Then you wrote me that you and Elmer were praying for me, and at first I was mad, and afterward kind of glad. At last I made up my mind to be a Christian, too. And it is so nice, Margie!"

Margaret had come over to the bridge, and sat down on the edge by Weston, and put both arms around his neck. "O, Weston!" she said again, "of course it is. And I am so glad." Her eyes were shining with tears of joy.

"Come, now," said Weston, "don't cry. We won't talk about it any more, only I just thought I'd tell you" — And he began to mow the grass about him vigorously with his hands — "now we'll surely have jolly times; we are all Christians."

A person of more dignity than Weston or than myself might have been shocked at his rather hilarious way of speaking, but, as he himself always said, "Who has a right to be more jolly, or hold their head higher, or have nicer times than a Christian?"

Then the brother and sister walked home. It was the same path by which they had come, but the sky was bluer and the sunshine brighter and the grass greener and the birds sang more sweetly than before, because of the new joy.

By the time they reached the orchard, their joy had bubbled over into singing, and these were the words they sang: —

"I've found a friend in Jesus, He's everything to me,
He's the chiefest of ten thousand to my soul,

He's the Lily of the valley, in Him alone I see
All I need to cleanse and make me fully whole.
In sorrow He's my comfort, in trouble He's my stay,
He tells me every care on Him to roll,
He's the Lily of the valley, the bright and morning Star,
He's the chiefest of ten thousand to my soul."

"It is queer," said Margaret, breaking off suddenly, "that Jacob Williams did not tell us about you."

"I presume," said Weston, "he wanted me to surprise you with my own story. He has a way of keeping still about things. Who is this Maria that you and Elmer talk so much about?" he continued, leaning against an old gnarled apple-tree. "You quite aroused my curiosity last evening."

So then the story of the forlorn berry girl, her fortunes and misfortunes, had to be told, and Weston grew as much interested as though he himself was favored with Miss Bunce's acquaintance.

"And now," Margaret finished, "Maria can sew quite a good deal, and walks straight, and talks — well, pretty nicely, although she will sometimes use rather peculiar English when she is in a hurry. And their house looks so much better, and old Aunt Polly is very cheerful, and Mrs. Sandford down in the village has taken Maria to help her kitchen girl, who has too much to do, and she — I mean Maria — is getting along real nicely."

"That's good," said Weston. "How much good you have been doing, Margie!"

"I!" said she, opening her eyes wide. "I have only helped a little." For Jesus had so fully answered her prayer as to make her forget how much she had been doing for Him, and she only remembered how much He had done for her.

Once at the house, Weston went up to the garret, at Mrs. Moore's rather mysterious suggestion, and finding no one there, sat down on the bed, which, however, suddenly began to roll and tumble under him, so that he arose rather more hastily than usual, to see the laughing face of Elmer peeping out from under a carefully-arranged comforter which he had not before noticed.

"Dear, dear!" said the submerged young gentleman, "you were a dreadfully long time coming, and I am reduced to a state of almost incandescence. Whew!" And looking like an Egyptian mummy, he arose from the bedclothes, and calmly seated himself, by one or two dexterous movements, on a cross beam just above the head of his host.

Weston laughed merrily, and had just climbed to his visitor's side, when Margaret put her head in at the door.

"Come down, you mischievous children. We have something to tell you, Elmer."

When he had heard the explanation of Margaret's even unusually bright face, and Weston's satisfied manner, no one could have been quicker than he to grasp the hand of the new soldier in the army to which he belonged.

"When two are agreed," he said, looking over at Margaret, who nodded back through happy tears.

The next few days were very happy ones; very soon the Moores would have to leave their "summer villa," as Weston merrily called it, and so rides and walks and family picnics became the order of the day, the "family" always including, when it could, Jacob Williams and Elmer, and occasionally Maria Bunce.

Some days later, just as the Moores were seated out by the rose-bushes in the yard, just at evening, to watch the rising moon, a step was heard on the path, and Jacob Williams' head appeared over the bushes. "Good-evening!" he said. "I came to see you about Aunt Polly. She is worse to-night; Mr. Wakefield and the doctor are both there. Mr. Wakefield sent me to town for Maria, and she would like Miss Margaret to come over. The doctor says Aunt Polly can live but a very short time."

Margaret rose hastily, and her mother followed her into the house to prepare to go over to the sick woman's cottage.

"Could I be of any use?" asked Mr. Moore. Jacob shook his head. "I hardly think there would be room for you in the house," he said, smiling gravely as he left with Mrs. Moore and Margaret.

Aunt Polly's room was still very bare, despite the recent improvements over which Margaret was so enthusiastic. On the bed lay the poor old woman, her thin white hair drawn back under a neat cap — Maria's last gift — her thin hands folded on the patchwork quilt, the shades of death creeping steadily over her face.

At the head of the bed stood the doctor, with his hand on the fluttering pulse, and beside him was the minister, while kneeling on the floor at one side, bitterly weeping, was Maria.

"Believe on the Lord Jesus Christ and thou shalt be saved," said the minister's clear voice. "The eternal God is thy refuge, and underneath are the everlasting arms." "Though I walk through the valley of the shadow of death, I will fear no evil, for thou art with me, thy rod and thy staff they comfort me." "And there shall be no night there, neither sorrow nor sighing, for the former things are passed away."

"Dear Maria," said Margaret, kneeling beside the weeping girl, "she will soon be at home."

"She is all I have in the world," sobbed Maria.

The door opened softly and Elmer came in and took his place with Jacob Williams, at the foot of the bed. Aunt Polly opened her eyes.

"She looketh for a city which hath foundations, whose builder and maker is God," murmured Elmer.

All was still. The moon shone in through the window as if to smile on the solemn group, and show them a glimpse of the light and glory into which Aunt Polly was going; it reminded Jacob of the night when he had bade his father good-by.

Once more the voice of the minister broke the stillness: "Thy sun shall no more go down, neither shall thy moon withdraw itself; for the Lord shall be thine everlasting light, and the days of thy mourning shall be ended."

Just a moment of solemn silence, and he added, "Her eyes have seen the King in His beauty: they behold the land that is very far off." Then the watchers knew that Aunt Polly was with Jesus.

An hour later they walked out in the clear moonlight. Margaret had persuaded Maria to come home with her, and the little procession wound over the hill.

"Do you know," said Elmer, taking Margaret's arm, "that to-morrow I must bid you good-by?"

CHAPTER 28: LIKE THE OTHER MORNING

MARGARET was washing dishes.

Do you remember, I wonder, how, months ago, I began her story with that sentence?

Whether you remember it or not, she remembered the fact; and on this September morning, thought of it and smiled. Things were so much the same, and yet were so very different.

To begin with, it was the same room, and the sun shimmered among the vines at the east window just as it did that morning which seemed to Margaret so long ago; and she set down the plate she had rinsed with careful hand, and a little recollective laugh over the thought that it was one of its mates which she had smashed on that troubled morning of the past.

Over by the window sat Johnnie, one arm around the neck of Pedro, while the other held a book on which he was hard at work. It was an arithmetic which Margaret had splashed with dishwater, she remembered, but Johnnie was studying algebra now.

Outside was Weston, whistling still; no boy ever loved to whistle better than Weston; he was mending a broken hinge of the blind, and the blows of his hammer kept time to the music.

Presently his voice sounded through the room: "Nearly done, Margie?"

"All but the knives and forks. Why\? Do you want me?"

"I thought we'd go over to the other house and nail up those vines if you are ready."

"Oh! I'd like to; but maybe mother will need me this morning."

"She'll fix it, if she thinks you have any plans," said Weston, with a pleasant laugh.

"Or you," said Margaret, as she joined in the laugh.

"Or any of the rest of us," declared Johnnie, without raising his eyes from his book.

"That is true," said Margaret. "I don't think anybody could be more unselfish than she is."

As she spoke she dried her hands to tuck a little corner of the bread-cloth back into place; and as she did so, Margaret smiled again. There had been bread set in this very spot to rise on that morning to which her thoughts kept wandering, and she had tipped the dishwater over on to it.

"What a dreadfully careless thing for me to do!" said Margaret to herself; "I wonder she didn't give me a whipping. She would if she had been some mothers, and I'm sure I must have deserved it." Even then I am not sure that she realized what a fearful storm of passion it would have roused in her heart, had her step-mother done any such thing.

Margaret knew that the people about her were very much changed; she did not understand how entirely different she was herself from the passionate little Margaret of that day.

There is something mysterious in the way in which one's thoughts can influence another's. Johnnie looked up from his book, and watched the bread-cloth being tucked back into place, then spoke his thoughts:

—

"Say, Margie, do you remember once when the dishwater tipped over on the bread?"

"Say-Johnnie, I remember it distinctly, and I remember that you were to remember that my name was not 'Say-Margie.'"

Johnnie laughed good-naturedly. "I forgot," he said, "but hasn't a lot of things happened since that morning?"

"'Quite several,' as old Joe says, which is really quite as sensible, I suppose, as saying 'a lot' of things. Among other things which have happened, John Stephenson Moore has been at the head of his class for three weeks, and his sister, Margaret Moore, is proud of him."

Johnnie laughed a pleased little laugh, then said, "There have more things happened to the Moores than that."

" So there have," said Margaret, coming to his side long enough to give a little pinch to his hard red cheek, then stooping suddenly, she kissed it.

"O, Johnnie boy! wonderful things have happened to us all. I was thinking of it this morning. If things had happened so that we could all go to Europe and live there together in a grand palace, and have everything we wanted, everybody would be talking about it, and saying what a wonderful thing it was. And here the whole Moore family are going to Heaven, and are having lovely times on the journey, and some people don't even know that it is wonderful."

"Some things happen that aren't lovely, though," said Johnnie, solemnly shaking his brown head. "There's my new knife gone, you know, with my full name on the handle; and there's that essay to write on Sir Thomas Moore, and I don't know a thing about the old fellow any more than I would if my name was not Moore."

"O, yes! " said Margaret, "and there would be car-cinders and dust and such things on the journey to Europe, and a storm on the ocean just as likely as not; but then we should take all such things as a matter of course, and not mind them much, because of what was to come afterwards."

"That's true," said philosophical Johnnie, "and I don't mind things much nowadays, not half so much as I used to — I don't really; but then I think — Margie, there's Aunt Frances stopping at the door in the little carriage."

He broke off to say this, and Margaret and Weston made haste to the side door to see what was wanted.

"Good-morning!" said Aunt Frances, leaning from the carriage. "I stopped to see if your mother didn't want to ride out with me; I'm going to drive past where her people live, and she might call while I am doing my errand a little farther on."

"Oh! " said Margaret, "I'm sure she does; at least, I'm sure she ought to; a ride would do her good."

"Mother!" she called at the foot of the stairs. "O, mother! "— as Mrs. Moore appeared with a pitcher in one hand and a lamp in the other, and Weston sprang forward to relieve her of both — "Aunt Frances has come for you to take a ride; she is going past Grandma's and you will have time to make a little visit there. Let me run for your things, and you won't have to go up stairs again."

"O, dear child! I don't see how I can go this morning; it was very kind in her, but there is the bread to bake, and dinner to get, and so many last things to see to about the moving."

"I'm equal to the bread, mother; and Maria and I can manage the dinner beautifully, can't we, Maria?" This last to a trim young girl in a neat-fitting dress of dark-blue calico, finished at the throat with a white ruffle, and her handsome auburn hair in beautiful order.

Without waiting for her eager, "Yes, indeed!" Margaret's voluble tongue went on: "It is just a splendid chance, mother, for you to get a little bit of rest after this hard week; and Maria and I will have dinner on the table, ready for you, when you come back."

"And as for the moving," chimed in Weston, "it is Saturday, you know, and father said the men couldn't come till Monday, and you said yourself that about everything was done that could be, unless we could eat our Sunday dinners right away, and have the dishes packed up."

"Hurrah for a ride!" shouted Johnnie, as he tossed his algebra in the air, and came out to the hall. "I've got every problem of them, mother, just on account of that hint you gave me last night. Hurrah! for a mother who understands algebra, I say. She's coming, Aunt Frances;

I'm going to bring her out in a minute on Pedro's back."

"O, what children!" said Mrs. Moore, half-laughing, and wholly helpless, for Margaret had bounded away for the various articles known as "things," and returning, was putting her mother's bonnet in place, while Weston folded the soft gray wrap about her, Johnnie volunteering the while to hold her hands, so she could make no resistance, and Maria earnestly explaining that she knew everything about the dinner. And at last the pony phaeton rolled away with "Aunt Frances" and "mother" seated side by side.

Wonderful things had happened to the Moores!

Margaret went back to the kitchen to take a scientific look at the bread and then to dust and otherwise set in order the pleasant room. Weston, meantime, had carried Johnnie off with him to do such things about the vines at the "other house" as could be managed without Margaret.

At this moment there came a light tap at the kitchen door, and then, without further ceremony, it was pushed open, and Hester Andrews entered.

Now Hester Andrews had been away from town for more than a year; it was only two or three weeks since that she had returned, and made an effort to renew her friendship with Margaret.

"Dusting, baking, and what not!" she said gaily, as she helped herself to a seat. "Poor child! such a lovely morning as it is, too; I came for you to walk, but she keeps you at it as usual, I see; I met her riding out in fine style, having left you at home to drudge. It is too bad!"

Hester had been talking very fast, and Margaret had turned to close the hall door, so Hester did not see the flash in her eyes until she turned them full upon her, and spoke quickly: —

"I beg you to remember that, besides imagining things which are utterly false and foolish, you are speaking of my mother."

"Bless me!" said Hester Andrews, "don't fly into a passion; I thought when you were sixteen you would get over that; I'm sure I meant no offence; I was only trying to sympathize with you."

Margaret walked back the length of the room, and stood quite still for a little minute before she spoke again in a much quieter tone:

"I beg your pardon, Hester; I needn't have spoken so sharply. I am trying to overcome that habit, but indeed if there is anything in the world of which I have not the least need, it is sympathy. If you could help me to be grateful enough, I should be glad; least of all do I need sympathy on account of my mother. I do not know how a girl of sixteen could have a kinder, truer, better friend than she is to me."

"I am sure I did not know," said Hester stiffly. "I did not suppose that girls forgot their own mothers, and took up with strangers so easily. People told me you were very much changed, and I see you are."

Poor Margaret felt the blood rushing into her face, and her eyes were full of tears.

"I have not forgotten my own dear mamma," she said. "It was she who helped me to see how wrong and false to her I was in rebelling and struggling and making papa's life miserable because God had taken her away. I know I am to blame for your mistaken ideas about my second mother. I remember how I used to talk to you, but if ever there was an insufferable little idiot, I was one. I want to" —

She was interrupted. Weston found that the particular sort of nail which he wanted was locked in his tool-chest that no one but himself could open, so he came back for it, and at this moment he pushed open the door and came and stood beside Margaret — her tall brother of nearly eighteen.

"Good-morning!" he said, bowing gravely to Hester. "I overheard some of your and my sister's words, Miss Hester. She says she was an idiot; if that is so, there were a couple of us. I think Margaret and I will both be glad of this opportunity to tell you that things are greatly changed with us; we both claim to have acquired a little common-sense, and we want you and all our friends to know that we respect and love our mother as we believe she deserves, and in doing this we feel that we honor the memory of the mother whom God took from us as we could not in any other way."

It was a long speech for Weston to make. Margaret had time to get herself into a quieter spirit, and realized presently that her strongest feeling was one of admiration for her handsome brother.

Hester seemed to have a little of the same feeling; the voice in which she replied was almost respectful: —

"I'm sure I beg your pardon; I meant no harm at all; things are changed, I see."

"Things are very much changed," said Weston, with a pleasant smile for their guest, and a quick glance of intelligent sympathy for Margaret. And then both these young people had tact and courtesy enough to change the subject entirely, and try to put their caller at ease.

Weston went away very soon, but Hester lingered, apparently fascinated with the many changes.

"We might adjourn to the dining-room," said Margaret. "I have promised to set the table for Maria; we have an ambition to have everything in immaculate order for mother when she comes back. That is, as immaculate order as can be managed with almost everything one wants packed up ready to move."

"I should think you'd hate to move," said Hester, as she followed Margaret into the pretty dining-room; "you have lived in this house all your life, haven't you? Though to be sure the other house is very handsome. Isn't it a great deal larger than you need?"

"It is pretty large; but then, our family is large, you know. Aunt Cornelia is going to spend the winter with us, and we wanted a room for Aunt Amelia to call her very own, and use as often as she can. And Maria had to have a room, of course. Oh! we shall manage to occupy the entire house. We are a great family to spread ourselves," concluded Margaret with a smile.

"Who is this Maria that you quote so often? Is she that bright-eyed girl I saw in church with you? What is she, anyway? Not your hired girl?"

"O, no! Maria is — why, she just belongs; she is one of us. She is an orphan, and lived with an aunt who died two years ago, and then she was alone in the world. She came to us to stay for a little while, and kept staying on until we can't any of us do without her, nor she without us. She thinks the world of mother, and has reason to."

" How queer! And does she do your work?"

"Why, we all do the work, together in vacations," said Margaret, with rising color; she knew very well that Hester was rude, but she did not believe Hester knew it.

"In the winter Maria and I are both at school. Mother got along alone last winter with what help we could give her out of school hours, but we don't mean she shall do it again; we have an excellent girl engaged who can come in October. Maria is splendid help, but her lessons will be harder this year, and mother thinks she ought not to have so much to do about the house."

"Anybody would think she was your sister, to hear you talk."

Margaret laughed pleasantly. "I'm glad of it," she said heartily; "I've always wanted a sister; and I shouldn't wonder if we thought as much of Maria as if she were our very own. I dread the thought of her going away to teach one of these days, as she will; she was born to be a teacher. She is an excellent scholar, and will be ready for High School in another year. Once she had an ambition to teach in that little red schoolhouse out at the Corners" — and Margaret laughed merrily over the thought — "but she has changed her mind. Nobody would have supposed who knew her only two yean ago, that she would ever"—and then Margaret suddenly stopped. Not for the world would she present to this cold-hearted Hester a picture of poor "Sallie Marier Bunce" as she appeared two years ago.

"That she would ever what?" questioned Hester, evidently much interested.

"That she would ever teach school at the Corners, and it is altogether improbable that she ever will," finished Margaret quietly. "She will be much more likely to be a preceptress in some young ladies' seminary. She has ambition in that direction; and she accomplishes whatever she undertakes. She was determined to learn to fit dresses, and she does it beautifully. She makes her own dresses and helps me with mine. I taught her in the first place, but she has gotten ahead of me."

"People say that Mr. Williams is going to marry her," said Hester, "and that you and Elmer Newton are going to be married."

Then Margaret's laugh rang out. "Since I am only a few months past sixteen, and Maria but a trifle ahead of me, and Elmer has reached the advanced age of twenty, people are undoubtedly correct, as they generally are. As for Mr. Williams, he is our good friend, certainly, but I don't think he has heard that remarkable piece of news; not that it would make any difference to him if he did. He knows that ignorant people will gossip."

"And people say," continued Hester, determined to give news, "that the reason your Aunt Frances took up with your step-mother is because your father has been received into the firm, and is getting rich, and has bought an elegant house, and she knew she would have to meet your step-mother in society, so she decided to make the best of it."

"As I said, ignorant people will gossip," repeated Margaret still quietly, though the flash in her eyes might have told her guest that she was presuming on forbearance almost too much.

"And it makes not the slightest difference to the parties concerned what persons of that class have to say. My Aunt Frances was prejudiced, I suppose, as even sensible people sometimes are, without reason, but when she had the fever last winter, and my mother watched over her night and day for six weeks, as my aunt herself says few own sisters could have done, she learned to know my mother's worth."

"Mag Moore!" interrupted Hester suddenly, "I want you to tell me honestly what has happened to you all to make you so different? I thought I knew you through and through, and when folks told me about your step-mother and you being so loving together, and she saying, 'my daughter,' and you 'my mother,' and all that, I said it was just put on for effect, and I could get to the bottom of it in ten minutes; but I must say I don't understand what makes the difference."

Which, I suppose, good friends, is precisely your state of mind. You think there have been wonderful changes in the Moore family; you do not understand why people who were so uncomfortable in their minds a few years ago, should suddenly grow into so much love and happiness. You are all ready to exclaim, "Oh ! that sort of thing will do for stories, but in real life it never happens."

Will you take my word for it that you are mistaken? That this "sort of thing" did happen "in real life?" That the difference in every member of the Moore family can be distinctly traced to the power of the religion of Jesus Christ, filling the heart, overflowing into the life, so that every affection, and motive, and action, are being transformed into

"His image," according to His promise?

There is much more which might be told about these lives; and I flatter myself that you are interested not only in the Moores, but in Maria and Jacob Williams, and Elmer Newton, and even in "Aunt Frances."

So it may be that in the years to come, I shall find time to tell you more of this story — how lives which seemed steeped in trouble sevenfold came out into the peace of God's own sunlight and shone for Him.

But, for the present, the written history of the Moore family is concluded.

ABOUT THE AUTHOR

Grace Livingston Hill was the foremost trailblazer of Christian Romance novels. She almost single-handedly built the platform for today's Christian Romance genre almost 130 years ago. Despite the passage of time and all of the changes that come with it, her novels endure and are read and loved by women everywhere. Her stories were filled with tales of good vs. evil and Christian redemption and almost always worked in a classic romantic relationship. Not only was she an influential Christian author, though, she was a person of great integrity, kindness and charity. She spent her life trying to help others both through her work as a writer and through her work with the Presbyterian Church. Until the day she died, she never stopped caring for people, always putting others ahead of herself.

On April 16, 1865, the second Livingston baby was almost lost at birth in Wellsville, New York, but after hours of hard work on the part of the doctors and hard prayer on the part of the family, she survived against all odds. Several years before, the Livingstons' first child, Percy, had died in infancy only one day after his birth and the family was grateful not to have to endure the sorrow of another death. They named their second child Grace as a constant reminder of what the Lord had done for them in sparing her life. Born to Presbyterian minister Charles Montgomery Livingston and his wife, Marcia Macdonald Livingston, both of whom were writers, Grace was destined to become a writer herself. It was in her blood. Grace was always bright and eager to learn. She was homeschooled before attending public school and always learned very quickly, earning high marks in class. While she wasn't in school, she would entertain herself at home for hours with nothing but pencil, paper and crayons. Grace soon developed a talent for painting, which was one of her favorite hobbies as a young girl and she sometimes sold her works of art to people in the church and in the community.

Grace began writing short stories at a very young age. She loved spending time with her aunt, watching her type out her stories on the typewriter and reading them fresh from the print. Having such a talented and intelligent role model in her life inspired Grace to start writing for herself. The Livingston family was delighted to see that she had inherited their love of the written word and would spend their evenings, after an hour of worship, listening to Grace read her stories aloud, along with other classic stories from Dickens, Bronte and other well-known writers. On her twelfth birthday her Aunt Isabella, the author, gave her a bound and illustrated copy of a story that Grace had written, The Esselstynes. As a favor to her "Auntie Bell", D. Lothrop Company, the same company which went on to formally publish many of Grace's novels, informally published the book as a gift. Grace was so enthused at seeing her work in such a professional presentation, it set off her determination to begin the journey as a published author.

As Grace's father grew older and suffered from vision problems, Grace began reading to him as well as helping him with Pastoral duties, playing the organ on Sunday mornings, helping with Sunday school and singing during the services in all of the nine parsonages that the family lived in between 1867 and 1892. Each of the places that Grace lived with her parents was small and cramped, even for the small family. After graduating high school, she managed to get out for awhile, attending Elmira College for one semester, but by Christmas break she was homesick. She determined that she missed her parents too much to continue and she moved back home to live with them. Grace later found herself enrolling in college again, at Cincinnati Art School. As before, it only took two terms for her to realize that she did not want to be away from her family for such a length of time and she returned home.

In November of 1886, while living with her parents in Winter Park, Florida and volunteering as a secretary at her father's church, Grace began working on her first full length novel, A Chautauqua Idyl. Her family was not able to afford a real summer vacation away from home as they always had in the past and her intention was to use the money from sales to fund the vacation to Chautauqua, New York. She finished the book in December and sent it to D. Lothrop Company to be published. It was welcomed by the publisher and received excellent reviews, followed by surprisingly high sales figures for a first novel. Grace was delighted at having succeeded in raising enough money to take the family to New York.

After her beloved Aunt Isabella past away in 1888, Grace compiled quotes and passages from many of her aunt's books and paired them with scriptures. Unlike many of the fiction novels Grace wrote in her lifetime, this was a daily devotional book dedicated to "Auntie Bell", called Pansies for Thoughts. Grace later claimed that even after her monumental career in Christian Romantic Fiction, Pansies for Thoughts was the one accomplishment in writing that was dearest to her heart. She realized that she did not just want to write, she wanted to spread the Word of God to her readers. Soon after publishing the devotional book and her stories began gaining popularity, she started including the message of salvation through Jesus Christ in the plot lines. Her tales became focused on the struggles of a Christian heroine, or in some cases a character who becomes a Christian during a crisis moment in the novel. Though her publishers removed much of the religious content in her earlier novels, they allowed it to pass in later works once they realized the level of popularity that her books were gaining. Grace knew that she had been blessed with the talent for writing and she was determined to make her faith the biggest influence on her work.

Grace Livingston married Frank Hill in 1892. Like her father, Frank was a God-fearing Presbyterian minister and helped to carry on the tradition of church in Grace's life. She had met Frank in Chautauqua, though he was a minister at a church near Pittsburg, Pennsylvania. She wrote to him from Chautauqua for nearly a year before seeing him again. Grace moved to Hyattsville, Maryland with her family for almost a year and finished a novel called The Parkerstown Delegate: A Christian Endeavor Story. All the while, Frank and Grace exchanged letters and two weeks after The Parkerstown Delegates was published, Frank proposed. They announced their formal engagement at Chautauqua where he presented Grace with an engagement ring. Grace Livingston became Grace Livingston Hill at Hyattsville Presbyterian Church on December 2, 1892, where her father served as the pastor.

Only a few days after her wedding to Frank, Grace became concerned about her husband's erratic behavior and mood swings. He confessed to her that when he was in Scotland, attending University, that he was diagnosed with severe headaches. The doctors had given him a prescription to manage the pain and side effects, but he had become addicted to the medication. As Grace tried to help Frank manage his addiction, they prayed about it together but kept the problem discreet. Aside from Frank and Grace, Frank's parents were the only ones who ever knew he had a problem with addiction until almost twenty-five years after his death.

Within the first year of marriage, Grace had given birth to their first daughter, Margaret Livingston Hill. Margaret was cherished and adored by both of her parents and the Hills were blessed with a second daughter in 1898. They named the baby Ruth Glover Hill (also known as Ruth Livingston Hill). Shortly after the birth of Ruth, Frank fell ill with appendicitis. There were serious risks involved in performing surgery so the doctors tried in other ways to restore his health but were unsuccessful. When his condition worsened rather than improving, his doctor advised emergency surgery but the decision was made too late and Frank died of appendicitis on November 22, 1899.

The loss was extremely difficult on Grace who not only had to raise two daughters by herself, but also had to find a place for them to live since she was residing in the parsonage of the church where Frank had been the pastor. Her mother, Marcia, came to stay with her through Frank's death and until she found a permanent place to live in Swarthmore, Pennsylvania. Despite her personal tragedy, Grace continued to write. She knew she had to write, had to make money, in order to keep food on the table for her children and a roof over their heads. Although she had made a decent amount of money on the novels she published in the first six years of her marriage, she knew she would need an ongoing source of income and in February of 1900, she published A Daily Rate. The novel earned her barely enough money to get by until she could pick up jobs writing articles for local magazines and newspapers, but she muddled through and went without food when she had to in order to give her children what they needed.

On July 6, 1900, tragedy struck again for Grace when her beloved father passed away due to old age and failing health. Grace's mother, Marcia, moved to Swarthmore to live with Grace and help in raising the girls. Marcia helped to educate Ruth and Margaret in their home while Grace wrote short stories for Christian publications such as "Christian Endeavor World", "The Golden Rule Press", "The American Sunday School Union" and "The Washington Star". Grace volunteered much of her free time to the women's groups at Swarthmore Presbyterian Church but was involved in four different churches, in various cities, while she lived in Swarthmore. Grace taught Sunday school to elementary aged children and help to direct church organizations. As a result of her devotion to the church, Ruth and Margaret became extremely involved in church activities as well and helped their mother with Sunday school when they could.

Between 1901 and 1904, Grace published six new novels. With the money she had earned, she built a house on a large lot she had purchased in Swarthmore. It started as a small, stone house, but over time, as Grace brought in more and more money with her novels, the house grew to the fourteen room dream-house that Grace had always pictured for herself and her family. She included a private study room where she could work on her novels, though she typically kept the doors open in a silent invitation to her family to enter without the fear of disturbing her.

In 1904, Flavius Josephus Lutz began showing a romantic interest in Grace. She had developed a friendship with him a year earlier when he became the music minister of music at Swarthmore Presbyterian Church. Margaret and Ruth had both been introduced to the piano at the age of five and as they practiced and studied at the church, Lutz frequently gave them advice and pointers about their musical abilities and complimented them on their talents. One day, after sharing a meal in the evening after church, Lutz asked Grace to marry him. She was hesitant to agree after friends and family advised against the union, but after giving it some thought she decided that it would be good for her daughters to have a father figure as well as a live-in music teacher. After a few weeks of deliberation, she accepted his proposal and they were married on October 31, 1904.

It was not long after the two were married that a tension developed between Grace and Flavius Lutz. According to Grace, Flavius refused to take a leadership role within the home and did nothing to help with raising the girls or doing work around the house. Whenever Grace would ask something of him he would either ignore the request or become belligerent. Even after Grace set up and in-house music school for him to teach music to children and spread the word that he was giving lessons, he never contributed his earnings to the family or household expenses and left everything up to Grace and her mother. He became unpleasant to be around and was argumentative and harsh with every other member of the family as well as some of his music students.

Grace continued writing and published another ten novels between 1906 and 1914. In May of 1914, Flavius Josephus Lutz left the family. After years of enduring his abrasive moods, constant criticism and refusal to work, he had begun disappearing from the house to be gone for a night or two before Grace would finally locate him at his parents' home or sometimes in the church. He would always return when she came for him, but eventually, he began missing Sunday Morning services in which he was supposed to play the Organ, forcing Margaret to take his place as an impromptu organist. Grace knew that she had made a mistake in marrying Lutz but divorce was never something she believed in or accepted as a possibility. She had made a commitment to a man before God and would hold fast to her beliefs, even if his behavior was hurtful and the relationship was complicated. Eventually, however, Grace determined, after much thought and prayer, that she could no longer live with him. He left again for several days and Grace asked him not to come back, thinking that he would apologize or promise to change but he was apathetic about her request and agreed to move back in with his parents. After several years, the marriage was annulled.

Grace published another four books between 1914 and 1917 under Lippincott Publishing Company. Though she was never unhappy with the services of D. Lothrop Company, Lippincott was nearer to her home in Pennsylvania and more easily accessible. However, The Witness was published in 1917 by yet another publishing company, Harper and Brothers. Grace decided to take her business to the new publisher because Lippincott was not receptive to the overt religious tones in her work and frequently made suggestions for alterations in her story lines. The Witness became her most popular and widely read novel causing Lippincott to see the error of their ways and eventually the company agreed to give Grace complete editorial power and publish whatever she wrote, regardless of content, without making suggestions for changes.

By the 1920's, Grace had written four more books (3 novels and one nonfiction book co-authored by Evangeline Booth). Two of her novels were made into films, sending her fame as a novelist skyrocketing. She decided to make some renovations on her home and build on some additions that she had been wanting for years, since she had the extra money. While her house was being worked on one of the men in the work crew, an Italian stonemason asked Grace if her family would come and play some music for the Italian community that he was from in Avondale. Her daughters had taken over the music school that Grace started for Flavius and had been so successful that they were able to move the business out of their home and into a studio making them a well-known entity in the community and the surrounding areas. Grace, Ruth and Margaret accepted gladly and after the concert, Grace asked some of the people of Avondale if she could come and teach a Sunday school class for children each week. She began holding weekly classes on the second floor of a vacant shop in Avondale but there were so many people attending her lessons that she was asked to start having the classes in an old Presbyterian church in Leiperville that had closed down many years before. For over twenty-five years, until her death, Grace ministered to the Italian community. She continued her Sunday school classes and Bible studies and even started English classes for the

Italian immigrants who were having difficulty assimilating. Whenever the church had difficulty meeting monthly bills, Grace was always there to lend financial support.

Between 1920 and 1940, Grace wrote fifty-one novels. Many of her short stories were published by Lippincott in book format and were later compiled into collections and published again. Grace was diagnosed with cancer in the early 1940's, but continued to write, though her strength was waning. She sometimes had to have someone type for her as she dictated her novels. Still, she managed to have eighteen more novels written and published by 1947. On February 23, 1947, the incredible writing career of Grace Livingston Hill ended when she passed away at the age of eighty-two. Her last novel, Mary Arden was finished by her daughter, Ruth and published in 1948.

In a testament to how much Grace Livingston Hill was admired and loved, not only for her writing but her gracious spirit and generosity, there have been three full-length biographies written about her life and work. Writing simply to entertain readers was never enough for Grace. Being raised in a Christian home, surrounded by ministers and brought up with the convictions of Biblical teachings, she always wanted to reach out to people on a spiritual level. She managed to do just that through her books, but also through the way she lived her life. By all accounts, Hill was a kind, generous woman who worked her entire life to help others. She taught the gospel of Jesus Christ, she taught English to Italian immigrants, she taught music; she donated much of her earnings as a novelist to various churches and charitable organizations and never accepted money from the congregations she was invited to as a guest speaker. Hill wrote over a hundred books in all, many of which are still in print today and have sold thousands of copies and changed the lives of readers everywhere. They taught that love and forgiveness, along with a relationship with God, was the way to a fulfilling life and lasting happiness. Even on her deathbed, Grace would not take credit for her own writings, claiming that whatever she had accomplished during her life was merely the Lord's work done through her.

Miranda Trilogy

By

Grace Livingston Hill

ISBN: 978-1-62943-003-4

This anthology consists of Marcia Schuyler, Phoebe Deane and
Miranda.
(3 Books in 1)

The Best Man (A Christian Romance)

By: Grace Livingston Hill

ISBN: 978-1-62943-007-2

The story is about the love between Celia Hathaway and Cyril Gordon. Cyril Gordon is a handsome Secret Service Agent who stumbles in upon a wedding ceremony while he is being chased by his pursuers. He is being forced to walk down the aisle as the best man as he was being mistaken by the people in the church. But to his surprise, he was not the best man, but the groom!

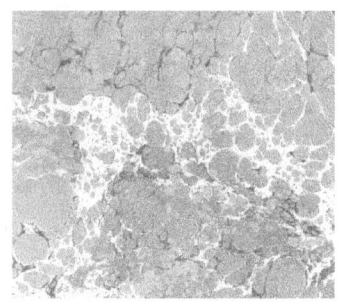

AUNT CRETE'S
EMANCIPATION

GRACE LIVINGSTON HILL

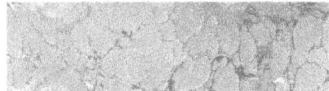

Aunt Crete's Emancipation

An Inspirational Christian Fiction

ISBN: 978-1-62943-008-9

Lucretia was short and dumpy, with the comfortable, patient look of the maiden aunt that knows she is indispensable because she will meekly take all the burdens that no one else wants to bear. Her sister could easily look over her head into the hall, and her gaze was penetrative and alert.

"I'm sure I don't know, Carrie," said Lucretia apprehensively; "but I'm all of a tremble. Telegrams are dreadful things."

"Nonsense, Crete, you always act like such a baby. Hurry up, Luella. Don't stop to read it. Your Aunt Crete will have a fit. Wasn't there anything to pay? Who is it for?"

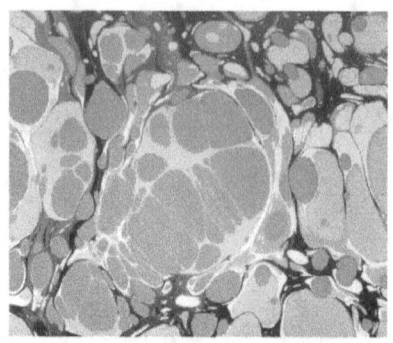

THE WHEELS OF TIME

Florence L. Barclay

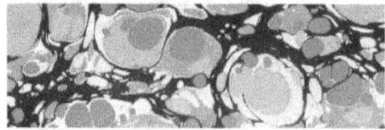

The Wheels of Time By Florence L. Barclay

ISBN:978-1491064948

A Charmingly touching Story

It is a prequel to The Rosary.

Dr. Deryck Brand stood, with his hand on the door-knob, looking back into his wife's boudoir.

There was nothing in that room suggestive of town or of town life and work--delicate green and white, a mossy carpet, masses of spring flowers; cool, soft, noiseless, fragrant.

Standing in the doorway, the doctor could hear the agitated clang of the street-door bell, Stoddart crossing the hall, the opening and closing of the door, and Stoddart's subdued and sympathetic voice saying: "Step this way, please." A heavy, depressed foot, or an anxious, hurried one...